DEATH AT THE TURLOUGH MUSEUM

A STAR O'BRIEN MYSTERY

MARTHA GEANEY

TURLOUGH, NOLAN PUBLISHING

DEATH AT THE TURLOUGH MUSEUM

Copyright © 2020 by Martha Geaney

Library of Congress Cataloging- in-Publication Data (TK)

Produced in the United States of America

10 9 8 7 6 5 4 3 2 1

First Edition

ISBN: 978-0-9600567-5-0 (print)

For requests and information, contact:—

Turlough, Nolan Publishing

PO Box 193

850 Teague Trail

Lady Lake, FL 32159

Attribution: John Armagh Photo of Turlough Round Tower

Email: *marthageaney@icloud.com*

Website: *www.martha-geaney.com*

Facebook, Instagram, Twitter: mgeaneyauthor

ACKNOWLEDGMENTS

Many thanks and shout outs to family and friends who support my career as an Indie writer.

In Ireland, there are "the cousins" who always amaze me with their abundance of love and support.

My cousin, Anne Hughes Kenny who serves as my "reading detective". Anne scours my manuscript for any errors regarding Ireland and County Mayo that I may have made.

In the United States, special thanks, again, to Nick Johns, fellow Indie author, who provides the first read and edit of my manuscripts. My writing is stronger because of tough feedback. At times, I think he knows Star as well as I do.

This book is dedicated to George W. Reichert, Jr. (my Bill). Bill has been the wind at my back through every step of life's journey. Although he can no longer read due to vision loss, he continues to urge me "don't give up". When the road gets tough, Bill is always there to take my hand. This one is for you, my Bill, my love, forever.

CHAPTER 1

It was one hell of a night to be on the greenway between County Mayo's capital town of Castlebar and Turlough Park Museum of Country Life. The gusting wind lashed cold rain into Jimmy Mahoney's face, but his armpits streamed sweat.

The Castlebar River had overtaken several areas along the seven-kilometer trail. Most days, especially Sundays, walkers, cyclists, and joggers crowded along the walkway's bridges, fields, and macadamed sections toward Turlough House's Rooster's Café. Upon arrival, a steaming pot of tea, complemented by a decadent chocolate Madeira cake, rewarded the energetic who finished the two-hour jaunt.

Well after 10:00 p.m. on a weekday evening, Jimmy didn't expect to encounter anyone other than his numbers-running boss. Anxious to get over what he was about to do, Jimmy took long strides. "Damn that woman," he shouted when the wind slapped a branch across his face. He swiped the limb away, allowing some of his anger toward Georgina to dissipate.

Then, he smiled. Georgina drove a hard bargain. He had to get out of the racket, or she'd report him to the authorities. He hadn't admitted it to her, but the ultimatum brought a sense of relief. He struggled every day with his motivation for participating in the shadow lottery gig.

After all, he was a successful entrepreneur—the owner of a pub in Neale. Money flowed. If he were honest with himself, money and success didn't drive him. No. His nature's dark side drove him into shady business deals.

Blast it. He sighed when the flooded path saturated his runners. He and Georgina hadn't been a couple for several months, but he still hoped she'd have him back. She was good for him. That was why he'd decided to quit the organization. Like no other woman before, Georgina deserved his effort to embrace the bright side of his character.

By the time he got to the meeting point, Jimmy's clothes clung to his body. Overheated and weighed down by his sodden jacket, he took it off, using a nearby tree branch as a hanger. He checked the time on his phone. His contact was late.

Jimmy wished he had a cigarette. Then he shook his head. Instead, he sent a text to Georgina: *looking forward to seeing you.* Smoking was another thing Georgina had made him give up.

Heavy breathing and rustling branches behind him warned that his meeting was about to commence. He shoved the phone into his pants pocket, took a deep breath, and turned to face the late arrival. For a minute, Jimmy was puzzled. The person he usually dealt with was fast-paced, but the approaching figure listed toward him as if on a collision course. *Maybe the boss sent someone else,* Jimmy thought. He didn't know every member of the secretive organization.

As the person drew nearer, Jimmy could see a dark stocking cap, black boots, and a puffer jacket. But the downpour made it impossible to see the person's face. Then the figure raised a hand. *Good,* Jimmy said to himself, *at least they sent someone friendly.* He stepped forward, offering a handshake.

Too late, he saw the ball-peen hammer just as the hand

holding it rained down furious blows, one after another, onto Jimmy's head. His body sank to the ground.

Jimmy's final thoughts swirled through his brain before settling on how much he'd miss the smell of the damp, mossy, Irish earth. Then the darkness took him.

CHAPTER 2

I accelerated the rental car up the steep, winding driveway to Lorcan McHale's ancestral home. When I'd gotten the call, I didn't pack much. The pre-owned and dented Renault, which I'd bought on an earlier trip, sat in the barn at French Hill cottage. Wanting to be in control at the wheel, I opted to rent a car at Shannon Airport rather than hire a limo driver.

During the two-hour ride north toward Castlebar, County Mayo, the frantic phone call from Lady Marcella McHale replayed in my brain like a recorder on loop. As I slowed the car to a stop in front of the massive double doors of the McHale estate, I rewound through our conversation for the millionth time.

"Star, this is Marcella McHale. Georgina's in trouble."

"What?" I'd pressed the iPhone against my head. Maybe I hadn't heard her correctly. Lorcan's mother, Marcella, normally exuded steely confidence. Instead, a whisper replaced her usual brisk tone.

Before we'd ever met, I pictured a gray-haired senior citizen sitting in her eighteenth-century stone house, reading and drinking tea with friends. Boy, was I ever wrong! When Aunt Georgina introduced me to the tall, slim, blond-haired

Marcella, I found an actively involved philanthropist who'd welcomed me with open arms into her circle of friends.

"I finally got her into bed. She's sleeping. She didn't want to call you, but I'm having none of that." Marcella's voice had seemed to regain some of its strength.

"What's going on?" I'd demanded.

"Jimmy Mahoney is dead, and Georgina thinks the murderer is stalking her."

"I'll catch the next flight," I'd said and ended the call. I had to get to Georgina. Until then, my questions could wait.

MARCELLA THREW OPEN THE DOORS BEFORE I REACHED THE TOP step.

"Thank God you came," she said, taking me by the arm and guiding me along a wide hallway toward the back of the house. "In here. I'm just about to make tea."

Ashford, the border collie I'd left in Georgina's care, rushed toward me, tail wagging like a welcome flag. I bent to rub his ears but stopped when my eyes glimpsed Georgina. My heart leaped into my throat. Georgina huddled on an oak chair in front of a monstrous open hearth, which seemed to engulf her frame. Instead of her trademark scarf, a knitted afghan embraced her shoulders. When her eyes met mine, she didn't bother to wipe the tears from her face. I rushed to her side and threw my arms around her.

"What's going on?" I demanded. I would not allow her to see how shaken I was to see this usually bustling, entrepreneurial Irish woman cowering by the fireside.

"Georgina, move over here, and we'll bring Star up to date." Marcella pulled one of the chairs out from a massive oak table, which sat in the middle of the kitchen floor.

Georgina complied, moving slowly from the hearth to the

table, where Ashford settled to lie at her feet. I sat on the chair next to her. Marcella positioned herself across from us.

Glancing from Marcella to Georgina, I said, "Okay, tell me everything," and waited for one of them to start. Georgina sat motionless. Marcella threw some tea bags into a teapot and poured the hot brew into three mugs. Then, she pushed one between Georgina's hands as if the heat would jump-start her emotional register. "Go ahead, Georgina. Tell Star what you told me," Marcella urged.

"Jimmy is dead. I killed him," Georgina said before she choked on the sobs that wrenched her chest.

"Yes, he's been murdered, but the rest of that statement is utter nonsense," Marcella insisted.

Her face mirrored Georgina's careworn look. I wondered what Georgina, or maybe both of them, had gotten up to while I was in the States.

"Okay." I turned my chair to face Georgina. "Jimmy Mahoney is dead. How did he die?"

"He was found—"

"I want Georgina to tell me what happened," I said, interrupting Marcella's response.

"I don't know," Georgina said. She turned her red-rimmed brown eyes to mine. "The garda claim he was killed on the greenway between Turlough and Castlebar because they found his jacket there on a branch and blood on the ground," Georgina said between sobs. "But his body was found in the Turlough Museum, draped over one of the exhibits."

"What did the paramedics say? Could he have had a heart attack or a fall?" I asked.

"I'm sure he was murdered, Star. His head was bashed in. And I had something to do with getting him killed. And now, I'm next on the list." Georgina shook her head. "I didn't want to get you involved. I don't want you killed too."

Marcella leaned across the table and touched Georgina's

hand. "Stop that nonsense, woman. Star is well able to take care of herself. We'll get to the bottom of this."

Georgina gave her friend a brief smile.

"So. Let's be sure that I have the facts. You believe he was killed?" I asked.

"Yes," Georgina replied. "The garda was on the scene for hours, taking evidence from the exhibit hall and interviewing the staff."

The guards, I groaned inwardly. No wonder Georgina was worried. Ever since the New York Police Department decided my mother's disappearance was a case of *child abandonment*, I'd never trusted them. My recent inadvertent involvement in some murder cases here in Ireland did nothing to change my opinion. Had the cops already accused an innocent woman?

"What did the police say? What did they ask you?"

"Well, they wanted to know where I was that evening. But, Star, I don't have an alibi. I was at the cottage alone. Jimmy sent me a message about seeing me. But he never showed up. I didn't think anything of it at the time."

"Then why, in heaven's name, are you blaming yourself for Jimmy's murder?" I couldn't imagine Aunt Georgina ever wanting to kill anyone.

"Jimmy ran numbers," Georgina stated.

"You mean an illegal lottery scheme?" I asked.

"Yes, I'm assuming he was low level but still. Why, in heavens name, did he think he had to make money through the mafia?" Georgina shook her head. "When I discovered his involvement, I pressured him to get out of the organization." She paused and pressed her hands against the mug she held. "I threatened to call the guards, Star. And now, he's dead." Georgina shuddered. "And I'm probably not long for this earth either."

Taking up the story for Georgina, Marcella said, "Georgina thinks someone is stalking her. I brought her to stay here with me. And then, I called you. And Lorcan. I told my son to get on the next plane home." Marcella sighed. "Your aunt and I need both of you to deal with this mess."

Georgina's and Marcella's words sent a chill up my spine. My hands moved to the cell phone clipped to my capri pants. But I quelled my usual need to take immediate action; instead, I stiffened my spine and said, "Let's take this one step at a time."

Georgina nodded.

"How did you get involved in Jimmy's nefarious deeds? I thought you'd broken up with him."

"I did. And don't ask me why," Georgina replied. In the tone of her voice, I heard the Georgina Hill I'd gotten to know when a widow-maker claimed my partner's life. His death not only left a gaping hole in my life but also left me a cottage and an aunt. Both in Ireland and both never mentioned in the years we'd been together.

"That's not a good enough answer, Georgina. You have some explaining to do."

"I just was uneasy with Jimmy for some time," Georgina said, pushing the tea mug away. "I thought he was lying to me about why he'd be late when we had a planned dinner date. He always said, 'something came up, that's all.' I didn't feel like we had an honest relationship."

Georgina stopped to wipe tears from her face before she continued. "Then, Star, you remember how he hid his business relationship with Jane Doherty from me. That was the end, there and then. I broke up with him."

"So, how did you learn he was running numbers?" I asked. Of course, Georgina's successful dress boutique, The Golden Thread on Main Street in Castlebar, was a part byproduct of her design capabilities and a part byproduct of her knowing everyone in the county. But how in the world had she happened upon underworld behavior?

"Well,"—Georgina's face grew animated as she spoke—I

was at the Old Turlough Cemetery. My family's buried near the base of the Round Tower. I'd just gotten into my car when I spotted Jimmy near a headstone up at the top of the hill where the tower sits. I saw him remove a stone brick from the tower's edifice and place a paper in the gap. After he put the stone back, he made the sign of the cross and pretended to visit a grave. *The very grave where my parents are buried!*"

"Did you ask him about it?" In my research about Ireland and the search for my mother, I'd learned that funerals and family gravesites formed a cornerstone of Ireland's cultural traditions. Catholic masses were often said on Sunday in church cemeteries during the summer months. It didn't take much for me to imagine how curious Georgina might have been about Jimmy's appearance at her parents' gravesite.

"I didn't approach him then. I knew for sure that he was up to no good. What, in heaven's name, was he doing at that particular grave? His own family is buried nearby in that cemetery. Surely, he should know the difference. So, I did a stake-out," Georgina admitted. By then, the afghan had slipped from her shoulders. She sat up straighter in her chair.

"How and where did you do this stakeout?" I asked. Although I was worried about what I'd hear next, I was happy to see Georgina's spirit return.

"Whenever I could get away from the shop, I drove out to the cemetery. It took a while before I figured out his comings and goings. I observed the times and days I saw him and noted them in a diary."

"Wait," I interrupted. "Is that the green-covered diary I noticed a few months ago?" I remembered being surprised that Georgina kept a diary. When I questioned her about the book, she said she used a diary occasionally to sort through decisions. I'd been even more struck by her answer because in the time I'd known her, she never seemed to have to sort through decisions.

I wished I'd asked her more questions then. Maybe I'd have saved her from her anguish.

"Yes, I've been tracking him for a while, Star. Always from the safety of my car," she emphasized when Marcella, who'd been listening closely throughout the entire exchange, threw her hands up in the air. Georgina smiled at Marcella and continued, "Anyway, one of the days, I decided to take a look at what was on the paper."

"When was this?" I asked.

"Not long after you flew back to the States. I waited until Jimmy left the cemetery. Then I approached my parents' grave. If someone saw me, I'd say I was visiting family. But the cemetery was deserted, so I pulled out the stone and looked at the paper. At first, I didn't understand. I didn't know what to make of it. Numbers, it just had numbers. I took a picture with my phone and put the paper back."

"What did you do with the picture?" I asked.

"Not picture, pictures, Star," Georgina emphasized the plural. "I kept taking pictures whenever I could until I figured out that Jimmy was involved in a numbers racket."

"You mean you went back more than once."

Georgina nodded.

"Did you show the pictures to anyone?" I asked.

"No, I decided to find out who was on the other end of what Jimmy delivered. So, I staked out the cemetery a few nights in a row. I saw someone retrieve the paper, but I couldn't tell whether the person was male or female, fair or foul." Georgina paused before continuing, "But I knew one thing for sure. I was going to confront Jimmy." Then she picked up the teacup, sat back in her chair, and drank the cold brew.

During the lull in the conversation, I recalled how I'd gotten Georgina involved in my amateur investigation when a good friend, Paul Doherty, had asked me to look into his mother's death. The very Jane Doherty that Jimmy had been a silent partner with in a yoga studio. I'd been nervous about getting Georgina involved then, but I relied on her knowledge of just about everyone in County Mayo. More importantly, I included her as my way of letting her know that she mattered in my life.

Although Georgina was Dylan's aunt, I'd come to think of her as my family. I'd spent most of my life building a tough, feisty, external shell to cover my vulnerability. I protected my independence. But with Aunt Georgina, I'd begun to feel some cracks in my emotional, defensive barriers. With all the losses in my life, I enjoyed the idea that someone cared about me again. But I wished I'd never encouraged her to be a part of *any* investigation, especially hearing she'd been running her own amateur investigation. *One that just might get her killed.*

No wonder Marcella contacted me. My profession as a researcher and information broker involved me in people's lives and, more often than not, disappearances and deaths. I'd found myself at the heart of a mystery more times than I'd like to count. But it was a mistake to label me a private investigator. While occasionally my research pointed the way to a murder, I was most definitely no Miss Marple! How was I going to keep Georgina safe?

CHAPTER 3

A doorbell chime cut into the silence. Georgina jumped, visibly shaken out of the reverie she'd sunk back into. Marcella glanced at the clock. "That must be Lorcan," she said. "I don't think he took his keys with him when he left for the States. I'll go let him in."

While we waited for her return, I prepared myself to see the man that I'd tried to put out of my mind since he said goodbye and left for the state of Wyoming regarding a problem with wind turbines, based upon one of his patents at a green energy plant. I touched my hair, wondering how many cowlicks stood up as a result of the rush from the airport. The man had a way of unnerving me. He always seemed to materialize when I looked my worst. Like when I hadn't showered or attained any semblance of looking like, or for that matter, *smelling* like a normal human being. *Forget your hair,* I told myself, *focus on keeping a cool, detached demeanor.*

I'd allowed Georgina into my emotional circle, but I wasn't about to admit that I was attracted to Lorcan McHale. Granted, he had saved my life after Jane Doherty was murdered. But still, I didn't want to like him. Anyway, that was what I told myself.

Marcella didn't return with Lorcan. Instead, two detectives

that I'd come to call the Hardy Boys, Irish edition, stood behind her. Marcella's grim visage foreshadowed what happened next. I rose and moved to stand in front of Georgina's chair. Thomas O'Shea circumvented me. He faced Georgina and said, "Georgina Hill, I'm placing you under arrest for the murder of James Mahoney. Follow me."

"I want to see your warrant," I demanded of O'Shea. The scar over his left eye deepened as he frowned at me. Then he nodded toward his partner. James Keenan stepped forward and handed an official document to me. Wanting to stall for time, I perused the paper, word by word. But I knew the form justified the action about to occur.

Georgina placed her hand on my arm. "Star, stop. I'll go with them. The sooner we get this settled, the sooner my life will get back to normal." With that, she stood and walked out of the kitchen, flanked by the two detectives.

"I'm going with you," I insisted.

"Miss O'Brien, you will remain here," O'Shea said in a stern voice. "When we've processed Ms. Hill, you'll be able to visit."

My hand clutched my phone's lime green case. I wanted to race to Georgina's side and throw my arms around her. Instead, I stood frozen in place, watching the detectives escort Georgina into their car.

Marcella and I remained in the driveway until the car carrying Georgina away disappeared from view. Then, Marcella wrapped her arms around me. Her grip was strong. "Don't worry, Star, we'll get through this together. In the meanwhile, why don't you get some rest? It's been a long journey for you."

"I guess you're right. I just wish there was something I could do now," I replied.

"Georgina would want you to rest."

I nodded as a wave of exhaustion hit me.

"Why don't you stay here tonight?" Marcella suggested.

"No, I'd rather go to French Hill. I'll get a better night's sleep there." I smiled, hoping I hadn't insulted Marcella, but the last thing I wanted to do was wake up in Lorcan's house, looking like a zombie. Ashford followed us outside to my rental car, which he hopped into when I opened the door. As I drove away, I glanced in the rear-view mirror and saw Marcella standing in the driveway, her arms wrapped around herself. I reached French Hill cottage in less than five minutes. I parked the car and turned the key in the cottage door. Ashford ran to the living room and his favorite resting spot. I walked into the bedroom and threw myself onto the bed, where I fell into a deep sleep.

THE NEXT DAY, THE POLICE RELEASED GEORGINA ON A STATION bail bond, provided she guaranteed to appear back before the court and formal charges in twenty-eight days. Her arrest became a sensational affair. And, in Castlebar, County Mayo's capital, news spread quickly.

With the media camped outside her cottage in Turlough, Georgina packed a bag and temporarily moved to the McHale estate, against my wishes. When I begged her to stay with me at French Hill cottage, she refused. "You have better things to do than catering to me, Star. I'll be fine with Marcella and Lorcan. And thank goodness Ashford is there to look after you."

Ashford more or less adopted me a few months ago. I'd been in the village of Cong, home of Ashford Castle, at the address of a mysterious female who called herself Evelyn Cosgrove. From a post on a missing persons' site, I'd determined the Cosgrove woman may possess information about my mother, who'd been missing since I was six years old. Frustrated that Evelyn was nowhere to be found, I'd taken a walk through the woods bordering Lough Corrib. Before long, a playful black and white border collie crashed out of the woods to join me. Then, he'd alerted me to the body of a woman.

Finding the unfortunate Jane Doherty began a cascade of events that ultimately led to the murder of another innocent person. After someone tried to kill me, I just had to get involved. Especially since the police, like in my mother's case, were willing to accept the easy answers.

When no one claimed the collie, I named him Ashford and brought him back to French Hill. I'd entrusted his care to Aunt Georgina when I returned to New Jersey for a consulting detective project. That was not the only thing I relied on Georgina to accomplish while I was gone, but I knew we couldn't have any detailed discussions until after Jimmy Mahoney's funeral. Georgina insisted she planned on attending. I agreed to go with her, not to pay my respects but because I was looking for a murderer.

Jimmy's bashed skull meant he wasn't waked in the usual Irish tradition, either at home or in a funeral parlor. The casket was closed and sent directly to the church. That circumstance, however, hadn't kept Midwest Radio, County Mayo's ubiquitous radio station, from announcing his death.

On the morning after I arrived back at French Hill, I sat at the kitchen table and tuned the radio to Midwest. I'd heard the daily death notices read on the air during my two previous trips to Ireland but listening to the announcer say, "the death has occurred of James Mahoney, very suddenly" struck me like lightning.

Georgina stood accused of this man's sudden death, and I had less than twenty-eight days to prove her innocence.

～

I STOOD NEAR THE KITCHEN DOOR PERUSING THE LUSCIOUS GREEN fields when Lorcan knocked. I'd gotten ready early so I wouldn't have to spend much time alone with him. The last time we spoke, he was on his way to Wyoming. I'd hidden my disappointment that a dinner he'd promised wasn't going to happen. In the three months since I'd seen him, he seemed to have enjoyed his time in the United States. For once, he wasn't wearing the timeworn leather jacket that usually covered a navy-blue button-down collared shirt and khaki pants. He still wore his John Lennon–style glasses over his blue eyes, although this morning, they were a somber reflection of his face. His tall frame looked slim in a black suit and tone-on-tone black tie. His thick blond hair, which typically scraped the top of his shirt collar, was shorter but blonder, I assumed from his time spent in the Wyoming sun.

"Star..."

I held up my hand. I couldn't bear to hear his voice, not at this moment. I stepped outside and walked to his car, where Marcella and Aunt Georgina waited for us.

CHAPTER 4

I nstead of a wake at the local funeral parlor, the death announcement instructed everyone to congregate at St. Joseph's Church in Parke, where the parish priest would celebrate the funeral Mass. When we arrived, the size of the crowd gathered to see Jimmy off worried me. How was I going to find a killer in this ocean of potential suspects? Of course, most of them were probably onlookers, curious about the man who'd been brutally murdered. As soon as Georgina emerged from the car, a surge of people rushed over to her.

"I know you didn't do this! I hope they find the blighter soon!" said one of the women with an angry toss of her head toward O'Shea and Keenan, who stood at the edge of the crowd.

"Georgina, how are you, love?" said another woman who embraced Georgina with a hug.

I moved aside and watched as this sixty-two-year-old woman hugged each and every person back, a smile illuminating her brown eyes. She wore a long-sleeved black dress with a rainbow-colored scarf that highlighted her olive skin. I'd noted the scarf as soon as I sat in the car. Aunt Georgina's trademark scarves were usually tossed casually around her neck, left to trail behind her like an exclamation point. On that day, she wore the scarf wrapped around her neck like a cocoon. However, Aunt Georgina's smile faded when Jimmy's specter materialized out of the crowd and approached her.

"Georgina." Jimmy Mahoney's identical ringer extended his hand in greeting. "We finally meet."

"You must be Flann," Georgina replied, taking his hand firmly in hers. "I knew Jimmy had a twin brother. I'm sorry we have to meet under these circumstances."

The man perused the crowd and said in a booming voice, "I don't believe for one minute that you had anything to do with Jimmy's death. Now, please. You were a friend. A good friend," he said, emphasizing the word good. Then he gestured to a woman standing on the sidelines, who came forward. "Please join me and my sister, Deirdre, as we pray for Jimmy's soul." With that, he led the funeral procession into the church, Georgina in tow.

"I plan to sit at the back of the church," I said to Lorcan and Marcella.

"We'll join you," Lorcan agreed.

I appropriated a vacant pew that provided a decent view of everyone in the nave.

"Can you see Georgina?" Marcella asked as she slid in next to me.

"Yes," I replied, noticing that Lorcan hadn't followed us. I glanced back at the church doors, where he stood, speaking to the two Castlebar detectives. *Good*, I said to myself.

Lorcan is the heir to a fortune through real estate owner-ship, several large businesses, and numerous patents for his inventions. When I'd first met Thomas O'Shea, he'd remarked that Lorcan assisted the guards on many an occasion. And, as native Mayo men, they knew each other from the football field. I hoped Lorcan's relationship with the two men garnered helpful information that the police might not share with me.

A bell tinkled at the top of the church, a priest appeared,

and the funeral Mass began. From my vantage point, I noted the congregation's stoic expressions with the exception of one woman who sat across the aisle from the Mahoney siblings. In between dabbing her eyes, she shot angry glances at the brother and sister.

I leaned over to Marcella and whispered, "Do you know the woman sitting across from the Mahoneys?"

"No." Marcella shook her head.

I made a mental note to learn the woman's name. Georgina probably knew her.

The flickering altar candles and solemn tones lulled me into a memory of going to Our Lady of Angels church in the Bronx with my mother. She'd pause at the statue of the Blessed Virgin and light candles. As I got older, she'd let me hold the taper to the igniting flame.

"Go ahead, Star. Light three candles," she'd say.

When I questioned why three, she always replied, "For me, you, and the one who isn't here."

I never met my father. My mother never spoke about him. But I like to think the third candle was for him. My mother disappeared two days after my sixth birthday without a word, a note, or a goodbye. Abandoned. *That was what the police said!* But I didn't believe it then, and I was determined to prove it wasn't true.

The remainder of the ceremony ended with the blessing of the casket. I'd been to plenty of Masses in my life but never to a funeral service. My church-going days ended when my adoptive parents, the O'Briens, were killed in a Cessna plane crash two months after my eighteenth birthday. After my mother disappeared, I'd spent time in a series of foster homes until I ended up in a foster-to-adopt care situation with the O'Briens. They completed the official paperwork when I was ten. Crushed by the pain of their loss, feeling abandoned all over again, I'd opted for cremation. In life, they'd surrounded me with love; in death, I mourned them quietly, sustained by my memories of them.

As the friends and family members processed behind Jimmy's casket to exit the church, Aunt Georgina broke away from Jimmy's siblings to rejoin Lady Marcella and me. Lorcan stood nearby in what looked like a casual conversation with several people. When the church finally emptied, everyone walked behind the family and coffin to the cemetery, conveniently located across the street.

I used the opportunity to get a closer look at the female who'd cast the aggrieved glances across the aisle. She had moved closer to the top of the funeral procession. She stood right behind the Mahoney siblings. Like everyone else, she was dressed in black with no real distinguishing clothing feature. But one thing did stand out. She no longer cast angry glances at Flann and Deirdre. No, her eyes threw daggers directed at Aunt Georgina. From my vantage point where I had sat in the church, I'd misinterpreted the recipient of the woman's stares. *She'd been watching Georgina all along.*

"Do you know the woman standing behind the Mahoneys? The one with the blonde hair swept up into a French bun?" I asked Georgina.

Before Georgina could answer my question, Flann Mahoney stepped away from the graveside and blocked our view. Then he addressed the crowd, "Please, everyone, I invite you to join us at Jimmy's pub in Neale after the service. Let's all have a hot cuppa or a whiskey. We can sit and share our memories of him as he'd want us to do." Flann's words hung in the cold, damp air.

Georgina turned to Lorcan, who'd caught up with us, and said, "I think I'd rather go home."

"Oh, no, we're not," I replied for Lorcan. "We've got a murder to solve."

CHAPTER 5

J immy's place boasted one of the lengthiest names I'd ever
come across. The Old Forge Restaurant and Gibbons' Pub
perched on the edge of what local people called the old
Headford Road in the village of Neale. A church, the bar, and
its restaurant were the sole occupants of Neale's quarter stretch
between Ballinrobe and Cross. The traditional Irish thatched
roof topped the building. The pub's red doorway hung sand-
wiched between signs for Paddy's whiskey and Player's ciga-
rettes. I'd been to the pub the night before I found a dead body
in Cong. That evening, the place burst at the seams with musicians, their instruments, and a crush of people at the bar.

Currently, the smell of stale beer seeped from the carpeting
into the air. Three large platters filled with sandwiches sat atop
the bar. Mugs for tea, along with sugar and milk, kept vigil at
the other end of the counter where the bartender stood ready
to pour drinks. The server I'd met during my first visit greeted
each person as they stepped inside.

"You must be famished. Please help yourself to a bite to eat
and some tea," she said, pouring for people as they gathered a
mug and waited in line for the refreshment.

Georgina and Marcella sat at a table. Lorcan stood at the

bar, talking to some of the men who'd gathered for a pint. I headed for the server.

"I'll take two cups of tea for my aunt and her friend," I said.

"No problem, love," the server replied. "Where are you sitting?"

"Over there," I said, nodding toward Georgina and Marcella. "And then, I'd like to talk to you about Jimmy."

The server shot a closer look at me and then over to where I'd indicated. Her pouring hand developed a shake when her eyes focused on Georgina. Tea spilled on the floor. "Oh, look at the mess. I'll be right back," she said. Then she moved over to the bar, grabbed a towel, and whispered something into the bartender's ear. She didn't return. The bartender took her place.

"I know you," he said when he'd wiped up the tea and poured two mugs for me. "I've seen you here before. And I know your reputation for digging into things. There's no need for you to be asking questions about Jimmy, especially today of all days. Now, if I were you, I'd finish my tea and get out of here. We've had enough grief for one day."

I stood there, pondering how little time I had to find Jimmy's murderer. But I realized I wouldn't get any leeway with the staff on this day. I nodded and said what all Irish say at a wake, "I'm sorry for your trouble." When I returned to Georgina and Marcella, Flann Mahoney had joined them.

"Now, Georgina. You've been through a terrible ordeal. I'll be in touch after we get Jimmy's affairs settled."

"We should go," I said to Georgina. Then I addressed Flann. "Have the police any new information about what happened to Jimmy?"

"No, none at all. Arrah, they'll figure it out with time, I'm sure." Flann shrugged. "I haven't met you before, have I?"

"This is my late nephew's partner, Star O'Brien," Georgina

said. "She's in Ireland to settle his estate while searching for her mother."

"Is that so?" Flann replied. "Mothers are special people, aren't they?" Then, he squeezed Georgina's hand and tipped his head toward me. "Well, you'll both have to come to the homestead for a visit. I want to know all about this search of yours."

I nodded and said, "Georgina, if you're ready, I think we should head home. It has been an exhausting few days."

I approached Lorcan at the bar and said, "We're ready to leave."

"I'm ready when you are," he replied with a smile.

"Please drop me off before you take your mother and Georgina back to your place," I stated as Lorcan escorted the three of us out to his car.

"Right, you first," he replied.

The ride back to French Hill was silent. Watching the stone walls and green fields slide by, I thought about funerals and closure. The rituals brought families and friends together in mournful and joyous ways. But this was one case in which closure for Jimmy's family or Aunt Georgina wouldn't come until Jimmy's murderer was brought to justice.

I, too, needed closure. Not just for Aunt Georgina's sake but also for the losses in my life. I'd lost my adoptive parents, my lover, Dylan Hill, and my mother. My heart and soul would never rest until I solved my mother's disappearance. Some people thought I was obsessed, but I disagreed. I'd rather describe myself as a relentless pursuer of hope. My entire purpose in life grew from the police's handling of my mother's disappearance. I was for the lost, the missing, and the dead. Evelyn Cosgrove came to mind. I hoped she could provide tangible information concerning my mother. But first, tomorrow, I must turn my attention to clearing Georgina. She would not be another lost soul.

CHAPTER 6

The day after the funeral, I power walked a few miles more than usual. A soft mist sweetened the air with the earthy smell of rain. Ashford didn't seem to mind because he ran circles around me in a joyful puppy dance. A glimpse of the cottage through some barren tree limbs reminded me I still hadn't decided about selling Dylan's family home. I'd come to think of French Hill as a cozy nest. When Dylan and I committed to our relationship, we bought an old colonial in Ridgewood, New Jersey. We'd installed separate home offices during the remodeling—mine, which I called my tree house, perched on the top floor just below the treetops. When the leaves took control of my view in the spring, the ceiling-to-floor windows and a deck along the back side of the house gave the impression that we lived in a secluded jungle.

When Dylan died a year ago, and I learned he'd left me a cottage in Castlebar, County Mayo, I'd been hurt and angry. We'd known each other for six years and lived together for half that time. He never mentioned an Irish address. But Aunt Georgina and Lorcan had filled in the missing pieces about why Dylan kept this place secret. Dylan had kept Ireland out of our relationship for two reasons. One, before we ever met, he'd had an Irish lover, Caitlin May, who died tragically. Two, he worried about my obsession with finding my mother. He'd thought it wouldn't come to any good.

At first, I didn't give a damn about claiming the cottage. All I wanted to do was use this place as a temporary base while I searched for my missing mother. But I hadn't counted on meeting Aunt Georgina, Dylan's aunt. Or finding a dog. Or, most of all, the feeling of continuity I got from knowing this place belonged to Dylan's family. His cottage, now mine, represented something I didn't have—roots. I still mourned his loss, but I also felt deep in my heart a connection to him that made me feel quite at home when alone there at night, safe, secluded, and far from the worries of the world.

As soon as I changed out of my wet clothes, I dialed Aunt Georgina's cell phone.

"I'm on my way to you now." Her voice sounded strong. "Put the kettle on. I'm bringing breakfast."

When Georgina walked through the kitchen door, she seemed like a different person from the one I'd seen just a few days ago. She wore one of her silk, olive-green blouses over beige linen pants. A loosely tied scarf billowed behind her.

"Now, get out of the way while I put these few things together." She waved me toward one of the kitchen chairs while placing a shopping bag on a countertop. "I didn't have time to make brown bread, but I stopped at Mulroy's. This will do for now."

Within minutes, she'd heaped our plates with bacon, or rashers as they were called in Ireland, vegetarian beans, and sliced McCambridge brown bread. A bar of Kerry Gold butter waited on the oak table. While I loved Georgina's brown bread more than anything, I gladly accepted McCambridge as a substitute. Lyons brand tea bags for Georgina and peppermint for me brewed in our cups while we ate our meal.

"I can see you didn't lose your appetite while you were back in the States," Georgina commented as I spread blackberry jam on another slice of bread.

"Definitely not for an Irish breakfast," I replied. "So, what has you out so early? Does Marcella know you're here?"

"Yes. She's not happy, but I'm returning to my own bed later tonight. And back to The Golden Thread this morning. I'm not hiding out."

My pulse quickened at the thought of her walking around Castlebar when whoever murdered Jimmy might target Georgina next. "Are you sure that's a good idea? This thing is far from settled."

"I have a business to run, Star. Beth, my shop assistant, doesn't get paid if the place is closed. The garda will find the culprit."

Ashford's bark signaled someone's arrival. I looked up to see Lorcan about to knock at the back door. I waved him in.

"Georgina, you're out early. I think mom was still in bed when I left the house. But she'll be worried when she gets up and learns you're gone," Lorcan said.

"I left her a note. I'm sure she'll find it when she's up," Georgina replied.

"And how are you doing?" he asked while she rose and heaped food onto a plate for him.

"I'm fine. Now, you go ahead and eat. Star can catch you up on things. I've got to go."

"You stay right there," I ordered. "We still have some things to discuss before you run off to town." Then, I turned my attention to Lorcan. "What did you learn from the police?"

Lorcan nodded. "Right, well, first off, they believe Georgina is Jimmy's killer." Lorcan looked over at Georgina. "I'm sorry to say the guards claim to have evidence with your DNA."

"What?" The word barely escaped Georgina's lips.

"What kind of nonsense have they come up with this time? What kind of evidence?" I asked.

"They took a DNA sample when they searched her cottage. The results matched a blood stain on the shirt Jimmy was wearing," Lorcan explained.

I glared at Georgina. "You *gave them permission* to search your cottage?" I asked.

"I didn't murder anyone." Georgina tossed one end of the scarf behind her shoulder.

"I know that, but the police don't. And, as usual, they've taken the easy way out." I pressed on with my questions. "Georgina, you said someone was stalking you. Could they have gotten a sample of your blood?"

Aunt Georgina shook her head. "I honestly don't know. The person was around the shop, not the cottage."

"That you know of," I reminded her. "What makes you think someone was around the shop and not your cottage?"

"The back door at The Golden Thread had scratches around the lock. It looked like someone was trying to get the door open." Georgina sighed. "There were some scratches on the window as well. I had the locks changed right away."

"Do the current locks look like anyone's been messing with them?" I asked.

"No," Georgina replied. "Look, I didn't kill Jimmy. And I don't like that I'm disrupting your lives. And I don't like that the guards went through my personal items. That's all the more reason for me to go home—to keep them out of my affairs as much as possible."

"I understand the desire to maintain as much control as possible over your surroundings and belongings. But keeping you safe and proving your innocence takes priority over all else," I replied.

"And, I have a plan for my security," Georgina said.

"What is it?" I asked.

"The security guard at the Turlough Museum. He moonlights outside of his work hours. I've asked him to keep an eye on the cottage for me at night."

"What's his name?" I asked.

"Terrence O'Shaunessy," Georgina replied.

"I know him," Lorcan added. "He's reliable. I've employed him a few times when I needed security around one of my projects."

"Okay, but I want to meet him. And I'll drop Ashford off at the cottage later. He's a good watch dog. Can the security guard meet us at your place?" I asked Georgina.

"I've already invited him for supper this evening. I'll see you and Ashford there at half six this evening." With that, Georgina exited the cottage.

For a few minutes after she left, Lorcan and I sat in silence. Finally, glancing at the time on the kitchen clock, I made a decision that I hadn't expected ever to make. But if I were going to save Georgina from a guilty verdict in the near future, I had to ask for assistance.

"I need your help," I said. "I've got to identify who this numbers person and stalker are. I also need someone to work with the police. That should be you."

"My mother and I are all in on this. I've known Georgina since I was a kid. And I know Dylan wouldn't want me doing anything else right now."

"Good," I replied firmly. "I already have a list of people and places to visit. Let's go over it now." I wanted Lorcan to remember I was in charge.

Lorcan cleared the dishes from the table, and Ashford moved to the floor in front of the hearth while I went to get my Mead composition book. With the book open in front of us, I started the list, including the server and bartender at Jimmy's pub and the angry-looking woman at Jimmy's funeral. I also planned to visit the Turlough Museum, where Jimmy's body was found.

"Can you get more information from the police about the murder weapon?" I asked Lorcan.

He nodded. "I'll try. They know the killer used something round and heavy, but the exact weapon hasn't presented itself yet. With the abundance of media attention on this case, O'Shea doesn't want this to go the wrong way." Lorcan's smile reached his eyes. "He'll talk to me."

"Can your mother identify the woman I pointed out to her in the church? She was throwing eye daggers at Georgina during and after the service."

"Maeve told my mother she wants to help as well. I'll get both of them working on that."

I stopped jotting notes. "What's Maeve Baldwin got to do with anything?" I demanded. In addition to not liking the local historian, who'd been on my suspect list when I'd investigated what happened in Cong, I didn't trust her. She'd thrown me a red herring about the search for my mother. I still couldn't figure out why Maeve, a woman I'd never met before, had shown an interest in me. Marcella may believe in Maeve's good intentions, but I didn't.

"She's a friend of my mother, and she's gotten close to your aunt while you were away. Maeve lives in Cong and thus near Jimmy's pub. We need all the help we can get." Lorcan grew silent. The smile left his face. His eyes studied mine from across the table. "Look, Star, I'm as worried as you are. I'm also leery about getting involved in this investigation. But for once, I understand why you can't leave things in the hands of the authorities. Promise me that you'll keep me informed about what you're doing."

"Being the son of English aristocracy doesn't mean you can tell me what to do," I replied. I needed his help, and yes, I was attracted to him, but I didn't want to risk another love in my life. I just couldn't let my feelings show. "I can take care of myself. Now, let's get back to work on this catalog of potential suspects."

"Right," he replied, his eyes crinkling with the broadness of his smile.

Before long, we had a list that included the staff at the Turlough Museum. Maybe someone had seen Jimmy when he set out on the walking path.

"I'll check in with you this evening," Lorcan said. Then he left to bring his mother up to speed and pay a visit to the police.

Soon after Lorcan left, the rental agency came to pick up their car. With that settled, I tidied up the kitchen and sent an email to Ellie and Phillie, my office staff back in New Jersey. My company, The Consulting Detective, primarily researched lost birth certificates and marriage licenses. Sometimes, I was called upon to find missing information about property and financial accounts so a will could be finalized. My work was accomplished by spending long hours scouring through public records, microfiche, and obscure online databases.

My business began in my junior year of college when I tried to find my mother. After paying a company that made big promises but returned little more than her name and our address before my series of sojourns in foster homes, I started an information brokerage of my own.

Having access to data unintentionally placed me at the heart of a mystery more times than I'd like to count. Private detectives and attorneys contacted me regularly to research documents and data related to divorce, adoption, family reunions, and missing heirs to estates and wills. Sometimes, a family wanted to make discreet inquiries—not wanting the particular relative to know the family had initiated a search—about the status of a long-lost relative.

Isn't it ironic? There I was digging into other people's lives, figuring out their personalities, getting into the heads of the missing, thinking about what drove them away from their families, and I hadn't located my own mother.

Recently, I'd had more than my share of getting involved in people's deaths, especially since coming to Ireland. Aunt Georgina was partially to blame. I hadn't wanted to do anything more than continue searching for my mother while I put the cottage up for sale. But Georgina reminded me, often, that my mission in life was to help other people, especially those who didn't have a voice. She was right, of course. The O'Briens had instilled in me the Irish trait of leaving the world a better place as a result of being in it.

"You have more than others, Star, and as a result, you carry more responsibility," my adoptive parents had said more than once. That was why I became an information broker—to be a voice for the people who were disillusioned by a private investigator or the police.

I still hadn't found my mother, and the cottage hadn't been sold. Several months ago, I'd been forced to choose between a pressing business matter at home in Ridgewood, New Jersey, and getting to Achill Island, where I believed my mother was born. I'd chosen to return to New Jersey. Ellie and Phillie depended on me to keep The Consulting Detective running. But I was hopeful. On the day I left French Hill for the States, I'd gotten a call from the elusive Evelyn Cosgrove, who claimed she had information about a Maggie O'Malley. Evelyn refused to discuss the matter on the phone, insisting we meet in person and then refusing to set a specific appointment.

Meanwhile, thanks to Lorcan, I had a list of names gleaned from the National Archives to hunt down when I finally got out to Achill Island. If I'd learned anything from my life-long quest to find my mother, it was never to give up. I knew I'd find her. But then, I needed to be Aunt Georgina's voice in this race against time. I packed up my knapsack, locked the cottage door, and put a leash on Ashford. Together, we went in search of answers.

CHAPTER 7

I drove to the Round Tower in Turlough, where Georgina had witnessed Jimmy's nefarious actions. Two roads led out of Castlebar to Turlough village. The N5, a national primary highway, connected most of Mayo to Dublin. The secondary road, referred to as the Old Turlough Road probably because it predated the N5, meandered and twisted along a series of fields, stone fences, villages, and parishes with names like Drumask and Ballynew.

I chose the old road because Aunt Georgina's cottage rested at its edge along a bend. I didn't stop but eyeballed as I drove by the place for suspicious-looking activity. Satisfied that the media had finally decamped, I continued to the Round Tower. Worried about attracting attention, I drove past the tower and parked along a byroad that connected Turlough to Parke. Then, Ashford and I walked to the hillside graveyard that surrounded the tower base.

Turlough's round tower hovered over the remains of what was believed to be the first church founded by St. Patrick. Sunken graves and crumbled headstones in the oldest part of the cemetery formed a labyrinthine warren of potholes. As a result of centuries of wind, rain, and sun, many of the grave markers no longer bore testimony to those souls the stones were meant to remember. Instead, tufts of wild onion grass waved in the wind, standing as silent sentries over the bones and dust of those who rested there.

The tower and others like it throughout Ireland bore testament to a time when they served as bell houses of churches. Other uses included watchtowers and places to hide people or valuables such as relics and manuscripts. And if you're wondering how I knew all this, it was because of the researcher in me. I was an information junkie.

Before I pushed through the rusted and bent turnstile gate, which squeaked like it must have been at least a hundred years old, I scanned the grid outline posted on a wooden board and pinpointed the section where Aunt Georgina's family was buried. I headed in that direction. After a few minutes, I sighted the pot of red geraniums at the base of a large headstone inscribed with the Hill name.

I paused at the spot for a few minutes, remembering that this couple was Dylan's grandparents. I knew from Georgina that he spent most of his growing-up years at the cottage in French Hill with his grandmother. But he'd chosen not to share this part of his life with me. In the last few months, I'd even come to accept his decision. But still. Didn't he think I'd have understood if he'd allowed me a glimpse into his losses and pain?

"You're deep in thought," a man's voice behind me said.

Surprised that I hadn't heard the gate, I turned to find Flann Mahoney. I had to admit that seeing the dead man's identical twin brother in a decrepit cemetery punched up my adrenaline. For a minute, I questioned whether Georgina had really seen Jimmy, or could the man in the cemetery have been Flann? *No.* Jimmy had admitted his guilt to Georgina.

On closer examination, I realized the facial similarities were all the brothers seemed to have in common. One of the last times I'd seen Jimmy, his pant cuffs and shoes sported red paint from some handiwork he'd been doing at his pub. Flann's immaculately clean and buffed nails indicated he did little to get his hands dirty. And the way he'd commanded the crowd at the funeral emphasized his standing and authority in the community. Jimmy, in contrast, had seemed to shy away from the limelight.

"I'm looking into what was probably the reason for Jimmy's murder. This seemed like a logical place to start," I replied. I didn't see any reason not to talk about Georgina's claims. I assumed the police had questioned Jimmy's family about his legal and illegal business dealings. "Is there a burial today?" I asked, looking around at the surrounding plots, wondering what Flann was doing there.

"Oh, no, no. There are no more burials here. Not for years. It's a shame, really. Too bad Jimmy had to be interred in the new cemetery, away from our parents." He paused to sweep his hands through his hair. His eyes shifted to gaze out over the fields below. "I guess I'm like Georgina in some ways."

"Oh, what ways are those?" I asked. I wouldn't have described Georgina as like anyone else.

"You know, keeping to the old traditions. My parents are buried here," he said, nodding to a well-kept plot not far from the Hill gravesite. "I visit occasionally. Now, enough about graves. How are you doing? Have you made progress in the search for your mother?"

"I have a few leads. Once I've cleared up Georgina's situation, I'll pursue them." Then I asked the questions I hadn't brought up at the funeral. "Did you know about Jimmy's involvement in a numbers scheme?"

Flann shook his head in denial. "But Jimmy did have a bad streak. I'll say that much. He always operated close to the edge when it came to his business dealings." Flann sighed. "He'd been complaining about his staff recently. I wouldn't trust them as far as I could throw them. But I'll get that straightened out soon enough."

"Do you think one of the staff could have killed Jimmy?" I didn't share that they were on my list of potential suspects. I remembered how secretive Jimmy had been about his business dealings when he and Georgina were an item. He'd been a secret partner in Jane Doherty's yoga fitness studio—information he'd kept from Georgina. Who knew what else he'd been involved in and the staff's connection, if any, to his schemes?

"Why would anyone risk their neck for a pittance like that? No, lass. Jimmy was probably into bigger things. Someone or something got the best of him. Ah, well, the garda will figure it out, I'm sure." His gaze settled on the road beside the cemetery. "Where is your car? I'll walk you to it."

"Thank you, but I'm fine. And, I have a canine friend with me," I said, glancing at Ashford, who suddenly appeared from around the other side of the tower.

"He doesn't look like much of a friend," Flann said, pointing at Ashford's pulled-back ears. "I guess you smell my cats, don't you, fella?" Flann continued, "Dogs and I are not compatible." Flann glanced at his wristwatch. "I have to get going, but it was good speaking with you, Miss O'Brien. Careful where you're walking. This place is full of hollows; many a person has tripped and broken an ankle."

I remained where I was until I saw him leave the grounds, climb into a Jeep, and drive away. Then I turned my attention to the tower's base. I examined every inch of the fieldstone without finding any loose blocks. I also didn't notice any spots with recent-looking mortar. Had someone tried to cover up the evidence? If so, they had done a good job of hiding their handiwork. I looked up at the tower's conical cap, enjoying, for a moment, the solitude. I imagined the sound of the bells ringing through the fields, calling the monks to prayer and currently spurring me to action.

From the tower's vantage point, overlooking the museum property, I watched several tour buses arrive. Visitors strolled on a path around the artificial, ornamental lake. A gardener turned over the earth around a greenhouse that occupied a section of the lawn in front of the manor house. From a distance, Turlough Park looked idyllic rather than the scene of a gruesome murder.

Calling Ashford to my side, I walked back to the car and drove the short distance down the hill back to Old Turlough Road. Then, I turned at the gates that opened onto the grounds of the National Museum of Ireland—Country Life. The next stop on my suspect list.

CHAPTER 8

Maneuvering along the narrow drive to the parking lot, I took in the magnificence that Turlough Park encompassed—the tower, the original landscaped Victorian gardens, the lake, and the greenhouse. Several of the park's buildings represented different historical periods and economic realities in Irish history. Now called Turlough Park House, the Fitzgerald House, built in 1865 by the Fitzgerald family, with its adjourning courtyards, stood front and center. A modern café and gift shop annexed to the house. Across and to the rear of the manor house's side entrance was the modern exhibition hall, where examples and artifacts of Ireland's rural life were on view. And where, according to what Georgina had told me, Jimmy's body had been posed in an exhibition area depicting rural craftspeople.

I began my museum visit there. The guard at the gallery entrance smiled as I strode toward him. I guessed his age to be somewhere in his fifties. He seemed in good shape. His shoulders broadened over his chest, and when he stood, he loomed over my five-foot-eight inches by about four. His name badge identified him as Terrence O'Shaunessy, the person Georgina had mentioned earlier.

"Good afternoon," he said. "Would you mind signing the guest book, please?"

I picked up the desk pen and said, "Sure, no problem. I'm surprised the museum is open to visitors. I heard someone found a body here not too long ago. What happened? Was it a heart attack?" I didn't reveal my connection to Georgina. This would be my only opportunity to check him out before we met formally that evening at Georgina's cottage.

O'Shaunessy's eyes surveyed the empty lobby. Then he leaned forward and lowered his voice to a whisper. "Unfortunately, the gentleman was the victim of a horrific crime."

"Is that so? Who found him?"

"I did. He gave me quite the fright, you know. Especially at that time of the morning." O'Shaunessy compressed his lips into a thin line before continuing, "You see, I open up and usually walk through the whole place, all four floors. You know, just to check for any critters or birds that might have gotten in. But I never expected to find Jimmy Mahoney. And him deader than the statues in the exhibits."

"I guess the police arrived quickly when you called them," I said, trying to elicit as much information as I could.

"Grainne Canny, the museum director, came along just as I spotted the body. She was checking on a new exhibit scheduled to open that day. Thank goodness. She went to call while I stayed with the deceased."

"Which one of the exhibits?" I asked.

"The one depicting the tradespeople of rural Ireland. Specifically, the exhibit with the figure of the postmistress." O'Shaunessy shook his head. "Now, that's a puzzle. Why would someone put him there?"

"You mentioned the victim's name. Did you know him?"

"Aye, his sister runs the museum café. In fact, I just saw him the night before going into the café. Probably for the event his sister was hosting." O'Shaunessy shrugged. "Arrah, I know the entire family. A nice bunch. Been living here for years. Their parents before them as well."

A rush of wind stirred the papers on O'Shaunessy's desk when a group of people pulled open the heavy glass doors and entered the lobby. He picked up a floor plan map and handed it to me. Then, he greeted the newcomers.

My gut told me O'Shaunessy was capable and would do as an extra set of eyes on Georgina's cottage, especially at night. With my concerns put to rest, I folded the map and placed it into the pocket of my capri pants. I'd been to the museum several times before, and each time, I'd come away with increased respect for my ancestors' way of life. I'd even spent a few afternoons sitting in one of the cozy nooks by a window, reading about Achill Island, the place where my mother might have come from.

On this day, I explored the building with a different focus. I located the exit doors and walked in and out of the bathrooms, searching for any clue why someone murdered Jimmy on the walking path and then draped his body in one of the display areas. I ended up in the trades and crafts section, which included the postmistress exhibit. Why here? What was the killer's message? Questions I'd have to sift through with little time to do so. I took a picture of the tableau and emailed it to Phillie back at The Consulting Detective with a note to find out as much as possible about the exhibit. Then I left the building and made my way to the café.

Rooster's Café, the modern annexation to the eighteenth-century Turlough House, featured a gift shop and two dining rooms. I breezed through the gift shop to the restaurant. I wanted to know more about Deirdre Mahoney and her relationship with her deceased brother. And whether or not she had access to the exhibit building.

I chose a table in the farthest corner, plunked my knapsack down to hold the space, and went to order food. When the staff behind the counter offered to bring the brown bread, butter, and pot of hot water to my table, I agreed. In the meanwhile, I perused the café's clientele and staff. Judging from their sneakers and cameras hanging from straps around their necks, I assumed most of the people at the tables were tourists.

A few minutes after I'd settled in, a group of individuals wearing identification badges and uniforms indicating the museum's name entered and walked by my table. Geez, my potential suspect list seemed to grow exponentially. I wondered how many had keys to the building during the off-hours. Following behind the staff, a female with the name Grainne Canny on her ID marched in briskly despite leaning on a cane. I wanted to speak with her at some point, but I'd decided to begin with Jimmy's sister.

The tourist crowd thinned out and Jimmy's sister, Deirdre, entered the dining room through a door from the kitchen. She hadn't seemed broken up about Jimmy at the funeral. Neither had she interacted much with anyone, leaving Flann to do the talking. Smaller in stature, Deirdre bore a slight resemblance to her brothers.

Looking around the room at the empty tables strewn with the dirty plates, cups, and napkins, Deirdre's eyes narrowed, and she slammed open the door to the kitchen. "Alisha, what are you doing? Clean these tables. Now."

A young server scurried through the kitchen door, cloth in hand. She quickly veered away from Deirdre and set to restoring the café's cleanliness. Deirdre walked over to the cash register, opened the drawer, and checked the receipts.

After rising from my seat, I approached her. The look she gave me wasn't much different than the glances she'd thrown at the server. "Yes, may I help you?"

"I'm Star O'Brien," I said, offering my hand in greeting. "I was at your brother's funeral with my aunt, Georgina Hill."

Deirdre glanced at her hands, wiped them on her apron,

and said, "Sorry, but I've been working in the kitchen and garden all morning. It's best not to shake right now." Her eyes, however, looked me over from head to toe. "Yeah, I remember seeing you at the church and then the pub. There's no need to offer condolences again."

I noticed a pile of register receipts on the counter and a spreadsheet with columns highlighted in red and black. Deirdre's eyes followed mine. She reached for the paperwork and turned it over.

"Was there a problem with your tea?" she asked.

"No. I have a few questions about Jimmy, though, and what happened the night he died."

"Really, is that what this is about?" Deirdre moved from behind the register and turned as if to exit through a second door, which seemed to lead back into the kitchen. But the museum crowd rose from their table and approached the register. Not able to escape, Deirdre cashed them out. I moved to the space between her and the door.

"I won't take much of your time," I stated.

"Who are you? And what do you have to do with that cursed brother of mine?" Deirdre asked.

"I'm acting on my aunt's behalf," I said, handing one of my consulting detective business cards to her. She promptly shoved it into an apron pocket. "I'm trying to understand Jimmy's movements the night he was murdered. In my line of work, I've found the police often focus on circumstantial evidence and not much else. I disagree with their conclusions about my aunt."

"You're not local, are you?" Deirdre asked.

"No, and I'm not a private investigator. You don't have to worry about anything you might tell me." Her shoulders relaxed when she heard my response, so I continued, "Did you see Jimmy here at the museum or café the night he died?"

"Sorry, but no, I didn't."

"Was it a busy night in the café? Could he have come in with someone, and you didn't notice?" I asked.

"The museum rented the café for a special event that night. I wasn't here, and I would have no idea if Jimmy attended." Her jaw clenched with a violent shake of her head.

"You don't seem especially shaken up by his death. Were you aware that he was into some kind of shadow lottery business?"

Her eyes shifted to the cash register. "Yeah, the guards told us about your aunt's claim. I don't know anything about it. But I'm not surprised. Bad cess to him anyway. I'm glad he's gone." Her gaze turned back to me. "I'm sorry. I didn't mean to say that. I'm just tired and have so much to do. I don't think I can help you." Deirdre jumped and almost collided with me when the kitchen door behind us sprang open. The young server who'd tidied up the tables appeared.

"Haven't I told you not to come up on me like that?" Deirdre's face flushed red.

"Sorry," the server replied. "It's just that Mrs. Flynn called. She wants the recipe for the lemon cream cheese carrot cake you served the other night."

Deirdre glanced at me as if to gauge my reaction to the server's statement. I remained silent. Finally, Deirdre's face relaxed into a smile. "Oh, goodness. Sorry, you'll have to excuse me, Miss O'Brien. I have work to do." Then, she moved around me and through the doorway, which had just scared the living daylights out of her.

What was that all about? And, why had she said she wasn't at the café when it was apparent she had been, at least at some point?

CHAPTER 9

I let myself out of the café through a door that opened onto
the courtyard. Deirdre may not want to admit she'd seen
Jimmy the night he was murdered, but there must be other staff
who could corroborate O'Shaunessy's statement. I set out
around the café building to explore the manicured lawns. I
intended to speak with the gardener I'd seen earlier from my
perch at the round tower.

Two greenhouses graced the museum's grounds. One, quite
small, sat alongside the outer wall of the café's courtyard.
Clumps of chives, basil, and marjoram occupied the tiny glass
house. A wheelbarrow, filled with tools and fresh potting soil,
provided a clue that the herbs and flowering plants were grown
for use in the kitchen. I opened the iron gate that led to a
narrow walkway adjacent to the glass structure. A few Aster
plants lined the cement path, but the beds mostly looked
forlorn and forgotten. I strode to the far end. Another gate led
to a rise of land occupied by several massive beech trees and a
thatched cottage replica. There, the landscape was wetter,
cooler, and darker. I imagined that someone could have
brought Jimmy's body back to the museum from this side of the
estate. But then, the terrain would have made it much more

difficult to get over to the exhibit gallery, especially with the ill-fated night's heavy rain.

I continued across the lawn to the Victorian Conservatory, the focal point of the gardens. Finding the main entry door unlocked, I stepped inside and examined the well-tended greenery and flowers. Back at the front of the building again, I gazed through the glass panes across the lawn at the Victorian Gothic Fitzgerald manor house.

"May I help you?" a male voice asked quietly.

I turned to the tall, blond-haired, slightly balding man. His hands held a bunch of cut Margarites. A Carhartt vest topped his khaki pants and flannel shirt. From my observation point up at the round tower, I had not been able to make out the face of the person mowing the grass. But the cuttings on his work boots and the dirt under his fingernails indicated he was the museum's gardener.

"I've interrupted your gardening," I stated amicably.

He gently laid the flowers atop a stone sundial. He removed his glasses and studiously cleaned them with a fresh tissue he pulled from his vest pocket. "Oh, I'm just taking these up to Deirdre in the café," he said, pushing the thick-lensed glasses back onto his face. "I'm sorry. I must have left the door unlatched. Tourists usually aren't allowed in here. Maybe we should step outside."

"The landscape is beautiful," I commented after he locked the greenhouse door behind us. "It must take quite a few gardeners to keep up with all this."

"Oh, no. I tend all of it." He smiled sheepishly. His eyes lit up as he surveyed the immense lawns and flower paths bordering the center lawn where we stood.

"I'm Star O'Brien, by the way." I offered my hand to him, but he didn't respond in kind.

"I'm Willem Block, master gardener," he replied. "I saw you in the café, speaking with Deirdre. We don't usually interact much with tourists. So, unless there's a gardening question, I must continue with my work for the day."

"I'm not here as a tourist. I'm here on behalf of my aunt, Georgina Hill. She was a friend of Jimmy Mahoney's, and unfortunately, the police believe she had something to do with his death."

Willem removed his glasses again and pulled another tissue from one of the pockets of his khaki pants. "And you were asking Deirdre about this?" His voice carried a questioning tone as if puzzled that Deirdre would be involved.

"Jimmy was here the night he was killed. It's only natural to ask Deirdre if she saw any shady-looking characters."

Willem's eyes squinted at me behind the glasses he'd restored to his face as if seeing me for the first time. "Yes, he was here but left soon after he talked to a few of the guests. Deirdre would have been too busy to take any notice." Willem's gaze turned to the café building. When he spoke again, he waved his hand toward the greenhouse. "It's sad what happened, especially that it happened so close to the museum. I heard he was mixed up in some bad things. Maybe they came back to bite him. But I don't think Deirdre would have anything to do with that. I have to get back to work. Don't worry, Miss O'Brien. I'm sure the guards will get their man or woman."

Willem pivoted toward the greenhouse and walked to the door with a slight drag to one of his legs. That was when I noticed one of his boot heels was higher than the other.

Willem's comments confirmed O'Shaunessy's observation that Jimmy had been at the café the night he was murdered. Maybe Deirdre was lying, or maybe not. I understood why a successful caterer might not want to get wrapped up in a murder investigation. But, in this case, the murder victim was her brother.

I decided the best path was to follow the money. As Willem

said, Jimmy's involvement in a money-running scheme might have bitten him in the butt or, to be exact, gotten his head bashed in. There was something else interesting that may or may not have factored into Jimmy's actions. O'Shaunessy said Jimmy's family, including Jimmy, were from Turlough. But Aunt Georgina had told me Jimmy lived in the Cong area, close to his pub in Neale.

The rosy-hued western sky reminded me I had better get moving. I wanted to get to French Hill cottage and pack up some of Ashford's food before heading over to Georgina's. I wanted to be there when O'Shaunessy arrived.

Before leaving Turlough village, I stopped at the Turlough Inn, situated about a quarter-mile from the entry gates to the museum grounds. The bartender, whose name tag identified him as "Owen," was in his sixties, tall, with hazel eyes. When I approached the counter, he was wiping down the bar and setting up glasses for the evening crowd. The inn was empty.

"What can I do you for?" Owen asked.

"Hi, I'm Star O'Brien," I said, handing a consulting detective business card to him.

He flipped the card over and threw it into a bowl brimming with other cards.

"I'm investigating Jimmy Mahoney's murder."

Owen's eyes widened. He glanced at the bowl of cards. "Were you hired by the family?" he asked.

"No. My aunt, Georgina Hill, is a suspect. I'm looking into what happened the night he was killed. Were you working that night?" I asked.

He stopped wiping the countertop and looked toward the door of the pub. "Well, I must have been. I'm the owner. I'm here every night."

"Did you know Jimmy?" I asked.

"Yeah, I knew him. He was an okay sort. Used to stop in once in a while for a pint." Owen paused to scratch his face. "I don't think I can tell you much about him, though, if that's what you're getting at."

"Did he stop in the night he was killed?"

Owen dropped his bar towel into a bucket behind the counter and wiped one of his hands over his mouth. "If he did, I didn't see him. There was an event over at the museum that evening. He might have been there. But beyond what I've already said, I can't offer much more."

"Do you remember what you talked about whenever he'd stop in?"

"Just some of the usual things that pub owners complain about. The price of supplies and such."

"Did he seem troubled about anything?" I asked.

"I don't remember anything in particular. Just the usual chit-chat."

"Any ideas about who might have killed him?" I asked.

"No. I'm sorry to hear about your aunt, though. She's a nice woman."

"You know my aunt?" I asked. His answer surprised me. I didn't think Georgina spent much time in pubs. Her dress shop, The Golden Thread, took up most of her time. When she wasn't working on a design for someone, she was organizing a fundraising event with Lady Marcella.

"I go to my share of galas. I've seen her around. Now, if you don't mind, the evening crowd will be here soon. I want to finish getting things in order."

"Well," I said, "thank you for your time. If you think of anything else, please call me. You have my card." I placed another one of my cards on the bar top.

"Sure, if I think of anything," he said.

~

ASHFORD, STILL CURLED UP ON THE BACK SEAT OF THE CAR WHERE
I'd left him earlier, barely lifted his head when I began the drive
back to French Hill. Until the police caught the real killer, I'd
feel better with him in residence at Georgina's. During the
drive home, I felt restless about the background information I'd
gathered so far. Based on what the groundskeeper and
O'Shaunessy had told me, Jimmy was at the museum the night
he was killed. Okay, so his sister said she didn't see him. That
made sense when you were the proprietor of a café, and there
were lots of people milling around the place. But why was she
so jumpy? Did it have to do with Jimmy or something else?
Other than what I'd learned so far, I didn't have much to come
up with any conclusions about the numbers-running scheme
Jimmy was involved in and whom he had bumped into along
the walking path.

~

THE TEN-MILE DRIVE TO FRENCH HILL AND THE GLIMPSE OF THE
setting sun over Croagh Patrick mountain in the distance
settled my nerves. As I drove the narrow byroad, which split off
from the Breaffy Road to the cottage, I anticipated the
surrounding sanctuary of the grounds. The hazelwood and ash
trees created a portal into the garden. I could see Aunt
Georgina's hand in the sweet Williams, day lilies, and geraniums blooming in every corner. Sometimes I felt as if I'd been
transported to some secret Celtic oasis when I returned to the
cottage. But at the moment, I didn't have much time to enjoy
the welcome breeze and the rose-scented perfume from the
bushes that grew on the lawn side of the cottage's wall. I had
work to do. So, I packed up Ashford's food and bedding and we
headed to Aunt Georgina's place.

CHAPTER 10

W hen I arrived inside the walled perimeter around her cottage, Georgina's blue Toyota Avensis was parked in the driveway. No other cars were there yet, which meant we could have a private conversation before anyone showed up. As soon as I opened my driver's side door, Ashford jumped out, heading directly to the cottage's green entrance. The door burst open, and Georgina scooted him inside. I followed behind into her open-space living room and country kitchen.

"You're just in time," she said, pointing toward the massive oak table in the kitchen. "Take a seat, and I'll put the kettle on." She moved toward the Aga cooker, which sat on the side of the cottage's original open hearth. The cooker produced the most delicious homemade Irish brown bread loaves I had ever tasted. Tonight, the smell of apples permeated the air.

"I've missed your brown bread," I said, anticipating the slices and homemade jam Georgina usually placed onto the middle of the table.

"Well, I'll send some home with you later. But since we're about to have company, I've made a few apple tarts for the guests. Pour the water into the tea mugs, Star."

I did as I was told and then watched while Georgina

extracted several oven-proof plates from the Aga. She cut two slices from one of the plates and poured cream from a crockery pitcher over the slices. We didn't speak again until we'd cleaned our plates.

"That was delicious. Thank you," I said and turned the conversation to something I wanted desperately to know before company arrived. "Margaret Hanlon, the woman who told Bridgett Sumner the story about a house fire and an orphaned child. You got to Achill Island and spoke to Hanlon?"

Georgina nodded. "It took some time to track her down, but yes, I finally met her. She verified what Bridgett Sumner told you, loveen. The story is true."

"Yeah, Bridgett's phone call surprised me, but she was so grateful for my help with solving what happened to her brother, Matthew, on Clare Island that she wanted me to know about Hanlon's house fire story and a lone female survivor. So, Bridgett's lead paid off?"

"Somewhat. The house fire killed everyone in the family, with the exception of the youngest child, a daughter. Her name was Margarite, like your mam's." Georgina's eyes widened as she continued her story. "Jesus, Mary, and Saint Joseph, I can't imagine the horror. They say the burning rafters fell onto the beds. How the wee one managed to crawl out is a miracle."

Whether or not the surviving child turned out to be my mother, I felt a pang of sorrow for how devastating it must have been for the child when she learned she was orphaned.

"How did it happen?" I asked.

Georgina tilted her head at the Aga cooker and thatched roof overhead. "The open fire hearths and the thatch. House fires were prevalent at one time."

I shuffled my feet, ready to take action. "What happened to the child? And how does Margaret Hanlon figure into the story?"

"Apparently, Mrs. Hanlon has lived on the island her entire

life. She was a teenager at the time. It's not something you forget."

"Did Hanlon know the girl or any of the family?" I asked.

Georgina shook her head. "I don't think so. Hanlon said a local family raised the girl until she became a teenager. Then, she just disappeared. Hanlon thought the teen might have gone to America. But Hanlon didn't recall ever hearing anything about the girl since."

"And the family who took her in? Did you speak to them?" I anxiously waited for Georgina's answer.

"According to Hanlon, they are long gone. Deceased. I asked around, but no one knew anything more. Although, you won't like what I have to say, Star. She was taken in by an O'Malley family."

I grasped the cell phone anchored to my capri pants to hide my frustration and anger. I couldn't take one more lead to someone with an O'Malley name.

"I'm sorry, agra. This might be a dead end. But you can't give up hope. Something will turn up." Georgina spoke softly as if even she didn't believe her own words.

"No need to be sorry. I have the names I identified when I was in the National Archive. I'll go out to the island myself and speak with Mrs. Hanlon and look for the others as soon as I can."

I'd spoken with Georgina several times after I returned to the States. But I hadn't mentioned the call I received from Evelyn Cosgrove before I left French Hill following the resolution of Jane Doherty's murder and the mysterious events in the Cong area. Then, seeing the shadows under Georgina's eyes, I decided this might be as good a time as any. Maybe my news would give her something to focus on other than this mess with the police and Jimmy's murder.

"I spoke with Evelyn Cosgrove."

"What! When were you going to tell me?" The smile on Georgina's face reached her eyes.

"How could I? We've got this mess with Jimmy Mahoney to untangle. I didn't want to seem selfish," I said.

"This is the best news I've heard in days. What did she say?" Georgina moved away from the table and put the kettle back on.

"Not much, Georgina. She refused to tell me where she is. But she did agree to meet me at a time and place of her choosing." I played around with the cell phone, which now lay on the table.

Georgina plunked a fresh tea bag into each of our cups, covered them with the boiled water, and sat back down at the table. "I thought the stalking issue was cleared up when Jane Doherty's murder was resolved."

"I did too. But Evelyn Cosgrove is afraid of something or someone, and I don't know which. Or maybe she just likes creating drama."

I didn't know much about the woman, other than she'd posted in an adoption thread six months ago looking for a Margaret O'Malley from Achill. Phillie had unearthed more information about Evelyn, including the news that Cosgrove was her married name, and O'Malley was her maiden name. And her husband had mysteriously disappeared while Evelyn was on a dig in England. I might have given up trying to find her, but then she'd called me. Why contact someone and then refuse to talk on the phone? Why all the mystery? Something wasn't right.

"I can't say that I blame her for being scared," Georgina said. "After all the shenanigans and murders in Cong, I'd be cautious too. When and where are you supposed to meet her?"

"That's just it. She said she'd be in touch and hung up."

"Then why, in heaven's name, did she even call you?" Georgina shook her head.

Before I could answer, the doorbell rang, and Ashford rushed toward the front entry. Georgina moved into the living room and pulled back a curtain to check out who was there.

"I'm glad to see you're being cautious," I stated.

"Lorcan's here," Georgina replied, unlocking the door.

Lorcan bent to rub Ashford's ears and walked into the kitchen. He sat down at the table next to me and smiled. "Star," he said. Then he proceeded to cut a large slice of apple tart onto one of the plates stacked on the table.

"Would you like some cream?" Georgina asked.

"No, I'm fine as is," Lorcan replied. "And what about you, Star? Have you tried Georgina's tart?"

Lorcan. The man was exasperating. He must have realized I was waiting to hear what he'd learned from the police about Jimmy's murder. Impatient for action, I rose and leaned against one of the kitchen counters.

"What do O'Shea and Keenan have to say about the investigation?" I asked. I didn't expect to learn much. As usual, the police were fixated on the wrong target.

"They haven't found the murder weapon yet. But from what the coroner told them, O'Shea believes it was something like a hammer." Lorcan paused to look at Georgina, whose face had blanched.

"What kind of hammer?" I asked. The police would have to come up with something more if they were going to find the murder weapon.

"The impressions on Jimmy's head indicated something round and heavy but not too big. They've ruled out claw. And, because of the size of the holes in his head, they've also ruled out sledge."

"That leaves what? Ball-peen or mallet?" I sat back down at the table and held Lorcan's eyes with mine. "They can't still think Georgina would be able to attack or kill someone in such a violent manner and then move the body."

"Star, O'Shea promised me he's looking at this case from all angles. He's got an open mind. They are searching all along the walking path and the exhibit building for the weapon. They will find it and the person whose fingerprints are on it."

"Yeah," I replied. "In the meanwhile, we can't leave this all with the police."

"I told O'Shea as much. He didn't like what I had to say. Told me to stay out of his way."

Bang! The unexpected crash from outside triggered Ashford's barks, which reverberated throughout the cottage. He ran toward the door, paws clawing at the wood. I jumped from my seat. "Stay put," I yelled to Georgina. Lorcan reached the door first. He whipped it open. I stationed myself alongside him. Ashford growled, rushed past us, and ran toward the cottage gate.

O'Shaunessy, hands raised midair, stepped back when he recognized me. "You. I thought you were a tourist. Where's Georgina? Is she okay?"

"What's that on your shirt?" I asked. The red splatter matched the stain that dripped down the cottage door.

"I don't know," O'Shaunessy replied. "I was about to knock when something was hurled at me."

"Stay with Georgina," I said to Lorcan. Then I ran down the driveway toward Ashford, who stood at the gate, uttering throaty growls. I opened the gate and ran out into the middle of the road. A vehicle's brake lights disappeared in the direction of Castlebar. Since it was too dark to see anything specific, I returned to the cottage where Lorcan and O'Shaunessy stood in the kitchen. Ashford followed me. O'Shaunessy daubed the front of his shirt with a damp cloth.

"It looks like beet juice," I said, grabbing a napkin and wiping some of the liquid from my finger. "Did you see anyone?"

O'Shaunessy's face paled when he noticed me staring at

him. He turned to Lorcan and said, "I'm not sure about this project, Lorcan. This isn't what I usually do, you know. Guarding someone who might be in serious trouble."

"Terrence, why don't you sit down, and I'll put the kettle on," Georgina said, indicating a chair at the table. "You look like you could use some sustenance."

"The guards are involved, and so are we," Lorcan said. He gestured to Ashford. "The border collie is an excellent watchdog. But if you're worried, I can...."

"No," O'Shaunessy interrupted Lorcan. "You are probably right. I don't like being lied to, though," O'Shaunessy said, returning my stare. "I thought you were a tourist."

"And I thought it best not to reveal who I was when we met at the museum," I replied. "Do you have a problem with me?"

O'Shaunessy moved over to the table where Georgina had placed a mug of tea and some ham sandwiches. "I'm taking a big chance here, and it's only fitting that I'm in on the game. That's all."

"Good." I nodded. "I expect you to keep your word."

"And, if I may, don't tell Grainne, the museum director, that I'm working with ye," O'Shaunessy said, in between bites of his sandwich. "She'll be madder than a wet hen. Doesn't want anyone or anything, for that matter, interfering with the museum. Runs the place like a general."

"Don't worry, as you've already discovered, I can be discreet," I said without moving a muscle on my face.

"I'll review Terrence's schedule with him, Star," Lorcan said.

"Are you okay with all this?" I looked to Georgina, who'd said little in the last few minutes.

"Of course, I am. I've nothing to be afraid of. And, I have known Terrence for ages. We'll get along just fine. Not to worry, Star."

"Okay, I'll call you in the morning. In the meanwhile, I think you should keep Ashford with you at all times."

Lorcan rose, walked me to the door, and stepped outside. "I'm going to call O'Shea and tell him about the beet juice. The vandalism may just be a childish prank, but it's best to report it."

"I hope so," I replied. I didn't want to scare Georgina, but Ashford and a rent-a-cop did little to alleviate my worries.

CHAPTER 11

I eased my foot from the accelerator when I turned from
Breaffy Road onto Cottage Road. The moonless night and
wet roads from an earlier shower reinforced my decision to
slow my speed. Cottage Road should really be called a lane
because it would be impossible for two cars facing opposing
directions to pass each other simultaneously. One car must pull
over and allow the other to go.

At first, I didn't pay too much attention to the lights in my
rear-view mirror. But then, the bright lights flashed. I ignored
them. I wasn't about to accelerate just to satisfy someone's
desire to speed through the lane. Then the other vehicle's
headlights loomed bigger, blinding me. I tilted the rear-view
mirror to keep the glare out of my eyes. The pursuing car's horn
blasted. And then, the car appeared alongside mine. I glanced
through the window at the other driver but couldn't see
anything. My hands clenched the steering wheel as I tried to
remain on the road. The honking blasts continued. Then, the
car swerved into mine, pushing me farther into the verge. The
vehicle kept advancing like a streak of light. I couldn't do
anything else. I yanked my wheel to the right, avoiding a collision. But not the ditch. My car lurched to a stop. I stared at the

other vehicle's back lights as they disappeared along the road toward French Hill.

Thankful for my seatbelt, I released it and stepped out into a wet and reedy drainage hole. I retrieved my cell phone from its holster and started to dial the police but then stopped. What could they do? What *would* they do was more like it? I hadn't gotten a glimpse of the other driver. The police would probably put it down to a Yank's inexperience at handling the narrow byroads of Ireland. Headlights, coming up behind me again, illuminated the road. I froze. Should I flag the driver down, or was it the same person come back to finish me off? I wasn't far from French Hill, maybe a mile. I could hide and then walk to the cottage. No. I wasn't going to hide. Instead, I stepped out of the rut in the grass. I turned on my phone's flashlight to signal the approaching car. The car slowed and stopped. The driver stepped out. *Lorcan!* I glanced down at my wet feet and shoes. From rain or cow muck, I wasn't sure. But for once, I was happy to see him.

"Star, are you okay?" He crossed over to my side of the road and touched my shoulder. "What happened? I've warned Seamus about the gates. His cattle are always getting out of the field."

"No, Lorcan. Cattle had nothing to do with this. Someone ran me off the road."

I couldn't see Lorcan's face in the gloom, but I heard his breath quicken. "Well, let's get moving before whoever it was returns." He reached into my car and retrieved the keys. "We'll have to leave your car here. I'll have someone rescue it in the morning. Do you need anything else out of it?"

"No, I have all I need. Let's get going."

Lorcan escorted me to the passenger side of his car and opened the door. I hopped in. We drove the short distance to French Hill in silence. When Lorcan parked alongside the cottage gate, I opened the passenger door and said, "No need to see me inside. I can handle it from here." I jumped out, opened the gate, and ran to the kitchen door. Before turning the key in the lock and entering the cottage, I glanced back at the road. Lorcan stood at the stone wall, watching me. I gave a quick wave and went inside.

I dropped my shoes in the kitchen and headed into the shower. After getting all the mud off, I changed into a pair of sweatpants and an old T-shirt. It was 9:00 p.m.

I picked up the phone and called Georgina.

"Is everything okay there?" I asked.

"I'm fine. I'm working on a dress design for a client. Ashford is sitting at my feet. And Terrence is outside, sitting in his car."

"Goodnight, Georgina. Remember, you can call me at any time if you need to talk to someone."

"Get some sleep, agra."

We ended the call.

I didn't tell Georgina about my near collision. She'd only drop everything and drive over here to take care of me. For once, I needed to mind her. I sat in the cottage's living room and closed my eyes, replaying the moments before I veered off the road. I still couldn't tell if the driver was male or female. All I glimpsed was a dark sedan and a streak of light. Nevertheless, I jotted down my account of the incident. Then, I wrote my impressions of the people I'd spoken with during the day. I made a list of the places I planned to go tomorrow morning. That was when I remembered I didn't have a car at the moment. Exhausted and more than a little frustrated, I went to bed and pulled the covers over my head.

~

AT 6:00 A.M., I GOT INTO MY RUNNING CLOTHES: A PAIR OF sweatpants and an old red flannel shirt of Dylan's. I holstered my phone to the sweats and headed out. During my short

sojourns in French Hill, I'd come to love my runs or power
walks along Cottage Road, with its abandoned stone houses
and occasional fox or hare standing on a rise. This morning, I
ran as a way to blow off the sleepless night I'd spent worrying
about Georgina, the meeting with Evelyn Cosgrove, and getting
to Achill Island. First, though, I had to get my car out of the
ditch. Once through the cottage gate, I turned in the direction
of where I'd last seen my car.

The car was gone! I thought I might have been mistaken
about the exact place I'd left it. After all, it had been a darker
night than usual. But an investigation of the grass and wet area
revealed a car's tracks in the wet drainage canal. *Lorcan.* Could
he have gotten there before me? I turned and ran back to the
cottage. By the time I arrived at the gate, my calves burned, and
my breath came in ragged puffs. Then, I heard the car horn. I
turned to see a Jeep, which pulled up beside me. Lorcan
stepped out. I wiped the sweat rolling down my face with my
shirt sleeve.

"You look like you had quite a workout," he said.

Why did he always catch me when I looked my worst? Like
now when I imagined my cowlicks stood on end. "My car is
gone. Did you have anything to do with that?"

Lorcan nodded his head and handed me a set of keys.
"These are the keys to my Jeep. It's yours until your car is
repaired."

I didn't want to accept anything from Lorcan, but I knew I'd
have to take him up on his offer. I had to take action. "Thank
you," I replied. "Where is my car?"

"I had it towed to the garage in Belcarra. It looked like there
was considerable damage. You might not have your car for a
while. But I know the garage technicians well. They service our
cars. You're in good hands with them." Lorcan's eyes smiled at
me from behind his glasses. "Are you ready now to talk about
what happened last night?" he asked.

He was right. I needed to tell someone. "Come on in," I said.

Once inside, I boiled the kettle and put a tea bag into each of the mugs I pulled out of a cabinet. Lorcan looked at the empty tabletop and smiled at me. "I guess there's no hope for a slice of Georgina's brown bread?" he asked.

"No, there isn't," I replied. "So, I don't think last night was an accident."

"Do you remember anything about the car or the driver?" Lorcan asked.

"Not much. I tried to rerun what happened in my head last night, but all I know for sure is the car was a sedan. Man or woman at the wheel? No way of telling."

Lorcan sat back in the chair. "I see. Well, we have to tell the guards."

"No." My hands reached for my cell phone in frustration. "I want the police focused on finding Jimmy Mahoney's killer. Besides I don't have much to tell them other than the car was a sedan. But I don't know the make."

"I agree with you. Still, I don't like what happened. This may have nothing to do with you, Star. What if it was a drunk driver? What if someone had been walking along the road? I live here, too, as does my mother. At least, we have to make the guards aware."

"Of course, you're right," I admitted. "I suppose it wouldn't hurt to have them take a look around. But"—I hesitated—"I don't have time to waste talking to them."

"I'll call. It's best to have the report on file. Just in case." Lorcan stirred more sugar into his teacup. "So, who do you intend to talk to today?"

"The staff at the pub in Neale. I think they know more than they're letting on. At least that's the impression I got when we were there after the funeral."

"I'll check in with O'Shea and Keenan when I go to the garda station. Maybe they'll have more information from their

sweep of the walk between Castlebar and Turlough. What time
do you think you'll be back?"

"I don't know. I want to check on Georgina, and I'm waiting
for a call from Phillie. I'll call you when I get back. Do you want
me to drop you home?" I asked, looking at the keys he'd
given me.

Lorcan laughed. "It's a short jaunt from the cottage up to my
house, Star. I think I can make it." He rose, walked to the back
door, and said, "Just be careful, Star."

Then, he was gone.

I SHOWERED, DRESSED, AND LOCKED UP THE COTTAGE WITHIN
forty-five minutes. Once I familiarized myself with the dashboard controls in Lorcan's Jeep, I started the drive through
Castlebar toward Ballinrobe and Neale. Along the way, I
considered my conversation with Lorcan, admitting to myself
that I was pleased to see him and grateful that he'd taken care
of my car and loaned me one of his. I didn't want to like him,
but I did. And that didn't sit well with me. I didn't have time to
get involved with someone. I'd lost Dylan, the love of my life. I
needed, *wanted,* to find the truth of my mother's disappearance.
I wouldn't, couldn't, allow myself to be hurt and suffer any
more losses than I had already. I shook my head. No, my focus
must be on proving Georgina's innocence and finding my
mother. I hoped the meeting with Evelyn Cosgrove would
produce tangible results—a real live link that I could follow.
Before long, I reached Neale and Jimmy's pub. I pulled into the
parking lot, exited the Jeep, and shut the door on my thoughts.

CHAPTER 12

The first time I ever sought out Jimmy, I'd gone to his pub in Neale at Georgina's suggestion. She'd thought a Cosgrove family previously owned the pub. That day, I delved into what he might know about Evelyn Cosgrove's whereabouts and whether she was related to the former pub owners. Today, I wanted to learn what the staff knew about Jimmy, his death, and his numbers-running gig.

A dark sedan with tinted windows pulled into the parking lot behind me. The bartender from the day of the funeral emerged. Lorcan had identified the guy as Ciaran Quinn when I'd asked about him.

"You again. Well, we're not open yet," he stated. He stepped in front of me and inserted a key into the pub door.

"I know," I replied and followed right behind him as he pushed open the door.

"Right. Wait here," he commanded and strode toward the bar area.

I stood still. Without any lights, the bar's interior appeared murky. Stale beer and whiskey odors hung in the air. The overhead lights flipped on. Ciaran stood behind the bar, cloth in hand. "I've already told the guards what I know about the argument between those two." He ran the cloth over the bar top as he spoke.

"Who was Jimmy arguing with?" I asked.

"With that Georgina Hill woman." Ciaran dropped the cloth from his hand into a basin of soapy water behind the bar. "I was here that day."

"You said you know who I am. Well, you should also know then that Georgina Hill is my aunt," I replied.

"She may be your aunt, but she marched in here like a north wind blowing in from the Barrclashcame Mountain with an icy stare, scarf billowing behind her. They went off into a corner, but I could tell whatever she said agitated Jimmy."

"How long ago was this?" I asked. I already knew the answer because Georgina had told me. But I wanted to gauge how valuable Ciaran would be as a witness for the police.

"A few weeks ago. After she left, Jimmy made a phone call. Then he took off in a huff as well." Ciaran started stacking cocktail napkins at random points along the bar top, talking as he moved. "I figured it was some kind of a lovers' spat. Whenever I've seen a woman that riled up, it's usually over another woman."

"Oh, was Jimmy seeing someone?" I asked. The blonde-haired woman who'd thrown angry glances at Georgina came to mind.

"He had been palling around with Nessa Bantry. She sings and plays here on our traditional Irish music nights. Maybe that's why your aunt argued with Jimmy."

"Does Nessa have blonde hair? Wears it in a French twist?" I asked.

"Yeah," Ciaran replied. "That sounds like her. Why?"

"I saw her at Jimmy's funeral. But she didn't come back here afterward with everyone else."

"No, she wouldn't. She keeps a low profile most of the time. Plays her gigs at the pubs and the arts centre in Castlebar."

"Was Jimmy here at the bar on the day he was killed?" I asked.

Ciaran tilted his head, and in my opinion, seemed to take a little too long before he answered. "I was here all night. Rosaleen can attest to that. He didn't come in that day. But that wasn't unusual. He often left things to Rosaleen and me to run."

"Has Jimmy had any problems with the bar recently? Angry customers? Disputes with distributors?"

By this time, Ciaran had reached the end of the bar closest to the door. He walked around from the back of the counter and stood in front of me. "I think it's time for you to leave, Miss O'Brien. I have a lot to do to open up. Customers will be showing up shortly. I don't want the pub's reputation to suffer."

"Oh, are you managing it now?" I asked.

"I may have an interest. Now, you will have to excuse me."

I pulled one of my business cards out of my knapsack and placed it on the bar. "Thanks for taking some time. Here's my contact information if you think of anything else."

I exited the pub and came face to face with the server who had assisted with the lunch after Jimmy's funeral. "Are you Rosaleen?" I asked.

She nodded. "I remember you. You were at Jimmy's funeral."

"Yes, and I ate in the pub one night, months ago.

I guessed Rosaleen's age to be late twenties. Her carrot-colored hair bounced in its ponytail tie when she laughed. "Forget me remembering anyone who's been here at night. This place is perpetually mobbed, especially when there's enter-tainment."

"Before you go in, I'd like to ask you some questions," I said.

She glanced at the pub's door. "I have a few minutes before Ciaran laces into me for being late. What do you want?"

"You know my aunt, Georgina Hill, is under suspicion of

killing Jimmy. I'm out to prove that isn't true. I'm talking to everyone who might have an idea about trouble Jimmy was in or potential enemies. Talking to you and Ciaran seems like a logical place to start."

Rosaleen pursed her lips and nodded. "I don't think Georgina killed Jimmy. I know everyone thinks she did. I was here the day she and Jimmy had an awful row, and I told the guards that. But I think Jimmy was involved with someone else, and Georgina found out and broke up with him."

I couldn't imagine Georgina killing a man over a woman. Not in a hundred years. "Were you here the night Jimmy was killed?" I asked, wondering if Rosaleen would confirm Ciaran's alibi.

She pulled the baseball cap she wore down to cover her eyes. "Well, I was here most of the night. But...sometimes, when Jimmy wasn't here, Ciaran and I would back up each other so we could run errands and the like."

"You didn't tell the police that, though," I stated, trying not to scream. How in the world would Georgina be proven innocent if people were lying about what happened the night Jimmy died? "You have got to tell me the truth. Were you both here that night?"

Rosaleen's eyes filled with tears. "We both took turns slipping out. Ciaran said he had to run an errand at the chemist in Cong. When he came back, I left for the evening. It was late, and I wanted to get to Castlebar before the pubs closed."

"I don't understand. What were you doing in Castlebar?" I asked, assuming she was local and lived somewhere nearby.

Rosaleen sighed. "My uncle owns the pub in Turlough."

"Wait, I've spoken with him. Is his name Owen?"

"Yes, he's interested in buying Jimmy's pub, this pub. But my uncle heard that Allen Skye was going to close a deal with Jimmy. I've been watching Skye's place and reporting his comings and goings to my uncle."

I stepped back at this revelation. "Did you see Allen Skye the night Jimmy was killed?" This could be the break that would prove Georgina's innocence.

Rosaleen hung her head and looked at the stones beneath our feet. "Yes, I did see him later. In Turlough. I was just going into my uncle's pub when I saw Skye drive past toward the museum."

"You've got to tell the police what you told me. An innocent woman's life is at stake. Do you want me to go with you to the police station?" I asked. As far as I was concerned, the sooner, the better.

Rosaleen's eyes widened. She stepped away from me. "No, there's no way I'm admitting I was in the vicinity. Skye is dangerous. If he thought I might be a witness to something, I'd be dead. No, I have to take my chances this way. I'm sorry," she cried and ran into the pub.

I opened the pub's door to follow her, but Ciaran blocked my path. Rosaleen stood behind the bar, arms folded over her chest. "You have got to tell the police what you know," I stated. "What are you going to do when they find out you lied?"

"Leave well enough alone," Ciaran said. "The guards will figure it out in time."

"Time," I almost exploded. "My aunt doesn't have time. Rosaleen, you have to come forward now." I pivoted to Ciaran. "You lied, too, when you said you were both here. Why is that? What are you hiding?" I turned back to Rosaleen. "Do you trust Ciaran? He said he was here all night. But you weren't here all night. This is going to look bad for you."

Rosaleen burst into tears.

"Rosaleen, get control of yourself," Ciaran shouted. "Let's take this outside. I can explain." He motioned me out the door. I nodded, and we faced off in the parking lot. "You're right. We lied. When Jimmy didn't show up that night, Rosaleen and I slipped out at different times. We agreed to give each other an alibi should Jimmy show up or find out."

"So, you've done this before?" I asked.

"Aye, Jimmy had no idea. Rosaleen and I have been covering for each other for ages. That night was no different."

"You're wrong. My aunt is facing an indictment. You have to come forward. I understand why Rosaleen is worried, but what are you afraid of?"

"That is none of your business. Just know that we didn't kill Jimmy. If I were you, I'd spend more time looking into your aunt's whereabouts that night," he said. Then, he turned on his heel and went back into the pub.

I didn't waste any more time talking. It was obvious these two were going to continue to back each other's lies. Instead, my thoughts turned to Allen Skye. I'd had a run-in with Skye, a known drug dealer, six months ago when I investigated the murder of Matthew Sumner, a young artist, on Clare Island. Aunt Georgina had asked me to help Matthew's sister, Bridgett, prove her brother's innocence when the police closed his case as a low-level drug deal gone bad.

Before leaving the parking lot, I dialed Ellie Pizzolato, my general office manager, who handles the schedules and contracts.

"The Consulting Detective, Ellie speaking."

"It's Star. I'm sorry I had to leave so suddenly, especially with the Southern Aircraft report still in draft form."

"Sheila Bixler called," Ellie replied. "She's satisfied with the contents of the draft report you sent to her. Do you want me to mark it final?"

"Yes, thank you. I don't know what I'd do without you. How are you and Phillie doing?"

"We're fine. But what about your aunt?" Ellie's voice sounded worried.

"She's back at work in her dress shop. She's innocent and

expects the police to find the real killer." I paused. "That's why I'm calling. They will need help to look in the right direction. I've got a research project for Phillie."

Phillie, Philomena Spring, was the technical guru who managed our databases and assisted me with research.

"Sure, let me put her on. And, oh, before I forget, Jim Hipple stopped by yesterday, and he said to say hi.

"Thanks, Ellie."

"Hi, boss, what do you need?" Like me, Phillie didn't waste time on the formalities; she was all about the task at hand.

"I want you to dig into Allen Skye."

"That guy," Phillie said. "Is he on the scene again?"

"Oh, yeah. Look into the ownership of his pub, the Wagon Wheel. Is he the sole owner? Is his name on any other properties? See what you can find."

"Right, will do. Talk soon, boss." The call ended. Then, I left Neale and drove directly to Georgina's shop in Castlebar.

~

I BARELY HAD THE GOLDEN THREAD'S DOOR CLOSED BEHIND ME when Georgina held up a dark-green wrap dress with bell sleeves and a V-neck. "Star, I was just thinking about you. I've got the perfect dress for you." She put the dress up against my shoulder. "Yes, this matches your eyes perfectly," she said.

I'd gotten used to Georgina's exuberance when it came to fashion and her efforts to take me out of my capri pants and put me into dresses. But I had work to do, and it had nothing to do with fashion. "It's pretty, but I need to talk to you. Seriously," I added.

"I'm earnest, too, Star. We've been invited to a fundraising event at Flann Mahoney's house."

"A party? I don't think that's a good idea," I replied.

"Look, Star. I'm innocent. And I plan to live my life as

normally as possible. Besides, some of the guests knew Jimmy. And people from the museum will be there. It's a good chance to get a handle on everyone." Georgina put the dress on a hanger and placed it on a rack. "I'll take care of getting the dress pressed and delivered to the cottage. You'll look beautiful!"

I agreed with Georgina on one point. Going to the event would give me a close-up view of people from the museum. But I still thought my best bet in finding Jimmy's killer was to focus on Skye. The dress? Well, I'd think about it.

"When is the party?" I asked.

"Tomorrow night. Flann rang to invite us. Marcella and Lorcan are invited as well, and Marcella said Lorcan will drive." Georgina tried to hide her smile but failed. Then, I realized what was behind the dress.

"I just came from Jimmy's pub in Neale. I spoke with the staff there, Ciaran and Rosaleen. Did Jimmy ever mention to you what he thought of them?" I asked.

Georgina shook her head. "No, not that I recall. They've been there a few years, and I imagine he trusted them. Otherwise, he'd have found a replacement. He wasn't the sort to put up with laziness. Why do you ask?"

"They are lying about where they were the night Jimmy died. Rosaleen, the server, admitted she left the pub early. She was in Turlough and saw Allen Skye."

"Then, why hasn't she come forward to the guards? I don't understand."

"Right, I told her as much, but she's afraid of Skye. And the bartender, Ciaran, lied as well. I don't know where he was that night, but he wasn't in the Old Forge Restaurant and Gibbons' pub the entire evening."

"This is good news, Star. All I have to do is tell the guards, and they will follow up."

"Will they?" I asked. "I'm glad you think so highly of them. Why haven't they already tracked down this information? They don't even have a murder weapon yet. But they are ready to put you in front of a judge and jury." I squinted at my phone's display as if it held the answers to my frustration.

"Star, I know you're angry, but the guards will find whoever did this. Has Lorcan talked to them?"

The bell over Georgina's shop door rang and interrupted our conversation. Two women walked in, and Georgina rose and went to greet them. I exited through the front door and stood on Main Street. In the distance, just past where Linenhall Street crossed Main, I stared at the "*Wagon Wheel Pub*" sign hanging over the building's entrance. I decided to delay a visit to Allen Skye until later in the day. In the meantime, there was someone else I wanted to interview about Jimmy.

The walk from Georgina's shop to the Linenhall Arts Centre took less than five minutes. One of the oldest in Castlebar, the building began life when Lord Lucan established the place as a clearinghouse for linen and flax. Currently, the structure hosts exhibitions, music, cinema, and theater. When I entered the ticket office, the woman in charge pointed to several display cabinets filled with brochures. "Are you looking for information about the walking tour?" she asked.

"Maybe," I said, taking a quick look around. I focused on the brochures promoting traditional Irish music. I picked a few out of the stack and walked over to her. "I'm interested in traditional Irish music. Are there any scheduled events this week here in town?" I asked.

"Oh, you have much to choose from in that arena, love," the woman replied. Then she shuffled through some papers on her desk and pulled one out. "Here's a list of all the pubs that offer traditional music." She glanced at the list, picked up a pen, and circled the names of three pubs. "These three have music this week—unfortunately, all on the same night. But"—the woman smiled at me—"you can create your own pub crawl and go from one to another. Does that suit?"

"It sure does," I replied and placed the list into my knapsack. "Thank you."

Back at French Hill cottage, I invested some time at my computer. Nessa Bantry's musical career meant she had a rich public profile for mining, including her address. A quick search using Google unearthed a husband named Pete.

CHAPTER 13

Nessa lived up on Staball Hill, famous for a battle during the 1798 rebellion against the British, just a stone's throw from Castlebar's Main Street. More than 200 years later, Staball Hill featured a row of dainty condominiums. The dark sedan parked in front had a scratch on the passenger side mirror and a bunch of decals plastered along the side panel. I knew I was in the right place when the woman I'd seen at Jimmy's funeral answered the doorbell.

"Yes, what is it?"

Her voice was low and raspy. Not what I would have expected from a singer of traditional Irish "come all yas."

"Nessa Bantry?"

"Aye, I am."

She was shorter than me but not by much, maybe five foot five, probably about a hundred and thirty pounds. Currently, her blonde hair hung down just above her shoulders. Her face bore no makeup, and dark shadows ringed her brown eyes. The colorful dress she wore stopped just above her bare feet. The hand she used to stifle a yawn boasted square-shaped, short fingernails.

"My name is Star O'Brien. I'm here on behalf of my aunt, Georgina Hill."

Nessa's face stiffened. "What brings you to my doorstep?"

"I'm looking into Jimmy Mahoney's murder. I'm talking to everyone who knew him. Ciaran Quinn said you and Jimmy were friends."

"Ciaran said that? I didn't think he knew what friendship looked like." She shook her head. "I don't need to talk to you. That Hill woman killed my Jimmy. I hope she gets life."

"Are you planning to testify at her trial?" I asked.

"I will do no such thing." She began to close the door.

"Is that your car with the scrape on the passenger mirror?" I asked.

She glanced out at the car and shrugged. "That's just a wee bit of a scratch. Probably got it in one of the parking lots in town."

"Someone tried to run me down last night. The person left some of their car's paint on mine."

Her face fell. She stepped back, opened the door, and waved me into the tiny room behind her. "I hope this doesn't take long. I have a gig tonight."

The living room furniture consisted of a blue leather sofa sitting atop a shaggy white area rug. Musical instruments lay scattered around the room, some on the floor, some on modern IKEA-like tables. Nessa sat on one end of the sofa, and I occupied the other end. She picked up a circular frame drum from the floor and held it in her hands—their muscular sinews stretched as taut as the instrument's skin.

"You are a musician?" I asked in an effort to diffuse her anger.

"You want to hear a song or what?"

I ignored her remark. I wasn't about to take offense. I had the feeling that anger was a natural part of her personality.

"So, I don't have much time. What do you want to know?" she asked, setting the drum back down on the floor.

"Did you see Jimmy the night he was killed?"

"No." She shook her head. "Maybe if I had, he'd still be alive. I had a gig that night at the museum."

"The one catered by the café?"

"Yeah, a big part of my income is supplemented by playing at fundraisers and galas. You know—I'm the one sitting in the corner playing harp music while everyone else is drinking and chatting."

"And you didn't see Jimmy there?" Either she was lying, or the security guard O'Shaunessy had misled me.

"No. I played until the end of the event and then drove home here."

"Why did you two stop seeing each other?"

"You're a smart Yank, aren't you?" She laughed. "Why do you think he broke it off? Georgina Hill came in on my patch. Jimmy and I were seeing each other since I'd left that lazy, lying husband of mine." Nessa stared at me. Her eyes narrowed. "I hope you don't think I'm rude," she said with a smirk. "But I've got things to do." She stood and picked up several wooden mallets from one of the end tables. She proceeded to drop them into a carrying bag labeled with the words *Dulcimer case.*

"I'd get that car looked at if I were you," I said.

"Thanks for the advice. You be careful too. Driving on Irish roads is an acquired skill." She seized one of the hammers and banged it down on the tabletop. Then, she opened the apartment door and waved me out.

I returned to the borrowed Jeep and headed back to French Hill. Nessa's anger at Aunt Georgina didn't sit well with me. Nessa had been at the museum the night of the murder. And if I had to choose whether Nessa or O'Shaunessy was lying about seeing Jimmy that night, I'd opt for Nessa. The information I'd found indicating a separated husband was interesting but may not be relevant. My conversation with Nessa hadn't eliminated her from my suspect list. Not yet. But she didn't top the list. Skye owned that honor.

When I opened the kitchen door, the silence hit me like a brick wall. Typically, I embraced the cottage's solitude, but on that day, I wished things were back to normal. I even wished Lorcan would appear with an update. I placed the keys to the Jeep on the countertop closest to the door in the event he came to collect his car. Then, I headed for my makeshift office to check emails and voice messages. I placed a call to The Consulting Detective. Surprisingly, Phillie answered the phone.

"Hi, boss, Ellie's out running some errands. Perfect timing for your call, though. I have some updates."

I picked up my composition notebook and pen. "Go ahead. I'm ready."

"That Allen Skye guy. He owns several bars in the county, all across a number of towns. Do you want the names?"

"How many?" I asked.

"Five, including the one in Castlebar. I looked at a county map, and all the bars are in towns between Castlebar and Neale."

"Is Ballintober one of them?" I asked, thinking of the towns I'd driven through, going and returning from Jimmy's pub.

"Yeah, Ballyhean, Ballintober, Partry, Ballinrobe. I'll email the list. And get this, the pub names all contain the word *wheel*."

I didn't know if the names meant anything, but the knowledge that you could draw a straight line on a map to connect all the pubs was interesting. Especially if Skye were involved in numbers-running. If Jimmy were about to take one of the nodes off the racket network, that would be a good motive for murder.

"Okay, what else do you have for me?"

"The museum exhibit where Jimmy was found is a loaner.

Seems it came from the national museum in Dublin. Do you think the subject of the exhibit had anything to do with why Jimmy was found there?" Phillie asked.

"I don't know," I replied. "He ran a pub, and his family is known around the area, but why someone chose that exhibit, I just don't know. I'm more inclined to believe the killer chose the tableau because of easy access rather than to make a statement. And to throw the police off the scent. Thanks, Phillie."

"Sure, anything else?"

"No. Say hello to Ellie." I ended the call, answered some business emails, and waited for the evening.

$\sim$

THE SETTING SUN LIT THE WESTERN SKY, SHOWERING A ROSY GLOW upon Croagh Patrick Mountain. The wind turbines that dotted the distant hills looked like fragile ballerinas, spinning in the evening breeze. I drove toward Castlebar for my showdown with Skye.

Inside the country-and-western-themed Wagon Wheel, the patrons, mostly male, stood near the bar, holding beer glasses and talking quietly among themselves. The kitchen door opened, releasing a waft of barbecue sauce into the dining room. My mouth watered as I remembered the thick French fries and meaty ribs I'd enjoyed during my last visit. But then, I hadn't met Allen Skye yet. Now that I knew who he was and how little time I had to find Aunt Georgina's stalker and potential murderer of Jimmy Mahoney, my stomach lurched at the idea of eating there. Instead, I intercepted the server on her way to another table.

"I'm here to talk with Allen. Where is he?" I asked.

She stepped back and glanced quickly at the bartender before saying, "I'm not sure, but I can check. In the meanwhile, can I offer you something to drink?"

"No. Tell him Star O'Brien is here. He knows who I am." I remained standing as she walked over to the bar and exchanged words with the bartender.

"He's in the back room," she said when she returned.

"Thank you." I didn't wait for her to show me the way. I headed for the kitchen.

Allen's physical appearance hadn't changed since the last time I'd seen him, and he still looked like an NFL wide receiver. When I entered the kitchen, his six-foot-plus frame was reposed on a bar stool. A few feet away from where he sat, the kitchen staff shuffled various pots and pans around gas flames of varying heights.

"I'm surprised to see you again, Yank. What can I do for you?" He didn't offer me a seat on any of the empty stools.

I took a breath and smiled at him. I needed information and knew I'd have to stroke his ego if I were to get what I wanted. "I need your vast knowledge," I said. "I understand there's a numbers racket organization in town. I'm sure with all your contacts, you might know whom I can talk to about it."

"Ah." Skye nodded his head. "I heard you've been around town asking questions. This has to do with Mahoney's death."

"Yes." I didn't say anything more, not wanting to reveal how worried I was about Georgina and the pending charges. I wouldn't give Skye an emotional cudgel to use on me.

"Yeah, there's been some rumors about his business dealings." Skye laughed. "I'm surprised you even thought of me. You know I'm out of the seedy side of my money-making ventures."

I didn't believe one word he said but continued to cozy up to him. "I'm happy for you, Allen. You've got a nice business here."

"A great chef and great food. It's a winning combination." Skye's eyes bore into mine. Then, he shrugged. "Okay, I knew Jimmy. We were competitors. Being in the same business, we had occasion to talk to one another once in a while. But a numbers organization? I got nothing to offer, Star."

I decided not to take offense at his sneer when he said my name. "Had you seen Jimmy lately?" I asked, looking around the kitchen. I wondered why Allen chose to sit back there instead of out in the bar area.

"Yeah, I saw him. He used to stop in here for a pint once in a while after he'd been out in Turlough visiting Georgina Hill. He liked to talk shop whenever he could."

"Was he worried about anything?"

Before Skye answered, another door leading to the outside opened. The gust of wind blew a pile of napkins from a shelf to the floor. The newcomer scooped them up, but not before I glimpsed a series of numbers written on some. I moved closer to get a better look, but he threw the papers into a nearby can. Then, he elbowed his way past me to stand behind Skye.

"The delivery truck is here, sir," the newcomer said.

"Good." Skye stood and beckoned me out of the kitchen back into the pub. Then, he escorted me to the pub door. "Jimmy always seemed to be up to something, but I wouldn't know what that was," Skye said. "But, hey, thanks for stopping by to see me, Star." He laughed before pushing me out of the pub.

I stood on the sidewalk in the drizzling rain. Glad to be outside, I turned my face up to welcome the distinct, fresh smell and took a few deep breaths. The conversation with Skye, especially his last words, didn't sit well with me. Maybe he'd been telling the truth, and maybe not. Allen Skye was a crook who used his pub as a cover. His revelation that Jimmy was involved in something could be a distraction thrown down a rabbit hole just for me. I wrapped my jacket around my shoulders and walked back to where I'd parked Lorcan's Jeep.

CHAPTER 14

E arly the next morning, I returned from my power walk to find Aunt Georgina's car parked at the barn. When I opened the kitchen door, the aroma of nutmeg hung in the air.

"Good morning, Star." Georgina stood at one of the counters, slicing a loaf of cake.

"Did you drive here by yourself?" I didn't want to think of her traveling around the countryside when a potential stalker lurked nearby.

"Of course, I did," she replied. "Please, sit down and have your tea. I'm trying out a few new recipes. This is a pumpkin bread. I think you'll like it."

I finally pushed my plate away after I'd scraped the last crumb of chocolate chip and pumpkin from my plate. "That was delicious. So, tell me what you're doing here so early in the morning."

"I had time before I needed to be in the shop and just wanted to see you. I miss being able to run out here at a moment's notice. And I figured you might like the dress I showed you the other day. I left it on your bed. The wraparound style will suit you."

"Thanks, but I'm able to dress myself." Georgina was always

trying to feminize my look, especially when she thought Lorcan might be at an event we were invited to attend. "Where's Ashford?"

"I left him in the cottage this morning. He looked so tired. He's been up and down several times each night."

"Really. Was there someone outside?" I hadn't heard from Terrence about any unusual activity.

"No, I don't think so. Just having Ashford and Terrence there might have scared off whoever has been skulking around the shop." Georgina tossed her scarf behind her shoulder. "Lorcan said he'd drive us to the party tonight."

"I'll take Lorcan's Jeep. I'm planning to head out to Achill this morning. I'd like to speak with Margaret Hanlon and whomever else I can find."

"You poor love. What with the previous nasty business in Cong and my current situation, you've put Achill on the back burner long enough. I'll tell Lorcan and Marcella that you'll meet us there." Georgina picked up the dirty dishes and placed them in the dishwasher. "I'll see you later. The party starts at nine p.m. Don't give me another thought. I'm on my way to the shop."

SHORTLY AFTER GEORGINA LEFT, I DROVE WEST THROUGH Castlebar onto Newport Road toward Achill Island. The sun hung on the horizon, highlighting the blue sky and pristine sea as I drove along Wild Atlantic Way. When I crossed over Michael Davitt Bridge from Corraun onto Achill Island, I headed directly to Margaret Hanlon's pottery shop.

Like a bad omen, the sky suddenly spewed a torrential rain as I pulled into the shop's parking lot. I waited a few minutes until the shower subsided and then entered the showroom. I paused at the door, taking in the beauty of the blue pottery pieces displayed on shelves in a glass-walled room. My breath stilled when I observed the view of the ocean from the vantage point where the shop perched. I couldn't help but wonder if my mother's love of blue pottery and her collection of blue willow teacups rose from her childhood on Achill Island.

A white-haired woman with piercing blue eyes entered the shop from the ocean side.

"What a day!" she exclaimed, wiping her hands on a towel. "One minute, the sun shines, and the next, the heavens shower us with rain. Ah, well, that's life on an island." She shrugged. "Can I help you?"

I handed her one of my consulting detective cards and introduced myself. "I'm Star O'Brien. I understand you spoke to my aunt, Georgina Hill, about a woman named Maggie O'Malley."

"Why, yes, I remember Georgina's call. I'm afraid I wasn't really much help." Margaret Hanlon tilted her head and raised her eyebrows as she looked me over. "So, you're the woman Georgina was assisting. Your aunt told me how you came by the name Star. Wait here. I have something I'd like to give to you."

Margaret Hanlon was back in a very short time. In her hands, she carried a pendant necklace from which hung a white stone accompanied by two white-stone earrings. "This is the Star of Achill," she explained. "The jewelry is made from stone taken from Slievemore Mountain. I want you to have this as a gift from me."

"Thank you, this is very kind of you," I said, reaching forward and taking the jewelry into my hands. As I looked at the stone, I remembered my mother's words when she'd told me about why she named me Star.

"You know where your name came from, don't you?" she'd ask. I knew the answer by heart. "Yes, I'm named after a star."

In my searching, I learned about the Star of Achill, a white crystal found on Achill Island. Local legend said that when people emigrated, they climbed Slievemore Mountain on the eve of their departure and cried. When they descended, they selected a piece of crystal to take with them for good fortune.

"So, have you had any luck in your search?" Hanlon asked.

"No, but I wanted to speak with you myself."

The woman pointed to a couple of stools. "Let's sit for a minute. I've been bending over a potter's table all morning, and I need a break."

I acquiesced, placed the jewelry in my knapsack, and then gently removed my mother's picture from my wallet, cradling the photo in the palm of my hand. "This is my mother. Does she look familiar to you?"

Maggie leaned over and took a long look at the picture. "No, I wouldn't know this woman. I told your aunt all I know about the poor lass, left an orphan after the fire. Funny, though, how things come back to you. After I spoke with your aunt, I remembered someone who came to Achill some years back, looking for a woman named Maggie O'Malley. I planned to call your aunt, but then, well, I don't know. I didn't have much to tell. Honestly, I didn't think I'd be much help."

"When was this? What was the woman's name?" I thought of Evelyn. Maybe she'd come to the island asking about my mother.

"Years and years ago. It was sometime in the nineties, but I'm not sure which year."

"Could it have been a younger version of this woman?" I raised the hand that cradled the picture closer to her.

"No, I'm certain it wasn't the person in your snapshot there. The one who came was sort of bossy. You know, snappy in her questions. She said she was looking for a long-lost cousin. I didn't like her. Not that I had much to tell. I told her I was busy here in the shop and couldn't answer her questions."

"What was her name?" I asked, feeling my heart crash

against my ribs in anticipation, like the ocean waves crashing against the shore.

"I don't remember. It started with an M, I think. One thing was for sure; she didn't fit in around here."

"Oh, why?"

"Well, her attitude for one, like I said. But surely it was the way she dressed—all in black and wearing pearls to boot."

"Did she sound like an American?" I asked.

"No. She was Irish. That much, I'm sure of."

"How did you know that?"

"Why, by the way she spoke when she said it was a wild, windy day."

I raised an eyebrow.

Hanlon continued, "When she said the word wild, it sounded like wile. That's a Donegal accent." The shop phone rang, and Margaret Hanlon hopped off her stool to answer it.

I peered at the ocean and thought about what she'd said. First Evelyn and then some other woman had been looking for a Maggie O'Malley. Somehow, these threads would come together. All I had to do was find why or how they joined. I propelled myself off the stool, waved to the woman still on the phone, and got into the Jeep. I had two more stops to make on Achill Island.

∽

I OPENED THE DOOR TO ST. JOSEPH'S CHURCH AND STEPPED inside. Silence and stained-glass trinity windows greeted me. "Hello, anyone here?" I asked. More silence, but I supposed an unlocked door meant someone had to be around. I sat down on one of the pews at the back of the church and retrieved the folded list of names from the inside of my phone's lime-green case.

"Mass is over," the voice behind me said.

I stood and faced the man dressed in his black cassock. "I'm afraid my church days ended long ago. But I'm hoping my prayers might be answered, Father. I'm Star O'Brien. Are you Father Mulligan?"

"Yes, I am. What can I do for you? I was just about to lock up the church."

"I believe we spoke on the phone several months ago about finding birth records for my mother, Maggie O'Malley."

"Ah, yeah. I remember. But sure, I told you then. A fire destroyed all the records. Did you check with the National Archives?" he asked.

"Well, that's the thing. I found a number of women named Margarite O'Malley but no one named Margaret. I wondered if maybe a mistake was made when the records were filed." I stepped toward him. "This is a list of Margarites I identified. Will you take a look? Maybe you know some of the relatives of the people on the list?"

His eyes scanned the paper. "No, I'm sorry. I'm not from this area." He shook his head and sighed. "Sadly, migration is a part of Achill Island's history. We've learned that sometimes we have to accept the things we cannot change." He handed the list back to me. "That may be the case for you, Ms. O'Brien. Now, I'm sorry, but I have sick calls to make. God Bless." He walked past me toward the altar.

I refolded my list and exited the nave through the oak door. Back in the Jeep, I pulled a map of the island from my knapsack and followed the road to Slievemore Mountain. From my research, I knew I wouldn't have enough time on that day to do the three-hour climb, but I wanted to look at the place that inspired my mother's name for me.

I parked to the side of the narrow curbless road and exited the Jeep. The sky, once again bright and sunny, seemed to dwarf the mountain. I turned my back on it and gazed out at the blue and green Atlantic, the sandy white beaches below, and the

Nephinbeg Mountains in the distance. The endless Atlantic Ocean stretched until it reached the horizon and disappeared. There was nothing more beyond.

I held the white Star of Achill in my hand. I wondered if my mother would agree with the priest's advice. I turned to look at Slievemore Mountain once again. Then, I got into the Jeep and drove east toward French Hill Cottage.

~

I ARRIVED BACK AT THE COTTAGE LATER THAN EXPECTED. THE dark green wrap dress Georgina had left for me was no fuss, and I gladly slipped it on after a quick shower. At the last minute, I retrieved the white-stone earrings and pendant necklace and slipped them on. Then, I headed to the party.

CHAPTER 15

J ust a few miles outside of Castlebar along the N5, I turned
right onto a narrow, tree-laden road beside the Turlough
Church of Ireland. The village signpost identified the area
as the parish of Drumdaff. Before long, I came to a gated driveway. A sign with the words "*Mahoneys Holsteins*" identified
Flann Mahoney's property. I turned onto the driveway and
halted at the gate. The box on the gate post issued a tinny voice,
asking my name, and I replied. The gate swung open, and I
drove through.

The bright, moonlit night filtered light through the dense
forestry, which lined the long winding driveway. I wondered
where Flann kept the dairy animals. I got my answer when the
forested area opened to fenced pastures, where I glimpsed cows
scattered across several fields. The paddocks closer to the
house were empty. Finally, the driveway gave way to stone slabs,
which formed a circular drive in front of the house.

The house surprised me. I'd expected a rambling farmstead
adjacent to cowsheds and milking equipment buildings.
Instead, the two-story Georgian building was stunning. Strands
of ivy snaked up trellises on both sides of the vibrant green
front door. Mature oak trees encircled the secluded grounds,

which blended into the forestry. I parked and then walked around to the back of the house, following the sound of voices. People stood about in small groups on a patio, which ran the length of the house.

"Star." Georgina's voice carried out of the house through the French doors.

I walked into the spacious, modernized, open-plan kitchen and dining room. Marcella and Georgina sat in an area under an expanse of skylights.

"Oh, you wore the dress. You look beautiful. Go ahead and get something to eat. Then, I'll show you around this gorgeous kitchen."

Marcella laughed at Georgina and winked at me. "Leave it to Georgina to take over when there's a kitchen involved. Did you see Lorcan when you came in?" she asked.

"No, but I wasn't looking for him. Getting something to eat is a great idea. I'll be right back." I walked over to a kitchen island lined with an assortment of finger foods. Deirdre Mahoney stood nearby, periodically moving empty trays off the island into a double sink.

"I imagine you're kept busy running the museum café and a catering business," I said.

Deirdre shrugged. "Hard work has its rewards. I enjoy the creative side of the catering business, and it affords me the opportunity to practice the art of baking and cooking. You could say it feeds my soul."

"Did Jimmy attend many of your catered events at the museum?" I asked.

Deirdre's eyes moved from mine to gaze at the crowd on the patio. "Yes, he did, but I wish he hadn't." She clattered together a few of the empty plates and started loading a stainless-steel dishwasher near the sink.

"Why not?" I asked, noting to myself how miserable Deirdre looked for someone who claimed to love being creative.

"I didn't always like his acquaintances." Deirdre's face reddened almost as dark as her hair. "Publicans and the like don't always appreciate the work that goes into preparing the menu and food for one of these events." Deirdre's eyes shifted to look past me.

"Here, I'll give you a hand with those," a voice behind me said.

Deirdre's entire body relaxed, and the joy I'd been looking for a few minutes earlier appeared at the sight of Willem.

I managed to enjoy a bacon-wrapped scallop and a few sips of Ballygowan water before Georgina walked over and took my hand. "Come on. I'll show you around."

The kitchen opened into a sprawling living room. The contemporary furniture created an interesting contrast to the oldness of the house.

"Ah, I see your niece has arrived." Flann Mahoney descended the spiral staircase and joined us. "I trust your trip to Achill was fruitful?" Flann asked.

Before I could reply, Maeve Baldwin appeared through one of the doors on the farthest side of the room. "That's an interesting necklace, Star. Is it something American?" she asked.

"Oh, no, not American," I replied. "An Achill native named Margaret Hanlon gifted the pieces to me. They are made from the Star quartz found on Slievemore Mountain. But, being an historian, I guess you know that already."

Maeve pursed her lips. Her hand moved to touch the ubiquitous opera pearls knotted around her neck. "What in heaven's name were you doing out there? You're not still trying to find your mother, are you?"

Before I could answer, screams erupted from the patio. I ran to the kitchen. Willem's arms supported Deirdre against his body, and tears ran down her face. I kept going to the patio, where a group of people surrounded a young woman. She gasped for breath. "Call an ambulance," one of the bystanders yelled. A broken platter and lettuce-wrapped hors d'oeuvres lay scattered around the woman. Lorcan knelt next to her, holding her hand. "Please, stand back. Give her air," he said to the onlookers. I moved closer and immediately recognized Rosaleen Nolan, the server from Jimmy's pub.

"How's her pulse?" I knelt next to Lorcan. Sweat soaked Rosaleen's ashen face. I didn't want to alarm her, but I'd seen this before. When the love of my life, Dylan Hill, suffered a massive heart attack.

"My purse. Shot." Rosaleen's words were barely discernable.

I jumped to my feet. "Where's her purse?" I ran into the kitchen, scanning the countertops. Deirdre pushed Willem away and reached down into one of the kitchen cabinets. "Is this it?" she asked.

I grabbed the purse and extracted the epi-pen, which protruded visibly from one of the bag's pockets. I ran to the patio and jabbed the pen into Rosaleen's outer thigh. Within seconds, her breathing quietened.

"Allergy?" I asked.

She nodded. "Peanuts."

I glanced at the tray of appetizers—shellfish wrapped in green leaves. I hadn't seen anything remotely resembling a peanut or peanut butter when I was in the kitchen. "How do you protect yourself?" I asked. In my mind, serving food would be the last occupation I'd practice if I had a food allergy.

She nodded. "I always check with the caterer before I agree to help out at a party. And, of course, I normally have an epi tucked into my apron. But tonight, when I saw Allen Skye out here, I got distracted."

"Skye?" I glanced around at the partygoers. I hadn't noticed him in the crowd. "What is he doing here?" Then, Rosaleen began to look much better. She sat upright. Some of the guests faded away toward their cars.

"I don't know." Rosaleen shook her head. "He's probably figured out that I've been keeping an eye on him for my Uncle Owen. I'd just seen Skye when Nessa, the musician, arrived, and she asked me to get her some food. By the time I finished with her, Skye was gone."

At this point, Rosaleen had recovered enough to stand. She shrugged.

"Did you ever leave the tray out of your hands this evening?" I asked.

"No. And even if I did, I wouldn't have eaten the food I'm serving." Rosaleen seemed insulted by my question. "Look, thanks for your help. But I have to go."

"If you like, I can drive you home," Lorcan offered. "My mother and Star's aunt will be with me, and we can drop you off."

"Thank you, but no," Rosaleen replied. "I'll stay with my uncle for the night. He's just down the road from here." She walked back into the house. I watched her have a brief conversation with Willem and Deirdre. Whatever she said, they shook their heads from side to side. Rosaleen left, and shortly after, Willem and Deirdre began tidying up the kitchen.

"I hope she'll be okay," Lorcan said to me.

"I've seen this type of thing before. The pen works. She'll be fine. What I want to know is what caused the allergic reaction." I walked around the patio, glancing at the dirty dishes and bits of food lying around. From there, I headed back into the kitchen.

Willem stacked clean dishes into a cabinet while Deirdre wiped down the counters. "Have you seen Rosaleen suffer an attack before?" I asked.

Willem didn't respond. Instead, he glanced at Deirdre. "No," she said. "But she's told me about her allergy, and she always asks about the menu." Deirdre looked at Willem. "Funny, she didn't mention the menu to me tonight."

"Did she sample any of the food?" I asked.

Deirdre's face flushed red. "I hope you aren't insinuating I served food without providing a list of potential allergens to the guests." She extracted a paper from a stack on the counter and handed the evening's menu to me. "See that grid. That's the menu, a list of possible allergens, and whether or not the menu item contains the allergen." Deirdre grabbed the paper back and turned to Willem. "I'm ready to leave."

Willem nodded, picked up a stack of clean plastic containers, and followed Deirdre out the French doors onto the patio.

Georgina and Marcella, flanked by Flann and Maeve, entered the kitchen.

"Star, is the server okay?" Georgina asked.

"I'm sure your niece and Lorcan got everything under control," Flann replied.

"Flann had us remain in the living room," Georgina said.

"No sense everyone rushing out there in an emergency. How does the old saying go? I don't like to buy trouble," Flann added. "I could see that you and Lorcan took charge, and that suited me."

"She's fine, Georgina," I said. "But I'm still wondering how she came in contact with the allergen," I said, annoyed that Deirdre had pulled the menu away from me before I had a chance to peruse it. I also wondered who invited Skye to the party, but I didn't say that. Instead, I asked Flann, "Do you have a guest list handy?"

He laughed in response. "Sure, we don't work off lists in this country, Ms. O'Brien. It's all word of mouth and relationships. I can assure you whatever happened to Rosaleen here tonight had nothing to do with any of the guests." He turned to Georgina. "Would you like me to run you home?"

Georgina looked at Marcella and Maeve. "No, I'm fine, Flann. Lorcan will drop me off on his way back to French Hill."

"We didn't finish our earlier conversation." Maeve's eyes stared at me.

"What conversation was that?" I asked. In my opinion, she didn't so much converse as bully her way into a discussion.

"What were you doing out on Achill Island?" she replied.

"I'm tracking down information about a Maggie O'Malley. Why, do you have information to add to my search?" I asked, remembering how Maeve had sent me on a wild goose chase to the Castlebar library archives.

She sighed. "I don't know why you're wasting your time, and others' for that matter. Everyone who crosses paths with you ends up hurt or dead. Maybe you should just leave Ireland."

Georgina and Marcella gasped and stepped away from Maeve.

"That statement is uncalled for. Star has every right to search for her mother. Anywhere Star chooses, for that matter," Lorcan said.

Maeve touched her strand of pearls. "Mark my words. She's trouble." With that, she stormed out of the house.

"Star, don't listen to that toxic slurry," Lorcan said.

"I'm so sorry. I introduced her to you," Marcella said to Georgina.

"Not to worry," Georgina replied. "I'm tougher than nails when it comes to dealing with gossip and innuendo."

Lorcan touched his mother's elbow and said, "Maybe we should all be going." Then, he turned to me. "Will you be okay?"

"Of course. Why wouldn't I be?" I replied. "I'd better get going also. Thank you for the invite, Flann."

Flann escorted us out of the house toward our cars. Then, his phone rang. "You'll have to excuse me," he said and waved goodbye. Lorcan stood by his driver's door until he saw me leave.

At that moment, alone in the borrowed Jeep, I felt a cloud of sadness descend upon me. Maeve's outburst reminded me that I'd lost everyone I'd ever loved—my mother, my adoptive parents, and Dylan. I'd spent most of my life building a tough external shell to cover my vulnerability. I protected my independence fiercely—from everyone. But inside, I hurt. Especially then when I thought I might lose Georgina.

CHAPTER 16

The morning after the gala, I awoke with a sole mission—determine whether Skye was connected to the numbers-running scheme and Jimmy's murder. I considered all the information I had in hand. First, no matter how much Skye claimed that he'd turned over a new leaf, I still remembered his involvement in drug-running. Then, there was Phillie's research report about Skye's string of pubs. Add to that Rosaleen's admission that she'd been watching Skye. He was too smart not to know. And the silly woman hadn't told the police she'd seen him the night of Jimmy's murder. I worried that it would only be a matter of time before he tried to correct last night's botched attempt at a second murder. Skye's story that he was trying to buy Mahoney's pub made for a good cover when he had to talk the numbers-running business with Mahoney. If he had murdered Jimmy, Skye would have had the strength to move the body. Everything seemed to add up, but there was only one way to know.

As I power-walked along Cottage Road, I thought through how I'd approach Skye. I decided on an ambush. Most pubs don't open until at least 10:00 a.m., so he wouldn't be expecting me. I'd enter the Wagon Wheel through the back entrance and confront him in the kitchen. I considered sharing my plan with the police. Finally, I decided against it. I needed tangible proof, like a recording of Skye's admission of guilt on my iPhone. With my mind made up, I turned around and walked back to French Hill cottage. Just as I neared the cottage, I spotted my Renault parked at the barn. Lorcan stood at the back kitchen door. He held my car keys in his hand.

"The garage called to say your car was ready. I hope you don't mind that I went to pick it up."

I glanced over at the used car I'd bought when I'd first arrived in County Mayo. For a minute, the sight of a familiar belonging gave me respite. I gazed up at Lorcan and simply said, "Thank you."

"I thought you'd be more comfortable rumbling along in your own car," he said.

When I first arrived in Ireland, I hadn't known how long it would take to settle the estate. So, I'd decided to buy a car. The older model car sported numerous dents. And it came with a manual transmission and no power steering. But I appreciated the turbocharged engine, which efficiently powered through the dips and twists of the narrow Irish roads.

Lorcan held up the key chain with the initials SOB on it. "I like your monogram," he added with a grin.

"Yeah, I often say it's a good indication of my personality."

Lorcan reached for a paper tucked away in his shirt breast pocket. "Right. I have the mechanic's report. There was a broken axle. That's why they had it so long. He also found some paint chips on the side. He took pictures. I'll share this information with O'Shea."

I nodded, but I doubted the police would pursue my car incident. "I'll stop by the garage later and take care of the invoice."

"No need for that. He didn't like hearing what happened, so he offered to do the work gratis. Besides, he's already working on several of our estate vehicles, and this was probably his way of showing gratitude."

"I'm the grateful one. Thank you, Lorcan. I'm relieved to have my car back," I said, unlocking the door and stepping inside. Lorcan followed and stood in front of the kitchen window.

"Any other updates?" I asked.

"None. My mother spoke with Georgina this morning, and all is well in that corner of the county."

"Yeah, I spoke with her earlier as well."

"I followed up with Rosaleen. She says she's fine. She put it down to a simple mix-up with some food or contact with a peanut."

"Is that so? A simple slip-up that might have had dire consequences. I don't believe in coincidences. You know Skye owns a string of pubs between Castlebar and Cong."

"The guards probably know that already," Lorcan, arms folded, continued. "I hope you're not thinking of confronting Skye yourself, Star. He's kept himself clean and away from guard scrutiny ever since Matthew's death. But it doesn't mean he's not dangerous."

I nodded but didn't respond. I had no intention of telling Lorcan what I was about to do. Not because I was some vigilante hero but because I didn't want any interference in getting Skye's confession. Time, like an hourglass, trickled away for Aunt Georgina.

"Maeve Baldwin called my mother this morning. She says she wants to help more. What do you think of having her go to Jimmy's bar and talk up Ciaran and Rosaleen? Being from Cong, the locals may be more willing to open up to Maeve, and she might learn something useful."

My thoughts turned to her hurtful comments about my visit to Achill Island. I couldn't put my finger on it, but I sensed there was more to Maeve's "wanting to be a help" overtures than met the eye. Maybe having her well away from me and Castlebar and would be a good thing.

"Sure," I replied. "I've got several phone calls with The Consulting Detective clients. I'm going to be glued to my office chair most of the day."

Lorcan pushed his glasses up the bridge of his nose and smiled. "I'll call back later after I've spoken with O'Shea." With that, he slipped out the kitchen door.

I didn't waste time. I grabbed my cell phone earbuds, swung my knapsack over my shoulder, and headed to my car. When I got to Castlebar, I parked in the lot behind Wynne's stationary shop. From there, I'd be able to approach the Wagon Wheel without Georgina spotting me from The Golden Thread's vantage point. I quickly walked from my car to Main Street, over the narrow walkway that crossed Castlebar River. Because I wanted to come at Skye through the pub's back entrance, I made a quick right turn onto Lucan Street. From there, I picked up my pace and turned into the driveway, which at the current moment had a beer delivery truck parked across it. When I wasn't able to wedge myself and my knapsack between the truck and cement archway, I dropped the knapsack on the sidewalk, popped in my earbuds for recording purposes, and wriggled through the remaining space. I'd just taken a deep breath when a voice commanded, "Stay right where you are."

I hadn't expected to find the police, but there I was, staring into the eyes of the uniformed officer who'd issued the warning. Behind him, I could see the flashing lights of the police panda cars. I also noticed the unmarked car I'd come to know, signifying that Keenan and O'Shea were somewhere in the vicinity. A small group of people huddled in a corner of the courtyard. I recognized one or two bar staff I'd seen the few times I'd been in the Wagon Wheel.

"I'm Star O'Brien," I said to the officer. "I've been hired to investigate Jimmy Mahoney's death, and I have business here with Allen Skye." I didn't care at that point whether or not my lie about being a private investigator got me into trouble. I wanted to get inside the Wagon Wheel and make sure the detectives had Skye in custody. I started to push past the cop. He stepped toward me and said, "I'm sorry, miss, but no one is allowed past this point."

"How many times do I have to tell you to stay out of garda business?" O'Shea's voice boomed throughout the tiny cement yard.

When the officer turned to look at O'Shea, I slipped by and strode directly over to the detective.

"You finally got it right," I said, glancing over his shoulder, hoping to catch sight of Allen Skye being escorted to one of the waiting police vehicles.

"I don't have time for you this morning, Miss O'Brien. Kindly move out of the way, or I'll have you removed. This is a crime scene."

"I know that. And I'm pleased to see you have discovered that Allen Skye killed Jimmy Mahoney. Did you catch Allen in the act of numbers-running?"

O'Shea's eyes widened in seeming surprise. Then, he nodded. "So, you think Allen Skye killed Mahoney? Is that your theory, Miss O'Brien?"

"Yes, I can walk you through why—"

"Enough of your amateur theories. Skye is dead— murdered apparently. We have a person of interest in custody. So, I think that shoots holes in your investigative abilities. So, if you'll excuse me, I'll see that you are safely escorted from the premises."

"What!" I stepped back. A sickening feeling, originating in the pit of my stomach, engulfed me. *Skye wasn't a good person but murdered?* Unexpectedly, I had a fleeting sense of grief at the loss of human life—even someone who may have been involved in another person's demise. But I also felt the breath I'd been holding since Georgina's arrest quietly release.

"This means the case against Georgina can be dropped," I pointed out to O'Shea.

O'Shea's brow furrowed. His eyes focused on me like a laser. "No such thing, Miss O'Brien. Georgina Hill's DNA is on Mahoney's shirt. That's more than enough evidence to support our suspicion of Miss Hill. On the other hand, Mr. Skye's demise seems to be related to an argument with a patron. We are still investigating what happened here. So, as I said at the beginning of this conversation, when are you going to learn to stay out of garda business?"

I didn't wait to hear any more. I turned on my heel, walked back to my car, and drove to French Hill. When I got there, I stopped the car, got out, and started running. For the first few minutes, all I could think of was how I'd failed Aunt Georgina. I felt like I was all over the place and yet nowhere in the case. I was so sure about Allen Skye that I may have wasted valuable time. Yet, just because he was dead didn't mean he hadn't killed Jimmy. But how would I prove that? When I finally stopped running, I turned back to the cottage, resolved to prove the police wrong about Georgina and maybe even Allen Skye.

CHAPTER 17

J ust as I neared the cottage door, Lorcan arrived. I could tell
by the look on his face that he'd heard the news.

"Star, I spoke with O'Shea—"

I interrupted him. "I don't want to hear anything about
O'Shea or his cohort of idiots. I just can't believe Skye is dead. I
didn't like him, but I didn't wish him dead. Despite what has
happened, the police still maintain that Georgina is their prime
suspect."

Lorcan nodded. "O'Shea sympathizes with your aunt's
predicament. But there is DNA evidence. He's got to pursue
this, Star."

"No, I've got to pursue this," I said, turning away from
Lorcan. I didn't want him to see the tears that threatened to
flood my cheeks. "I've failed Georgina. I trusted my instincts,
and now here we are. No closer to finding who killed Jimmy. I
just know it wasn't Georgina." I straightened my shoulders,
looked at Lorcan, and asked. "Do you want to come in for a few
minutes?"

"I'd like that."

I opened the door and stepped into the meticulously clean
kitchen, due in part to its current state of disuse. Lorcan quietly

closed the door behind him and looked around at what was usually a bustling scene of activity whenever Aunt Georgina was there. He might have sensed my loneliness because he moved farther into the room and said, "If you grab some mugs, I'll rustle up some tea. Then, we'll talk."

I nodded and pulled some large coffee cups out of the cabinet along with sugar and creamer from the refrigerator. "I'm sorry, but there's no Aunt Georgina brown bread in the house."

"Not to worry, she'll be here soon enough, Star," he said, pouring the boiling hot water into the mugs and tossing a few different varieties of herbal tea bags onto the table.

Minutes later, we sat quietly, sipping the hot brews. My Mead notebook sat on the table in front of me, opened to the notes I'd jotted down at the end of each day. I'd been so sure Skye was the killer. What next? I wondered.

Lorcan broke the silence first. "I'm afraid I have more bad news, Star."

I stopped perusing my notebook and looked up at Lorcan. "What could be worse than the current situation?" I asked, bracing myself for whatever Lorcan was about to say.

"Ashford's owner has been found. I delivered the pup back to him this afternoon."

My heart stopped. My eyes filled with tears. What had Lorcan done? I'd begun to think that Ashford was rightfully mine. I'd done everything to find his owner. What would Georgina do without him as a guard dog? He was part of our family—my family. I got up from the table, opened the kitchen door, and stared out at the green hills.

"He had to go back, Star. That's the way it works in this country. Those dogs are valuable."

"Oh, yeah. So valuable his owner lost him."

"The owner's been in hospital and didn't realize the dog was missing. When the owner got home after a long stay in rehab, he put out flyers. Someone in Cong recognized the dog and contacted the vet offices. Somehow, I got a call." Lorcan came and stood beside me by the door. "I'm so sorry."

I shook my head—Georgina and then this. I felt like an orphan all over again, but I wouldn't be defeated. I closed the door and sat back at the table.

Lorcan joined me. "Are you going to write anything in that diary?" he asked, pushing his glasses up his nose.

"I was just so sure."

"I trust your instincts, Star. I want you to know that. Don't give up. I'm in on this with you. And so are my mother and even the caustic Maeve. With everyone's help, we'll get to the bottom of this." He stopped and looked at me as if he weren't sure he should continue. "And I'll keep working O'Shea. He has to follow the evidence wherever it leads. He doesn't have any other recourse at the moment. I'll continue to press him about sharing information with me."

As Lorcan spoke, I clasped my hand around the cell phone holster clipped to my pants. When he was silent again, I nodded and said, "Okay, let's get going."

I pulled the notebook toward me and began writing questions as fast as I could. If Allen Skye hadn't killed Jimmy because of the numbers-running racket, then who had? And what other possible motives existed? Or maybe the numbers-running was still the motive? Maybe Allen had hired someone to kill Jimmy? Perhaps it had something to do with getting his hands on Jimmy's pub? I needed to check with Flann and Deirdre about the pub's ownership as a result of Jimmy's demise.

Next, I drew a circle in the middle of a blank page and wrote Jimmy's name in it. In the spokes and circles emanating from that center circle, I added the names of everyone who could have a motive for his murder. As I added names to the page, I knew I'd have to revisit Jimmy's timeline the night of the gala at the Turlough café.

"That's quite a list," Lorcan said when I finally dropped my pen onto the table.

"Yeah," I agreed. The bar staff, Ciaran and Rosaleen, topped my roster. They had a history of lying to give each other an alibi. Also, Rosaleen was at the gala, and, by her own admission, she'd seen Allen Skye in the area that night. And Nessa provided the entertainment that night. She definitely had motive, especially if she knew Jimmy was planning to get back with Georgina.

"Grainne Canny?" Lorcan's raised eyebrows said it all.

"Yes. I'm not certain the museum director belongs on my suspect roster, but she's definitely on my interview list. Jimmy was killed on the walking path. Why carry his body all the way back to the museum and place it in one of the exhibits? There's got to be a connection there."

Lorcan nodded. "Then whoever killed Jimmy had to have the physical strength to get his dead weight into the building. I think that eliminates some of the women on your list."

I shook my head. "No, I don't think the police found drag marks, but I've noticed at least a dozen wheelbarrows around the museum grounds. Anyone could have used one of those to transport the body—or a car. The path runs along the N5."

"Yeah, but..."

"You're sounding like the police. We have to consider every motive and every option including that more than one person is involved. Georgina's life depends upon it." I looked back at the mind map I'd drawn and added three more circles with spokes linked to Jimmy's name. In the circles, I placed Deirdre's, Flann's, and Georgina's names.

Lorcan looked surprised and said, "No, I don't think his family had anything to do with this. And Georgina—what's her name doing there?"

"Yeah, Deirdre was in charge of the event, so she was there, and so was Flann. I don't think she'd have been able to murder her brother along the walking path and be in the kitchen at the same time. I haven't sensed a motive on the part of the siblings to murder their own brother. But digging deeper into Jimmy's life means having to interview them."

"And Georgina?"

"She and Jimmy had a relationship. It might have ended a while ago, but she still cared about him. She might not like it, but I intend to interview her. In fact, she's my next interview."

Lorcan's blue eyes sought mine. "So, what now, Star O'Brien, information broker and apparently a mind-mapper?"

I couldn't help but smile at his teasing tone and the realization that this was the first time I'd ever shared my notebook musings with anyone. For once, though, I was glad to have some help, as long as Lorcan knew I was in charge. I stood up and stacked our empty mugs in the sink. Then, I pointed to the door. "I'm going to talk to Georgina. You should go talk to O'Shea again, and see what you can dig up about Allen Skye's assailant."

CHAPTER 18

"Really, is this how seriously you take your own security?" I asked Georgina when I found her turning the latch and lowering the closed sign on the front door. I'd entered through the unlocked back door.

"Star, you look exhausted. I guess Lorcan told you about Ashford," Georgina said as if she hadn't heard me.

"Yes, Lorcan explained, and I'm adult enough to understand that Ashford had to go back to his owner. But that doesn't negate how losing Ashford has made me feel like an orphan again."

"Ah, Jesus, Mary, and St. Joseph, you poor girleen. I wasn't thinking about your years as a foster child. Sit down, agra. I'll make us a cup of tea."

"Thank you. That would be nice," I replied, watching Georgina walk toward her storage room.

"For someone worried about a stalker, you seem very composed," I remarked, following her into the tiny back room, which housed a hot plate as well as the shop's inventory.

"I am. Allen Skye is dead, and they've arrested his killer," she said while carrying steaming mugs of tea toward the chairs she provided for shoppers. "I'm relieved to get back to normal, which means I leave my back door open."

I shook my head. Aunt Georgina was a smart business-woman and a wonderful dress designer. I couldn't believe she would dismiss the danger she faced so easily. "No, Georgina. The police still consider you a suspect. They are building their case on blood trace. In the words of Detective O'Shea, he 'plans to follow this conclusive DNA evidence to its end.' *You* are the prime suspect. And as such, you cannot let down your guard. Not until I've gotten to the bottom of what's going on here."

Georgina tossed one end of her scarf over her shoulder. "When clients came into the shop today and told me about the scene at the Wagon Wheel, I'd hoped the horrible nightmare was done and dusted."

"I'm curious. What were people saying about what happened?"

"Apparently, Skye was in the pub when a drunk customer pushed one of the servers. Skye took over and ordered the customer out of the pub. That's when the customer went crazy, jumped behind the bar, and assaulted Skye with a knife." Georgina sighed and straightened her shoulders. "But I'm not going to live under the thumb of the garda or whoever the evil person is who killed Jimmy if it wasn't Skye. I have a life to live, and I'm not going to waste my time with fear or recrimina-tions." Then she reached for my hand, the one clutching my phone. "And neither should you, Star O'Brien."

"I agree," I replied, squeezing her hand in return. "So, let's not waste time. I have a few questions about your relationship with Jimmy."

Georgina sat back in her chair, silent for a moment before she said, "What do you want to know?"

"I think you are hiding something from me."

Georgina's smile froze on her face. "What?"

"No, don't try to stop me. I thought you were all about truth and being direct. But I don't think you've told me everything regarding Jimmy."

Georgina nodded. "The last time I saw him, we had a terrible fight. And the next thing I knew, he was dead. I was in a panic, and I ran to Marcella's house. She had just convinced me to turn myself in when the guards appeared. Star, you were there when they arrived."

"What was the argument about with Jimmy?"

"Character," Georgina replied. "I believe he was a good man, underneath it all. But he was running the numbers. I've told you that. When I confronted him, he lost his temper. He claimed I didn't know whom I was messing with. 'Stay out of my business,' he said. And then, the letter arrived at Marcella's." Georgina's face lost its warm tone and blanched. "It came to Marcella's. Someone knew I was there. I was frightened."

"What letter?" I asked, feeling both angry and disappointed. I thought Georgina and I had a deeper relationship—one that didn't include secrets. Her nephew, Dylan, had kept secrets from me, but I never expected similar behavior from Georgina. I took a deep breath. "Okay, so where is the letter now? And what did it say? Have you shown it to the police?"

"No, I didn't give it to the garda! Jesus, Mary, and St. Joseph, Star. Whoever wrote the letter threatened Marcella and me. They told me to stay away from the guards. I couldn't put Marcella's life in danger or get her into trouble with the guards. I hid it. I knew you'd come. So, I hid the letter, knowing you'd find who was behind all this."

"Do you still have it?"

"Of course, I do." Georgina untied the belt she wore on her olive-green shirtdress. Then, she revealed a secret pocket sewn into the cloth belt. From there, she extracted a small sheet of paper and handed it to me.

"That's a clever hiding place," I said. "What other secret hiding places do you have stashed around your shop?"

"Well, I am a seamstress," Georgina replied, retying the belt around her waist. "I've got a few tricks up my sleeve," she continued with her usual breeziness.

"I'm glad to see some of the Aunt Georgina I know resurfacing. So, let me see that threat." I didn't have the heart to reprimand her about keeping this information from me. All I could do was move forward. I examined the single sheet. The paper looked like it came from one of those spiral notepads. The top of the paper was jagged as if it hadn't ripped cleanly. The background had an image of a tree imprinted on it, and one of those sayings that everyone thought were so cute: *the true meaning of life is to plant trees.* The writing, in pen, was slanted and scrawling as if someone had hastily written the message and quickly ripped it from its pad.

Stay away from the guards if you know what's good for you.

"Does anyone else know about this?" I asked.

Georgina shook her head. "No, it was slipped under Marcella's front door, and I hid it before she had a chance to see it."

"When was this?"

"Before you arrived back in Ireland. When I was staying at Marcella's."

"Where's the envelope?"

"There was no envelope. That's what was so frightening. It was delivered in person. Someone was right outside the door." Georgina stood up and collected our tea mugs. "Star, I'm expecting Flann to call for me. Can we continue this later?"

"Flann?"

"Yes, he checks in when I close up the shop each evening just to be certain I get into my car safely."

"Oh, does he know about the note you received?"

"No, but there was something else." Georgina's voice faltered. "I should have told you, but I didn't know if it mattered or not."

"Tell me what?"

"A few times lately when I've arrived at the shop, there has been a dead animal at the back door. The first time, it was a bird, and I put it down to maybe a baby falling out of a nest. But then, the next time, it was a rat."

"What!" I exploded. "With all that's going on, you decided not to say anything."

"Well, Flann stopped by the morning I found the rat, and I told him about it." Georgina reached out her hand to me. "I'm sorry, Star; I should have told you. That's why Flann has been coming by when I close up the shop."

"I'm angry that you didn't tell me, but I'm also relieved that you aren't locking up alone each evening." I tucked the note into the case that held my cell phone and then rose. "You know I have to give this to the police."

Georgina nodded. I checked the front door's lock and then proceeded to the back door. "I'll wait with you until Flann arrives."

"Have you heard anything more from Evelyn Cosgrove?" Georgina asked. We stood outside the back entrance to the shop.

"Not a word," I replied.

Flann suddenly appeared, sporting an oversized black umbrella. "Georgina, I see you have your niece with you. Would you like to join us for dinner, Star?" He opened the umbrella and held it over our heads.

"Flann, you're getting wet yourself," Georgina said. "Maybe I should just go home. We can get together another time."

"Not at all, Georgina. Come on, let's pop in over at McCarthy's restaurant. It won't take but a few minutes."

"That's a great idea," I said and scooted out from under the umbrella. "You two share. I'll meet you in the restaurant. I don't mind getting wet."

Normally, I'd have opted out of any so-called dinner plans Georgina might have with a male friend. But this was an oppor-

tunity to pump Flann about Jimmy. Ten minutes later, we sat at
a table for four with a pot of hot tea for Georgina, an herbal for
me, and a large glass of full-fat milk for Flann.

The restaurant was empty except for us. Probably because
most of the shops were closed, and the continuous stream of
people who came into town from the countryside each day
had dissipated. Although I'd said I didn't mind getting wet, I
was thankful for the bit of heat emanating from a gas-lit fireplace. I embraced my herbal tea mug to warm my hands.
After the server went into the kitchen to place our order,
Flann peppered me with questions about my business, how
long I'd been in Ireland, and if I'd found a buyer yet for my
cottage.

"I haven't made a final decision about French Hill," I
replied. I really didn't want to discuss this with anyone apart
from Georgina. She had enough on her plate other than
worrying about my plans for what had once been her ancestral
home.

Flann nodded. "I understand completely. When I was a
young sprout, we moved around, and it took its toll on the
family."

"Oh, I got the impression your family has been on the local
scene for several generations," I said.

"Ah, sure, my parents met in London, and we lived in
central London until they got the place here. It was my mother's family home. When her father died, she came back, and my
father followed."

"Jimmy never mentioned that to me," Georgina
commented.

Flann's eyes narrowed, and his lips formed a grim line
before he responded to Georgina. "Aye, Jimmy was an
ungrateful one at times." Flann shook his head. "You know he
bought a pub in our London neighborhood. He called it
Mahoney's Smithfield Pub. We were all young at the time. Mam

and Dad staked some of the funds to him. But he sold out after a few years and ended up back in Cong."

"Why Cong?" I asked. I'd been wondering why Jimmy lived in Neale, especially when his entire family seemed to dominate the Turlough area.

"Who bloody knows?" Flann, sounding exasperated, replied. "He always was secretive. Never talked to me about anything much." Flann shifted in his seat and turned his attention to Georgina. "Are we still on for tomorrow evening?"

I glanced from Flann to Georgina. Tomorrow evening? This was beginning to sound more serious than I'd even considered.

"Yes, if the material arrives tomorrow. I'll ring you and let you know," Georgina replied. Then, she looked at me as if she'd guessed what I was thinking. "I'm helping Flann with some redecorating. He wants to replace the slipcovers on his living room furniture."

"That's nice." I'd already seen Flann's place, and I didn't think he needed new slipcovers. I assumed this was just a ruse so he could be with Georgina. I decided to leave. "You'll see that Georgina gets home to her place," I stated firmly to Flann.

"Not to worry. I'll follow her and make sure Terrence is on the premises before I leave."

"Good. Please call me later, Georgina." I rose and walked out of McCarthy's onto Main Street.

I didn't feel too much like going home, so I turned right and walked back to Lucan Street and around to the backside of the Wagon Wheel pub. Police tape crisscrossed the back-alley entrance. The yard was empty save for a police car that, from my vantage point, looked unoccupied. Darkness lurked within the pub's kitchen windows. I wondered what would happen to the place. I wasn't finished with Allen Skye yet, nor with my hunch regarding his connection to Jimmy's demise. I pulled my cell phone out of its holster and called The Consulting Detective. Ellie answered on the first ring.

"We've been wondering when you'd call." Her voice sounded tired.

"Is everything okay there?" I'd dropped all our client work in Ellie's and Phillie's laps when I'd gotten the call from Marcella. I trusted in the team's abilities, but I also didn't want to burn them out. We'd been together since I founded The Consulting Detective. Ellie and Phillie held my hand when Dylan died and cheered me on in my search for my mother. I reminded myself often that I owed a lot to these two wonderful women.

"Yeah, everything is under control. How goes it there with your aunt?"

Ever since I'd returned from Ireland and told Ellie and Phillie about Aunt Georgina, they'd both taken an interest in her.

I sighed. "Nowhere near clearing this whole mess up yet. But you and Phillie can help." I didn't wait for Ellie to answer. I knew she'd already have her steno pad and pen ready at hand. "I want you to dig around and see if you can find out more about Allen Skye and the Wagon Wheel. Check out things like the credit bureau and the local business bureau. Highlight anything that looks suspicious."

"Got it. His name sounds familiar. Phillie was doing some research on him the other day, right?"

"Yeah, he was on my suspect list, but now he's dead."

"Oh, so you need this data as soon as possible."

"As always," I replied.

A human shadow fell across the pavement, and I looked up at its owner to see the cop who, I assumed, belonged to the police car.

"Move along, miss," the shadow's owner said.

I held up my free hand and nodded. "Look, Ellie, I have to run. I'll call you later."

I holstered my phone and walked closer to the cop. "What

happened here?" I asked. There was no way he knew who I was or what I knew.

"This is the scene of an investigation. Move along, please."

"Oh, the pub? Did something happen there?" I asked.

"Yes, miss. And it's my job to make sure this location is secured. So, please, move on."

"Did the police get the guilty parties?"

"Yes, although, with the recent demonstrations concerning the pork industry, we want to make sure nothing untoward happens. There's been a lot of strangers in the town." The cop moved closer to me. "Now, please, show me your identification. It's getting late in the evening for an American to be lingering around here."

"Oh, no need for that, Officer. I'm just out for a walk. Thank you." I didn't waste time getting back to my car.

Once back in French Hill, I sat down in my away-from-home office and googled the Irish pork industry. Interestingly, there'd been some recent demonstrations regarding pork and dioxin. I didn't think the issue had any bearing on Allen Skye or Jimmy, but I'd ask Flann about it. When I checked my email, I saw a note from Ellie stating she hadn't found anything untoward in Skye's records. She'd attached the report for me to review. After a few minutes, in agreement with Ellie, I closed the PDF file. There was nothing there. I pulled out my list from earlier in the day and put the staff from Jimmy's pub at the top for tomorrow morning. When my cell phone rang, I expected to hear Lorcan's voice on the other end. "Hello," I said.

Instead, I heard another voice. One with which I'd become familiar. "This is Evelyn Cosgrove."

"I've been waiting to hear from you." My hand pressed the phone against my ear. "I don't know what you want, but if you can't meet in person, you should stop trying to contact me."

I'd had enough of this cat and mouse game. I had no idea

what Evelyn was up to, and I'd gotten to the point that I almost didn't care whether or not I ever met her.

"I'll meet you at my house in Cong tomorrow. Say ten-ish."

More of this "ish" stuff. I certainly didn't have time for it. "I'll be there at ten a.m. But I'm warning you; I don't have any more patience left for whatever it is you are about."

I hung up, got into the shower, and washed away my anger and frustration. I'd lost everyone I ever loved, and now I stood a chance of losing Aunt Georgina. I couldn't let that happen. Nor could I afford to let Evelyn's games keep me from the search for my mother.

I'd just towel-dried my short bob when I heard the knock on the kitchen door. Lorcan stood in the doorway, a covered plate in his hand. "Come on in," I said.

He handed the dish to me. "My mother sent this. It's one of Georgina's homemade brown breads. Mom has several in the freezer. She knows how much you love it." Lorcan looked around the kitchen. "She also knows that you aren't much of a cook."

I tried not to look into Lorcan's blue eyes or notice his hair where it brushed his collar. "Well, what are you standing there for? Put on the kettle, and we can discuss tomorrow's plans. I want to know what you might have gotten from O'Shea."

Lorcan smiled and got to work slicing thick slabs of bread and boiling the water. In the meanwhile, I took some mugs and dishes out of the cabinets. In no time, we filled up on bread, butter, and blackberry jam.

"So, what have you got?" I asked when the last crumbs of the loaf were cleared from our plates.

"O'Shea is firm in his belief that Allen Skye's death is in no way related to Jimmy's. Although he does admit that he's open to considering any threads we might come up with."

"Wait a minute." I pushed away from the table. "He's willing to consider information we might provide?"

Lorcan nodded. "Yes, he knows it looks bad for Georgina because of the blood on Jimmy's shirt. O'Shea also admits there could be other reasons for that." Lorcan sat back in his chair and casually stretched. "My guess is he knows it's all circumstantial at this point, and he realizes that anything we come up with helps him in the long run."

"Is he doing anything else to solve the case? Other than his misguided focus on Georgina?" I knew I sounded sarcastic, but I couldn't help myself. Lorcan's friendship with the detectives went back to their school days and included Dylan. But I didn't feel like this was a situation where I wanted emotional ties clouding my judgment.

"I'll keep the conversation with O'Shea open. What are you planning to do tomorrow?" Lorcan asked.

"Drive over to Neale and Cong to talk with the pub staff and meet with Evelyn Cosgrove."

"So, you've heard from the Cosgrove woman. Any more leads?"

A few months ago, Lorcan had set up an appointment for me at the National Archives in Dublin. I wouldn't admit it to him, but I will be forever grateful. I hoped the information I gleaned in the archives would contribute to the search for my mother.

"I won't know until I talk to her. I understand her reticence because of what happened in Cong. I get it. But at this point, that's all over with."

"Everyone is different, Star. Sometimes, it takes a while to get over bad experiences. Are you sure her behavior stems from the Cong murders?"

"Well, she's agreed to meet with me tomorrow morning in Cong." I picked up my cell phone from the table and looked at the display. "It's getting late, and I want to get started early tomorrow."

I don't know why I said that. I just knew I didn't want to

show my emotions to Lorcan. Not because I didn't think he'd understand, but because I didn't trust that I wouldn't break down completely. He was that kind of listener. I could see it when I looked into his eyes.

"Yeah, you're right." Lorcan got to his feet and walked to the back door. Then, he turned to face me. "Goodnight, Star. Sleep well." He opened the door and was gone.

I locked up and glanced out through the glass panes at the moonlit, star-studded sky. I smiled, turned out the lights, and slept better than I had in a long time.

CHAPTER 19

The night sky surrendered to a dry Irish morning. The sun, breaking through my bedroom window, warmed my face. I jumped out of bed, donned my yoga pants, laced up my sneakers, and went for a walk along Cottage Road. The morning was quiet except for the birdsong emanating from the shrubs bordering the byroad.

I didn't know if I wanted to remain in Ireland for any amount of time. But I did know that I loved the solitude that came with the cottage's setting. When I was there, I felt cloistered from the cares of the world. The scent of pink roses, growing up the stone walls, surrounded the garden and filled the air with a sweet aroma. At the back of the garden, hazelwood and ash trees observed my coming and going like silent sentries, ready to offer protection. I chuckled at the russet-colored fox running for cover under a thicket of hedgerows. The car horn blasted me out of my reverie. I turned to see Georgina's Avensis parked near the cottage's barn. I waved and ran to greet her.

"Is everything okay?" I asked.

"Of course, it is. Aren't I allowed to visit?" Georgina pulled a bag of groceries out of the car and handed them to me. "Here you go. I figured you needed some supplies. So, what are your plans for the day?"

I jostled the bags on my hips to take a closer look at Georgina. I'd never noticed the puffiness under her eyes before. She may put up a good front, but she wasn't fooling me. She had to be worried. Not wanting to add to her anxieties, I didn't tell her about my planned visit to Jimmy's pub. "Evelyn Cosgrove called me last night. I'm heading over to Cong to meet up with her."

Georgina's lips blew out a breath. Her shoulders relaxed. "That's great news. I'm hopeful for you, Star. Are you taking anyone with you? Is Lorcan available? Maybe he could pilot you over?"

I laughed. Even a murder investigation couldn't keep Georgina from matchmaking. "No, I'm not going with Lorcan," I replied, remembering the last time Lorcan had taken me to Cong. We'd flown in his piper airplane, and I'd loved the experience of gliding over the green fields and stone walls. I moved the groceries from one hip to the other. "I have to go, Aunt Georgina. Thank you for the goodies. I'll call you later."

She nodded. "That would be good, agra," she said, climbing back into her car. She waved as she pulled away from the grassy verge. It didn't take me long to stow the groceries in the fridge. Forty-five minutes later, I was showered, dressed, and on my way to Cong Village. The road to Cong led me through Neale and past Jimmy's pub. The parking lot was empty. I didn't know what time the staff arrived on the premises but assumed they would be there on my return trip.

～

MY ARRIVAL IN CONG COINCIDED WITH THE VILLAGE'S MARKET day. Vendor stalls offering fresh baked goods, vegetables, meats, and dairy products lined the main street. I headed down Abbey

Street toward Evelyn's house and pulled into the church parking lot. I sat in my car for a few minutes and then walked across the street to St. Mary of the Rosary Church. I stood outside the church doors and observed Evelyn's house for signs of movement and life. Baskets, filled with Fuchsia, sat on both sides of the front door. From my vantage point, the plants looked healthy and watered. Three women emerged from the church. They glanced at me but didn't say anything. I thought about the last time I'd stood outside Evelyn's house with the same purpose. On that day, I'd gone for a walk in the Cong woods and happened upon a murder scene.

Once again, I strode across the street to Number One Abbey Street. I knocked and waited. A few cars sped by over the small bridge that crossed the River Cong on their way up the drive to Ashford Castle. I knocked again—nothing. I felt one hand ball into a fist. The other grabbed for the cell phone in my holster. A few more cars passed by, but Evelyn Cosgrove was a no-show.

I pulled my phone from its holster and called The Consulting Detective. I knew they weren't in the office yet, but I left a voice mail, instructing Ellie to send me the address of the dig in London where Evelyn Cosgrove worked when her husband disappeared. She wasn't going to get away with this again. If I had to follow her to the ends of the earth, Evelyn Cosgrove and I were going to have a heart-to-heart.

I turned on my heel and looked over at the church door. *No,* I said to myself. Prayers weren't going to help in this instance, just good-old persistence and hard work. I left my car parked where it was and continued to Main Street.

I headed directly to the former Jane Doherty Fitness Vitality studio, which had been renamed Sarah's Yoga Place. Sarah, Jane, and Jimmy had been business partners at one time. Jimmy had been a silent partner. He'd sold his stake to Sarah after Jane was murdered. According to Georgina, he'd wanted to make amends for not telling her about the partnership with Jane when he and Georgina were dating. But Georgina hadn't budged. In hindsight, I wondered what else Jimmy had concealed. Of course, he must have had secrets; otherwise, why was he dead? Some secrets, I had learned, lived parallel and undiscovered lives of their own.

On the way to the yoga studio, I passed the Quiet Man Café, and I couldn't help but think of Paul Doherty and our lunch there. Across the street from the café, Ben's Rarities sported a fresh coat of paint and a new name. I looked away and increased my stride. I wouldn't dwell on a past that I couldn't change.

Sarah was at her desk when I entered the studio. She extended her hand in greeting. "I never thought I'd see you again," she said, looking a bit puzzled. "I'd heard that you returned to the States."

I nodded. "Well, here I am again. I guess you heard about Jimmy. The police have mistakenly focused on my aunt as the prime suspect in his murder. I'm digging into Jimmy's relationships, and I thought you might be able to fill me in."

Sarah's smile faded. "Oh, I don't know what to tell you. I had to buy him out of his portion of the yoga studio." She glanced around the room and then said, "I'm glad of that. I had to beg and borrow funds from my family, but I'm now the sole owner of the place. Do you want to sit for a few minutes? I don't have a class for another thirty minutes."

"No. I'm wondering if you've spoken to him recently. Did he have other business deals that he was involved with? Did he seem worried about anything?"

"I don't know about other business deals, but he was worried about the pub in Neale. I think that's why he was so amenable when I approached him to sell me his share of the studio. He needed the money."

"Oh. I thought the pub did pretty well for itself." I recalled the first time I'd gone to the place and could barely move through the tightly packed crowd.

"Things have been a bit tight recently. Really for everyone because of the economic downturn, you know, the mortgage-backed securities issue. Jimmy mentioned that he'd owned a pub in London ages ago, which had gone under. He didn't want that to happen again, especially in County Mayo. He admitted he wouldn't be able to bear the embarrassment of going broke in his own country."

"Then he must have felt relieved to get out of your partnership," I said.

Sarah shook her head. "I don't know. We agreed to the deal, and my lawyer handled all the paperwork. I knew your aunt ended the relationship with him, and that broke him up pretty badly. He told me he planned to win her back but didn't say how. That's the last time I spoke with him."

"When was that?"

"Oh, not too long ago, really. I ran into him one of the days that the market was on Main Street. He was buying supplies for his pub."

I thought about the vendor stalls I'd passed. I didn't think there'd be anything that Jimmy would need from a street market. "Really? I'm surprised that he'd get supplies from a market event."

"I'm not. Jimmy was really into the buy local idea, and that's one of the reasons he chipped in on the yoga studio. He wanted to support the region's economic activity." Sarah's look at me seemed surprised. "You didn't know that about him?"

I shook my head. "I only spoke to him a few times, and our conversations were about the Cosgrove family and then the unfortunate events here."

"Check the meat vendor stall. Jimmy always bought his meat from a local producer. Maybe he can tell you more."

I noticed Sarah's appointment book open on top of her

desk. "Has Evelyn Cosgrove been in lately?" I asked.

"No." Sarah shook her head. "She seems to have disappeared off the face of the Earth. I heard about the university colleague who was stalking her. But with him in jail, I'd think she would feel safe being around town again." Sarah pulled some towels out of a basket that sat at her feet and began folding them. "The village is just getting over the murder and everything we learned about one another. I don't mean to sound selfish, but for everyone's sake, I hope Evelyn is okay. We couldn't take another killing."

"I hope so too," I replied, but I didn't like this disappearing act at all. I'd already had a life-changing disappearance in my life. "Thanks, Sarah. Take care," I said and left the studio.

I took my time walking along Main Street. I paused at every stall, trying to see the products on display through Jimmy's eyes as a pub owner and entrepreneur. He'd been a silent partner with Sarah. Maybe I was missing some other special agreement that had gone bad. There was only one meat vendor stall. A banner advertised local free-range beef, and I stopped to read the menu and prices.

"How are ya?" said the six-foot-tall, sandy-haired man standing behind the display table. "We've got some prime rib steaks on sale today. Good stock. Raised right here in the area. What can I get for you?"

I pulled a consulting detective business card out of my pocket and placed it on the table. "I'm interested in a local publican, Jimmy Mahoney."

"And who are you that you're asking about a recently departed man?" The vendor picked up my card. After a cursory look, he slipped it into a jacket pocket. Then he moved out from behind the table. Although he stood directly in front of me, his stance didn't seem threatening. I surmised that he wanted to separate himself from his business and my questions.

"My name is Star O'Brien. Georgina Hill is my aunt.

Currently, she's under suspicion of Jimmy's murder. But she's innocent, and I'm going to prove it. So, I'm interested in learning more about Jimmy and motives for his murder."

"I'm Paul." He passed me a card with the words *Life has more meaning with meat* printed under his name, Paul Shephard, Meat Purveyor. "Ah, yeah. Jimmy went with her for a while, didn't he? Poor lad. He always fell for the ones who left him in the end. I've met her, your auntie. She's a good egg. What do you want to know?"

"How well did you know Jimmy?"

"He bought his meat from me every market day. A good customer. That's the extent of it other than the odd time I had a pint at his pub, and we talked about life in general."

"I'm curious as to why he bought his meat here. Why not have it delivered from a distributor?"

"Jimmy was very into the organics and knowing the origins of your food, especially his meat." Shephard pulled at his beard. "You know we had a big scare recently about the levels of dioxin in the pork, and Jimmy swore he'd never buy pork from a distributor again." Shephard chuckled. "I don't know how long Jimmy could keep that up. We Irish love our bangers and sausage rolls."

The cop guarding Skye's pub had mentioned concerns related to the pork industry. But I dismissed the idea that it had anything to do with his death. As far as I was concerned, the shadow lottery racket provided a much bigger motivation for murder. "Did Jimmy ever get into hassles with anyone at the market?"

"No, he was a quiet guy. Ran into his sister here once in a while, and I'd see them chatting with each other for a few moments."

"Deirdre?" I asked. "Gee, that's curious. Cong seems like a long way to come to a market from Turlough." I made a note to ask Deirdre about it.

"Yeah. And speaking of the devil, there she is." Shephard pointed toward a cluster of vendor stalls selling vegetables, herbs, and spices. Deirdre's back was turned to me but her companion, Willem, spotted me at the same time I saw him. I turned back to Shephard. "You said Jimmy didn't have luck in his relationships with women. Anyone in particular?"

"Ah, yeah. The musician, Nessa. The one who plays the bodhran. She wouldn't leave Jimmy alone, and I warned him she'd be trouble. I can tell you this much. Her husband, Pete, wasn't happy about her getting chummy with Jimmy. I've heard Nessa and Pete are in the middle of a separation period. But I've seen him around when I've been in Jimmy's place, especially when the wife was in the pub with Jimmy."

Out of the corner of my eye, I caught movement where I'd last seen Deirdre and Willem. I turned to see Willem nudging Deirdre and steering her in the direction opposite from where I stood.

"Look, I've got to go. But you've been helpful. May I contact you if I have any more questions about Jimmy?"

"Aye, sure. He didn't deserve what happened to him. Anything that helps find the murdering devil who bashed his head in."

I hadn't seen Shephard at Jimmy's funeral, but I surmised everyone in the county must know about Jimmy's head injuries. Although I wished the police had kept the information under wraps, I accepted that it would be impossible. After all, the police couldn't keep people like Terrence or Grainne from talking about what they'd seen when they found Jimmy's body.

I caught up with Deirdre and Willem just as they were putting bags of produce into the back of a navy-blue, four-door sedan. I didn't know any other way to begin other than diving right in.

"Hey, I'm surprised to see you here. I'd have thought you'd do most of your shopping for the café in Castlebar."

Deirdre slammed the trunk of the car shut and frowned at me. "We aren't as insular as you might think, Miss O'Brien." She glanced behind me. "What are you doing here?"

"I'm looking into Jimmy's friends and what has been going on in his life. You know, what might have been the reason someone wanted to murder him. Because it wasn't Georgina Hill."

Willem glanced at his watch and opened the driver-side door. "Deirdre, we have to get going. The event begins at half seven, and we need to prepare the food."

Interesting. I thought Willem's purview was the grounds and flower beds, but he seemed to be everywhere Deirdre was when an event involved her or the café.

"Why don't you leave Jimmy and the case to the guards, Miss O'Brien?" Deirdre pulled at a strand of hair that had fallen out of the headband she wore. Her eyes searched the crowd behind me again, almost as if she were looking for someone. I glanced around but didn't notice anyone or anything untoward. Unless, of course, she was worried about the meat vendor, but then I didn't think she had seen me speaking with him.

"I didn't get the impression that you and Jimmy were close. Yet I just spoke to someone who claims you often met up with your brother here in Cong. Why here? Why not at his pub or in your café?"

Willem's face twisted as if he were in pain. His hand went to his forehead, and he rubbed his eyes.

"Willem, let's go now," Deirdre commanded while she jolted open the dinged-up passenger door and jumped in. Willem gave me a sad glance. Then, he did as he was told.

I watched the car as it left town. Deirdre was hiding something. That much I knew. But what and from whom? I'd have to talk to her again, but next time I'd make sure she didn't have Willem in tow.

CHAPTER 20

The sun hung close to the horizon, painting the evening sky with a rose hue. I straightened the knapsack on my shoulder and checked for my cell phone in its holster. Then, I returned to Evelyn Cosgrove's house.

The 6:00 p.m. Angelus bells rang out from St. Mary of the Rosary church as I walked back to Abbey Street. Once again, I stood at Evelyn Cosgrove's door—the third time since last September. But nothing had changed since earlier in the day. The silence deafened me. The church bells rang again, sounding like a death knell. I said a silent prayer for answers. Then I got into my car and headed for Jimmy's pub.

The empty parking lot didn't surprise me as much as the newly painted door. A weekday evening at 6:30 p.m. accounted for the empty parking lot. But I couldn't think of any reason why the pub's previously red door sported a freshly painted coat of green. The sign hanging over the pub door had also gone the same way. Green with a new name. Ciaran's Pub and Grill. I hadn't heard who inherited the business. I'd naturally thought it would pass to one or both of Jimmy's siblings. I wondered if it had and was already sold or if it had always been destined to land into Ciaran's hands.

The few men sitting at the bar gave me cursory glances before turning their attention to the television suspended on the back wall. That, too, was something new. The few times I'd been in the pub, I'd noted the traditional musicians who'd gathered in front of a cozy fireplace. I wondered how long the business would last if it moved from its traditional roots to a run-of-the-mill sports bar.

One thing hadn't changed, though—Ciaran's angry glances. He came around from the back of the counter and met me inside the door. In a hushed voice, he said, "If you're not here to enjoy the atmosphere or have a drink, you should leave. Now."

A door from the kitchen swung open, and Rosaleen joined us. She placed her hand on Ciaran's elbow and said quietly, "Let's not get excited. It isn't a good way." Then, she turned to me and said, "May we help you, Miss O'Brien?"

"Yeah, I'm starving. How about a bowl of vegetable soup, brown bread, and a basket of sandwiches?" Then I pushed past both of them. I wasn't about to be frightened away, but I conceded to their concern and chose a table near the back of the pub. There was no cozy fire and no musicians. A few bodhran drums and sticks lay on a bench near the cold fireplace.

When Rosaleen arrived with the food, I invited her to sit down. She glanced nervously over at Ciaran, who'd retaken his position behind the bar. "I can't. We're under new management, and I don't want to lose my job."

"I noticed. So, when did all this happen? I would have thought one of Jimmy's siblings would be in charge."

"I have no idea. Ciaran came in yesterday and said he's the new owner." Rosaleen sighed. "I'd hoped it would go to auction. My uncle was dead set on buying the business. He's disappointed and a little mad at me that I didn't tell him what was happening." She looked over at Ciaran, who was laughing at something one of the customers was saying. "But I didn't know.

So, it's a closed issue now. Signed, sealed, and delivered without a peep."

I didn't doubt her words. For something to have changed hands this quickly, it must have been very hush-hush. I'd have Phillie do some digging on the deal. I moved on to another topic. "I'm curious. Did Jimmy ever talk about the bar he owned in London?"

Rosaleen nodded. "Sure, all the time. He warned us about not getting in over our heads if we ever wanted to manage our own business."

"I'm surprised he talked about it at all. Most serial entrepreneurs more or less leave their financial disasters buried in the past, never to be resurrected again."

"I don't know. Maybe he thought of himself as a mentor."

I nodded. By this time, a few of the other tables were occupied. Rosaleen shoved her order pad into her pocket and said, "Look, I have to get back to work. Now that Ciaran is the owner, our relationship has changed, and I don't want to lose my job."

In between drinking my soup and eating slices of brown bread, I kept an eye on Ciaran. If he was still nervous about me being on the premises, he didn't show it. Rosaleen bustled in and out of the kitchen, bringing plates of food to the tables filled mostly by couples. Some of the men walked up to the bar to place drink orders and then carried the glasses of beer back to their tables. Rosaleen chatted with several as she moved in and out of the kitchen.

Ciaran continued to work the people at the bar, wiping it from one end to the other, stopping along the way to talk with customers. I had to admit that his outgoing personality would probably keep the place going. I finished up my meal, rose, and walked to the end of the bar to settle up with Rosaleen. A tip jar stood at the edge, filled to capacity. I wasn't surprised. From what I'd observed, Rosaleen knew most of the customers, and they all seemed to like her. I decided to catch up with Ciaran another time.

~

AS SOON AS I GOT BACK TO THE COTTAGE, I PICKED UP THE PHONE. Ellie answered on the first ring.

"Star, how are things going? Any answers yet related to your aunt and the police?"

"No, but I have something for you and Phillie to research. Find out how probate in Ireland works when someone is deceased. Jimmy's pub in Cong has already changed hands, and I don't know how that could have been possible. Also, did he have a will, and if so, can you find out the details? If he did and the pub was left to someone, I want to know to whom. And I need that information as soon as possible."

I could hear Ellie scribbling on her steno pad as I spoke. "Anything else?" she asked.

"Yeah, can you send me any clippings about a pork toxin issue here in Ireland?" I stopped talking and looked at my notebook. "Oh, and have Phillie email the article she found about Evelyn Cosgrove and the London dig. Also, any articles about her husband's disappearance."

"Okay. We'll be right on it. Talk later."

I sat at my computer and gazed out the cottage's window. I didn't think Evelyn's husband's disappearance had anything to do with my mother, but I wanted all the details I could find for my trip to London tomorrow. I walked into the kitchen and stared at the house phone attached to the wall inside the kitchen door. I picked up the antiquated phone cord and twisted it in my hand, and I wondered if Lorcan would call with any updates from his discussions with the police.

My computer's notification alert sounded, and I returned to my office. Phillie had sent four emails with PDF attachments about the dig in London and Evelyn Cosgrove's husband. I spent a few minutes studying the documents before googling the address. Then I booked a flight from Knock Airport. Next, I logged into Ryan Air's website and booked myself on a morning flight from Dublin to London's Stansted Airport. I'd just finished up when the house phone rang.

"Good, you're home. I was worried about you. Why haven't you called me?" Aunt Georgina's voice sounded muffled as if the scarf she typically wore covered her face.

"I was about to do that, and I'm fine. I just booked a flight to London for tomorrow."

"London." Georgina's scarf had moved. Her voice came across loud and clear but sounded worried. "What, in heaven's name, is taking you to London?"

"Evelyn Cosgrove. She was a no-show again, and I'm going to try one more time to pinpoint her. If I can't do it in London at the dig, well, then, I'll just write her off as some kind of crank."

My words reminded me of Dr. O'Dowd. She'd described Evelyn as flighty. I made a note to call Dr. O'Dowd this evening.

"It's been ages since I've been in London. I'm afraid I can't give you any advice about traveling. Maybe Lorcan could help. He's got the Piper Cub that he likes to take up all the time."

I shook my head. "No, I'm going on my own. Lorcan is more valuable here in Castlebar, keeping tabs on the police. Which reminds me, are you home? And is Terrence there with you in the cottage?"

"Yes, Star. He's outside. And Flann is stopping by with some take-out food. We're going over swatches for the furniture that he wants re-covered. You just worry about yourself and getting a good night's rest before your trip."

"Okay. I'll call when I get back." I hung up the phone just as a knock came at the back door. Lorcan stood outside with a plastic takeaway bag from Dunne's stores.

"Something for me?" I asked when I opened the door.

"Thought you might like some decent food while we catch up on where we are." Lorcan placed the bag on a counter next to the sink. Then, he reached for the dinner plates stacked up in one of the cabinets. My stomach growled as the smell of cooked chicken wafted through the kitchen.

"Oh, and my mother sent her special mashed potato salad with scallions," Lorcan added.

I didn't waste any time. I sat down and allowed him to fix a plate for me while I reviewed my notebook and suspect list.

"Okay, what did you learn from the police today? Any new leads or suspects?" I asked as I devoured most of the chicken thigh and mound of salad Lorcan had placed in front of me.

Lorcan shook his head. "At this point, the guards are pretty wedded to their theory."

I slammed my notebook shut. "I knew it. They can't get out of their own way, can they? I just hope tomorrow's trip isn't a waste of time."

Lorcan raised his eyes from his overflowing dinner plate. "What are you planning? I thought we'd go back to Neale. Maybe we can get more information from Ciaran or Rosaleen that could point us in the direction of the numbers-runner."

"No need. I was already there earlier."

"Did you learn anything useful?"

"Well, for one thing, Ciaran now owns the pub. That's curious, if not downright unusual. I didn't think probate happened so quickly. And, I was in Cong and happened to run into Deirdre and Willem, and something doesn't seem right there either."

Lorcan's blue eyes crinkled into a smile behind his glasses. "Do you always suspect everyone, Star O'Brien?"

"I do when an innocent person is at the mercy of the bungling police. I've asked Phillie to follow up on the probate process and how Ciaran came into ownership of the pub so quickly. But there is something you can do for me while I'm in London tomorrow."

"Why London?"

"Jimmy owned a pub there, once upon a time, and it went bankrupt. Maybe there's a connection to someone who might have wanted him dead. Oh, and I'm chasing down Evelyn Cosgrove. One last time."

Lorcan pushed away his empty plate. "Looking into Jimmy's background in London makes sense, but what do you hope to accomplish with Evelyn? If you can't meet with her here, what makes you think you can find her in London?"

"I know what you're getting at. But she is leading that dig in London. There isn't anything else I can do at the moment. It may all be a waste, but while I'm there, I'll visit Jimmy's former pub."

Lorcan nodded. "What do you want me to track down for you?"

"I've been hearing about an issue with dioxins and pork. The cop outside Allen Skye's place mentioned it. I don't think it has anything to do with Jimmy, but it's a thread to follow. I want to know if Jimmy was having any issues with people, potentially for refusing to order pork supplies from distributors. Do you think Flann can shed some light on the issue?"

"Flann is a dairy farmer, Star, but I'll call him. However, in my opinion, the environmental issues were done and dusted a while ago. It seems like quite a stretch for Jimmy to be that involved in the issue."

"You're probably right, but when I was digging into what happened at Ashford Castle, I recall hearing Jimmy on the phone arguing with a distributor. Maybe there is a connection."

Lorcan pushed his glasses up on the bridge of his nose. "Okay. Not to worry. I'll follow up with Flann. So, how do you plan to get to London?"

"I've booked flights from Knock to Dublin and then on to

Stansted. The dig isn't far from there." I paused, realizing that when I'd looked at the map to pinpoint the pub and the dig site, they were within blocks of each other.

"I can drive you to Dublin."

I shook my head. "No, I'm fine."

Lorcan stood, gathered up our dishes, and proceeded to set them in the sink. "Well, then, I'd better get going. You're going to be on the move early in the morning." His eyes sought mine before he continued, "Just be careful. All this numbers-running intrigue isn't just nefarious. It's dangerous. I wouldn't want anything to happen to you, Star."

"Thanks, Lorcan. I'll be okay."

With that, he exited the cottage. I rinsed off the dishes and left them on the counter to dry. Then, I made a quick mental checklist of what to wear and pack for my one-day trip. I decided this was a fitting way to procrastinate and keep from thinking about Lorcan.

CHAPTER 21

When I arrived at Stansted, I visited a banking kiosk to change euros to pounds. From there, the friendly attendant at the information counter provided a train schedule to Central London's Smithfield district, the location of the Charterhouse Square dig. While the train moved along from one stop to another, I considered how I'd approach the current pub owner. First, though, I'd go to the dig site. My frustration with not reaching Dr. O'Dowd the night before had worn off by the time I'd arrived in Dublin. Each time I spoke with her, she continued to protect Evelyn's privacy. So, the conversation would probably have hit a brick wall.

The walk from Smithfield's train station took me past London's oldest market. I took a quick peek inside at the meat-laden storefronts and butchers ready to serve the public. After the market building, a series of trendy-looking restaurants, bars, and professional buildings occupied the avenue. When I reached the dig, its enormity surprised me. I'd expected something the size of a postage stamp, given my impression that older areas of London were filled with narrow Victorian row houses. Instead, I found yellow tape, fences, and warning signs surrounding an enormous-looking circular pit:

CHARTERHOUSE SQUARE DIG SITE. NO TRESPASSING.
CONTACT: DR. COSGROVE, UNIVERSITY COLLEGE
DUBLIN FOR FURTHER INFORMATION. PHONE: 011 353 93
658 5424

I was writing down the phone number when I sensed a pair
of eyes on the back of my neck. I quickly glanced around the
sidewalk, which was filling up with lunchtime shoppers. Just as
I turned my attention back to the dig, I caught sight of Grainne
and Deirdre walking toward me from the direction of the
market. Not sure I was seeing correctly, I looked again. But, yes,
there they were. What were they doing in London? It didn't
seem plausible that they just happened to be there on the same
day I planned to visit Jimmy's old pub. Deirdre certainly
seemed to get around—first Cong and then here. I placed the
paper with the telephone number into my knapsack and strode
in their direction.

"Hey," I shouted over the sounds of the traffic. I could see
Deirdre, shifting a bag with the words *"London Central Markets"*
on it, raise her hand toward the street. Before I could reach
them, Deirdre and Grainne climbed into the back of a taxi.

At that moment, a familiar-sounding voice behind me said,
"Are you following me?"

I turned toward the voice's owner, a young female with
hazel eyes, freckles, and creamy white skin. I immediately
suspected the short blonde hair was a wig. She was about my
height. And, from the looks of her, she was short on pounds.
Her clothes hung on her thin frame.

The woman continued, "I said I'd be in touch."

For a minute, I was dazed. Could this tiny, dreadfully thin
wisp of a woman be Evelyn Cosgrove? And how did she know
I'd be in London? How did she even know who I was? Finally, I
said, "So, you're the mysterious Evelyn Cosgrove."

"How did you know you'd find me here?"

"I didn't, but now that bit of business is settled, how do you know who I am?"

"I'm a researcher, not too different from you in some ways. I've seen your picture in the newspaper archives back in New Jersey."

I nodded, accepting her answer. Dylan and I had attended many of Ridgewood's events. "Let's talk about my mother," I said.

Evelyn's face flinched at my words, and she scanned the area around the dig site. She shook her head. "No, it's too risky. Why didn't you listen to me?" she asked as she untied a scarf from around her neck and dropped it into her tote bag.

"I did listen. I went to your house in Cong for the meeting that you asked for. But you were a no-show," I replied.

Instead of answering me, Evelyn reached to unclasp a gold chain that hung from her neck. She thrust the piece of jewelry into my hands.

I gasped. My feet cemented to the ground. I stared down at the dented and scratched, tiny, heart-shaped gold locket. I already knew what I'd find when I opened it. Nevertheless, I placed my thumbnail into the worn notch. The front opened and revealed two pictures—one of me and the other of my mother. Two smiling faces posed in such a way that it appeared as if they regarded one another. For a minute, it seemed as if the ground beneath my feet fell away.

"My mother. How did you get this? Where did you get this? Who are you really?" I choked on the words. I remembered my mother wearing this locket when I was about six years old. But then it disappeared.

Evelyn reached forward and closed my hand over the locket. "Your father. Our father. He wanted you to have this, and I promised him that I'd find you." Evelyn stopped speaking, pulled the scarf back out of her tote bag, and wrapped it around her neck. "I have to go." She turned and hurried into the bustling crowd.

Too emotional to move at first, I remained riveted in place for a few seconds before throwing my knapsack to the ground and hurtling myself after her. Desperate to catch her, I shoved my way through the crowded sidewalk, but by the time I got beyond the throng, she'd disappeared. I turned back to where I'd left my knapsack.

"Is this yours, Miss?" a senior-looking man said, holding the knapsack in his hand.

"Yes, thank you. You're very kind."

"Are you okay? Can I get you a water or something? Maybe you should sit down. You look a little bothered." He pointed to a bench outside one of the restaurants.

"I'm fine, thank you," I replied.

Tipping his baseball cap at me, he walked away. But I took his advice, walked to the bench, and sat down in an effort to collect myself. The first thing I did was pull the phone number from the dig site out of the knapsack. Although I didn't expect a human to answer, I called and left a message.

"This is Star O'Brien. I'd like to speak to you. Please call me as soon as possible." I didn't say much else. I didn't have the words, really. I'd come this close to actual information about my mother, only to have a complete stranger intimate that she was my half-sister or maybe sister. And then she ran.

I pulled my notebook out of the knapsack and poured my heart and soul out onto the lined paper.

Why didn't I know my father? How had he ended up with the locket my mother had worn? And why did he ask Evelyn to give it to me? Why didn't he look for me himself? And what about my mother? She must have been the one to send him the locket. Why had she kept me from him? What had happened to my mother? I wanted to scream as I wrote the question that had haunted me all my life. Didn't she know I'd spend years in foster care? I had so many questions. And then there was one other person on this planet, Evelyn Cosgrove, who might hold the answers to some of those questions. She had to tell me what she knew.

While I wrote, I got my emotions under control. When I finished, I placed the diary back into my knapsack and stared at the locket I'd wrapped around my wrist. I unwound it and then opened the clasp, gazing again at the smiling faces from a time in the past. I wondered if I'd ever regain that smile. I closed the locket, placed it into the pocket of my capri jeans where my cell phone was holstered, and refocused my efforts on clearing Georgina's name. I resumed my walk to Jimmy's former pub.

The Smithfield Pub looked exactly like Jimmy's pub in Cong. It seemed to me that he might have had to leave London and his business behind, but he had taken his memories with him. Once through the door, I immediately approached the bartender, whom I recognized as the owner, Donna Adams. Phillie had provided her name and a picture from a recent news article, so I didn't waste much time with introductions.

"Hello, my name is Star O'Brien. I'm investigating the death of a former owner of this pub named Jimmy Mahoney." I placed one of my consulting detective business cards on the bar, where the owner leaned on her elbows, watching an afternoon talk show.

"Now that's a name I haven't heard in quite a while. He's dead, is he?"

"Yes, he was murdered, and my aunt is the number one suspect, according to the police. I'm checking into Jimmy's past because I think someone he knew killed him. Maybe someone from his time here in London."

Donna nodded her head. "Let's move to the back of the pub. We can chat in one of the booths there." She pointed to a dark corner of the room. "Liam," she called.

"Yeah, love." The voice belonged to a tall, lean, and

muscular man who popped his head out of a doorway behind the bar.

"Take over here for me, will you, love?"

"Sure thing." He walked to where Donna had been standing and propped his chin in his hands to watch the same show she'd been absorbed in when I entered the place.

She noticed my puzzled look and laughed. "What can I say? The husband. We share the same astrological sign."

We quickly settled into the corner she indicated. "I don't want anyone to hear what we have to discuss. Bad for business," she said.

I waited patiently.

"Have you heard about the missing woman?" she asked.

I felt my eyes widen as I leaned forward in the chair. "No, who is it, and what do Jimmy and this pub have to do with it?"

"He owned the place when the girl went missing."

"When was this?"

"Lord, it must be almost forty years ago. No one was ever arrested. And the lass was never found."

I nodded my head when I heard no one was arrested. The police, as usual, probably chalked up another missing woman to something other than kidnapping or murder.

"Who was the woman? Did anyone come forward about what happened?"

I thought of the female victims of Retinol in bars and pubs in the United States. I was sure London or Ireland hadn't been exempted from similar issues.

"From what I was told, the place was packed to the gills that night. It was a traditional Irish music night with bodhrans, pipes, and fiddles. I doubt if anyone saw or heard anything. Supposedly, the girl was with a group of friends. They parted ways outside on the sidewalk, and the lass was never seen again." Donna paused to sip from the glass of lemon water she'd brought to the table. "The bobbies may not have found what happened, but word got out around the neighborhood. Business dried up. Mahoney closed up and left for Ireland."

"How do you know all this?" I asked. I estimated her to be about my age, too young to have known Jimmy back in the day when he owned this pub.

"Ah, I grew up near here and heard all about the stories. This place was boarded up for years. I went to culinary school but couldn't find a restaurant kitchen to call my own, so my husband over there suggested we buy this place. And here we are."

"Were you in touch with Jimmy when you transacted the purchase with the bank?" I didn't think she would have been but asked anyway.

"No, most people around here thought he got a bad rap. What happened here could have happened in any pub, especially when there wasn't as much education about the things evil people do. We've got cameras all over the place and bouncers who mingle with the crowd to make sure everyone gets home safely. We live here in Smithfield, along with everyone else, and we want to keep our neighborhood safe."

"Did you ever meet any of his family members? I understand the entire family lived in London for a while."

"No, I'd have been too young to remember. As I said, I never met him. I just grew up hearing about the pub, and then when I bought the place, I learned his name." Donna paused and tilted her head to look closely at my face. "You don't sound Irish, and may I ask what makes you think this pub has anything to do with the bloke's murder?"

"I'm American, and it's a long story," I said in response to the quizzical look that passed over her face. "I'm not looking to make trouble for you. I had another reason to be in London and thought I'd look up Jimmy's old establishment while I was here."

She nodded and pursed her lips as if she had something

she wanted to say but wouldn't or couldn't. I waited, but she said nothing. I pulled another one of my business cards from my pocket and placed it on the table. "If you think of anything else I should know, please give me a call. Time is short for my aunt. I'm determined to find Jimmy's killer." I stood and walked toward the exit door. "I guess you get a lot of workers from the dig site?" I asked quietly.

"Oh, boy, do we. A lot of our dinner trade comes from the crew. They like to have a few in the evening before they head to wherever they come from. That place has had its share of mystery and not just what they've dug up." She shook her head.

"Really? What do you mean by that?"

"A missing man. Husband of one of the dig people. That case hasn't been resolved either." Donna shivered. "I hadn't thought of it in a while, but it makes me wonder if we have some kind of serial killer in the neighborhood." She shrugged. "Well, I have to get going. Good luck with your aunt." She walked over to her husband and whispered into his ear. He glanced at me and nodded.

I didn't wait around. I headed toward the dig site. The place was empty, which seemed odd. The pub was empty, too, when I left. So, just how many of the dig site workers frequented the bar? From my observation, I'd say hardly any at all. This time, I didn't feel as if anyone was watching me. I pulled my cell phone from its holster and dialed Aunt Georgina.

"Star, are you home already? Are you coming by for a cup of tea on the way from Knock? I miss seeing you." Georgina sounded upbeat for someone who was living under the threat of at least thirty years in prison.

"I'm still in London. It will be late when I get home. I'll see you tomorrow."

"Oh, how did the trip go? Did you learn anything more about Evelyn?"

I reached into my pocket and touched the locket. "Yes, I did. I have a lot to tell you but not now. I have a question, though."

"Yes."

"Did Jimmy ever mention his pub in London? Did he tell you about the woman who disappeared while he still owned it?"

Georgina didn't reply immediately. In fact, the silence lasted so long that I began to think I'd lost the call. I heard her take a deep breath.

"Georgina? Did you hear me?"

"Oh, yeah, that place. I don't want to talk about it, Star. Look, I've got to go. Give me a ring when you get to the cottage. Goodnight." Georgina ended the call.

What a strange reply and so unlike Georgina to rush off the phone, I thought, staring at the empty dig site. I debated whether to remain in London for another day. But considering Evelyn's behavior thus far, I decided nothing would be gained by staying. I pushed my phone back into its holster, straightened the knapsack on my back, and made my way toward Ireland.

CHAPTER 22

I managed to ignore the heart shape burning a hole in my pocket and my brain until the wheels on the Ryan Air flight rotated. I then held the tiny, open piece of jewelry in my hand and gazed at my mother's face. The last time I'd seen the locket, it was around her neck. When she'd tuck me in at night and kiss my forehead, I'd reach up and touch the gold case. I could still hear her voice:

"When you grow up, Star, this will be yours one day. Until then, I'll wear it close to my heart, which is where you will always be. Just remember, courage and strength. That's what this means to me, and one day, I hope you will find the same."

I'd been too young to know what my mother might have meant when she said those words. And, honestly, I still didn't understand completely what all this was supposed to mean. I closed the locket and squeezed it in the palm of my hand. Courage and strength—I needed it then more than ever.

"That's a cute little trinket," the woman sitting beside me remarked.

"Yeah." I nodded and put the locket into my pocket. Then, I retrieved my notebook from my knapsack and forced myself to process what I'd learned about Jimmy. Maybe the horrific case

of a missing woman in his pub had something to do with his
murder or not? If so, it meant that someone in his life knew
about what had happened and, in some way, might have
blamed him. The question then was, who knew? I didn't like
Aunt Georgina's sudden reticence to talk about Jimmy's
London pub. That wasn't like her. Did Flann and Deirdre
know? I definitely needed to talk to them again. And what
about the police? Did they know? And did they have any
threads that connected to his past? Lorcan had promised to talk
to them, but I had to see O'Shea myself. And what about the
numbers running? That might have started in London. Did the
missing woman see something she shouldn't have? Lastly, I still
hadn't given Nessa a pass. I put my notebook away when the
flight attendant announced preparations for landing. Courage
and strength—I'd need it for what I had to do.

EARLY THE NEXT MORNING, I EMAILED PHILLIE TO DIG INTO ANY
murders or missing women cases reported in London around
the neighborhood and time that Jimmy owned his pub. That
done, I called Lorcan and asked him to meet me at the Mayo
County Library in Castlebar. I planned to visit O'Shea as soon
as possible but wanted any information Lorcan had before I
walked into the police station. Then, I called Georgina before
she left home to open The Golden Thread.

"Aunt Georgina, it's Star."

"Certainly, I recognize your voice, agra. So, you're home.
That's grand. When will I see you? I'm not too busy in the shop
this morning. Why don't you come in for a cuppa, and we'll
chat? Beth will assist any customers who might pop in."

"Later. I have a few things to run down this morning. But I'll
be there as soon as I can." I didn't mention her shyness
yesterday when I'd asked her about Jimmy's London pub. That

was something I planned to do in person when I could see her reaction. "Is everything working out with Terrence?" I thought of the feeling I'd had of being watched. "Any more signs of someone watching you?"

"No, I'm fine. I'm feeling much more secure, especially with Terrence here when I'm home. Don't you worry, Star. Everything will come right in the end. Now, I've got to go. See you later."

I wish I had Georgina's same sense of optimism, but I knew from experience that life didn't always go according to plan. After a quick run along Cottage Road, I showered, grabbed a few slices of the bread Lorcan had brought by, and wolfed them down. Then I bolted out the door to town.

Luckily, I found an empty parking space on the road that ran between the library and the police station. As I neared the buildings, I spotted Lorcan standing outside the large glass doors to the library, speaking to a willowy-looking young woman with long red hair. A medium-sized dog sat at her feet; its head cocked as if listening intently to their words. Oddly, I felt a pang of regret, seeing him there, looking relaxed and engaged in conversation with a beautiful woman.

"Hi, I didn't expect anyone else to be with you," I said when I reached the two of them.

"Star, this is an acquaintance of mine. She owns a private investigation firm called AP Braxton. And, this is her pup, Turlough. Penny, this is my friend Star, whom I was telling you about."

Penny and I shook hands. Then I said, "Are you investigating Jimmy Mahoney's murder?"

Penny laughed. "Oh, no, I was just talking to Lorcan about his wind project in Wyoming and some of the issues we've been having in Blacksod Bay. That's where I live."

At that moment, Penny's phone rang. Glancing at the display, she said, "I've been waiting for this call. I have to go.

Nice to meet you, Star. I'll catch up with you again, Lorcan."
Penny walked away, and the little black dog with a face like a
fruit bat followed her.

Lorcan and I entered the library and sat at a desk in one of
the reading rooms.

"You look tired." Lorcan's blue eyes scrutinized my face
from behind his glasses.

I didn't want to admit it, but I was exhausted. I'd sat in the
cottage living room most of the night, staring at my mother's
locket in the hopes of finding the answers I just didn't have.

"That pub that Jimmy once owned in London. Well, a girl
went missing from there when he owned it."

Lorcan leaned forward in his chair. "What?"

"Yeah, seemingly he lost the place after business died down,
and then he came home to roost here in Ireland. I spoke to the
current pub owners. The girl was never found, and the case was
never solved."

"Do you think there's a connection?" Lorcan asked.

"I hope not."

"No wonder you look so fatigued. Are you sure you're up to
this today?"

"I'm fine. Let's get to work."

I pulled out my notebook and showed Lorcan the diagram
I'd drawn with circles and arrows from the pub in London to
Cong. My current suspects were in the circles. I'd tried to determine if there was any overlap between London and Cong. I'd
already eliminated anyone on the list who was in my age range.
They would have been too young to be involved. That list
included Nessa and Grainne, the museum curator. I left
Jimmy's siblings on the list, although they claimed they hadn't
had anything to do with his business. It was curious, though,
that Deirdre had been in Cong and London. Places that I'd
been in at the same time. When I'd finished explaining it all to
Lorcan, I dropped my pen onto the paper.

"So, what do you think?" I asked.

Lorcan laughed and pushed his glasses up the bridge of his nose. "I'm surprised that you want my opinion. Did something else happen that's caused this sudden change in attitude?" Once again, his eyes studied me.

I pulled the locket, which hung around my neck, from under the collar of my pink cardigan.

"Among other things? This happened." I raised the locket so he could see it. "It's a picture of my mom and me. I was about six when this picture was taken. You know I went to London to dig into Jimmy's previous business dealings, but I also went to the dig site that Evelyn is running. While I was there, I had a feeling that someone was watching me. Just at that moment, Evelyn found me." I shook my head. "I also saw Deirdre and the museum curator at the same time. They jumped into a cab just as I tried to catch up with them. And then Evelyn came along. I'm feeling like my notebook here with the circles and arrows is a little defense against getting to the bottom of what's going on. I almost need a little artificial intelligence to figure this all out." I stopped talking, realizing I'd just about spilled my guts to Lorcan. Once again, my mother's words came to mind—Courage and strength. I straightened up my papers and said, "So, I'm heading over to the police station to talk to O'Shea. What about you? Were you able to speak with Flann?"

Lorcan nodded. "I rang him several times but kept going to voice mail. I stopped by his place. It turns out he was in his wine cellar and didn't hear the phone."

"What did he say about Jimmy and the recent pork industry tensions?"

"Flann dismissed the whole idea. Said Jimmy was always getting involved in hopeless cases but never committed to anything. Flann was surprised, though, that you'd gone all the way to London to track down info about Jimmy."

"Really, he doesn't know me very well, does he?"

"That's for sure. He seemed hurt that you'd gone to London rather than asking him about Jimmy. But I smoothed things over and told him you were primarily there gathering info on Evelyn Cosgrove."

"A tie between what happened to Jimmy and the pork industry tensions the police mentioned was a long shot. But thanks for following it through." I picked up my notebook and stood to leave.

"Star, wait, don't leave yet," Lorcan said, taking the notebook from my hand and putting it aside. "Are you okay?" he asked. "I can't imagine what it's like for you to have lost everyone you've ever loved."

I hesitated at the loaded question. I didn't feel I had the time or the heart to get into it.

Lorcan looked up at me carefully for a moment before adding, "I can see you carrying the world on your shoulders. Everyone does. Please, tell me, how are you feeling?"

I sat quietly back down before I answered. "I'm scared. I don't want to lose Georgina."

Lorcan reached across the table and took my hand in his. "It's okay to be afraid once in a while, but you're not alone anymore. I'm your friend, and I care about you."

I didn't pull my hand away; instead, I chose to let it rest in Lorcan's. Finally, I said, "Thank you."

"Star, just know that when you need me, I'll be there," Lorcan said, handing back my notebook.

I nodded, gave him a brief smile, and reluctantly removed my hand from his to take the notebook. Then, I set out to confront Detective O'Shea.

~

I'D BEEN IN THE CASTLEBAR POLICE STATION SEVERAL TIMES before, so it didn't take me long to make my request to the person on duty at the entrance desk. A few minutes later, I entered O'Shea's office.

"Miss O'Brien, what can I do for you?" Compared to the other times I'd seen O'Shea, he looked relaxed. A smug smile crinkled the scar on his face. He offered me a seat. I didn't like to think about what that might mean.

"I was in London yesterday and discovered a missing woman case connected with a pub Jimmy owned there. Have the police looked into any connections between that event and Jimmy's murder?" I watched his face to gauge his reaction.

A shadow moved across the bridge of his nose, momentarily eliminating the smug look I'd seen a few minutes earlier. "Now, Miss O'Brien, we've talked before about your interference in garda matters. What you found or didn't find has no rhyme or reason connected to this case in the here and now." He narrowed his eyes and pursed his lips, causing the scar to disappear. Then, he said, "We have the murder weapon."

I froze in my seat, and my breath escaped quickly as a flood of relief washed through my body. "Thank goodness. So, you can make a public statement regarding Georgina Hill's innocence."

O'Shea shook his head. "No, Miss Hill remains a suspect. It was her blood that we found on the deceased's shirt. Unfortunately, the murder weapon doesn't bear any fingerprint or DNA evidence that would exonerate her."

"That's ridiculous, and you know it." I leaned forward in my chair. "You grew up in this town. You knew Dylan Hill, and you've known Georgina all your life. She's innocent. Don't you believe in justice?" I couldn't help myself. Police blindness that led to wrong judgments angered me.

O'Shea's face flushed red. "I agree with you. I have known Georgina all her life. Unfortunately, it is her blood on the victim's clothes. Therefore, she is the prime suspect." O'Shea pushed a pile of papers on his desk to the side and leaned forward. "Look, I get it. And I know we haven't seen eye to eye before, but maybe if you shared whatever information you have, it might help our case. It might just clear Georgina."

I sat back in the chair and perused O'Shea. Lorcan had vouched for him in the past, and Georgina's life was on the line. "What is the weapon?"

"A ball-peen hammer."

"That's a specific kind of hammer. And not something found in every homeowner's tool kit. Where was it found?" I asked.

"In a wheelbarrow just outside Turlough Park House. Unfortunately, the weapon's been wiped clean. But the medical examiner has determined that the nature of the wound matches with the hammer. Microscopic blood stains matched Mahoney's as well."

My stomach spasmed. The possibilities were astronomical. Droves of people came through the museum each day in tour buses and family camping vehicles. Same with the greenway, especially on weekends when people went for walks and ended up at the café for tea and cake.

"So, what are you doing about it?" I asked. I didn't think anything I'd learned so far could be helpful to the police other than the information about the London pub and the numbers-running.

O'Shea shrugged. "We're doing what we can with the evidence we have, and that's all we can do."

"No. Whoever killed Jimmy must have known him. To strike someone with a hammer and bash their head in—that's a crime of red, searing, hot anger. It's got to be someone he knew. Most likely connected to his businesses, either here or in London. Have you questioned the bar staff in Cong?"

O'Shea nodded his head in the affirmative. "They are all accounted for during the night of the murder."

"Are you sure? A witness told me they weren't at their stations in Jimmy's pub on the night of his murder."

"Ah, yes. The amateur Detective O'Brien." O'Shea smirked. "We know about their whereabouts—all documented and witnessed."

"What about the numbers-running racket?"

"That case is closed, Miss O'Brien." O'Shea stood up to indicate that our conversation had ended.

But I wasn't ready to give in so easily. "I don't agree." I pulled the threatening note Georgina received from my pocket and threw it onto O'Shea's desk. I pointed at the paper and said, "She is a victim, not a murderer."

O'Shea leaned forward and read the note. "You don't seriously expect me to accept this as any kind of evidence. I thought you were brighter than that, Miss O'Brien."

Of course, I knew he was right. Nothing would be gained from analyzing the paper. Nevertheless, I continued Georgina's defense. "That may be so, but when I was in London yesterday, I saw Jimmy's sister, Deirdre, and the museum curator, Grainne. It seems like an eerie coincidence to me. Have you talked to them about their relationships with Jimmy? Numbers-running isn't just exclusive to men."

"We are interviewing everyone who knew Mr. Mahoney and following up on all leads. But again, I have to reemphasize that we have physical evidence tying your aunt to the shirt the victim was wearing when he was battered to death." O'Shea glanced at his watch and moved from around his desk. He opened the office door. "Now, if you'll excuse me."

"What about the person or persons who wrote the letter? I know Lorcan reported the vandalism incident at Georgina's cottage. And someone has been leaving dead animals at her shop door. She is in danger from someone. What are you doing to protect her?"

"Thank you, Miss O'Brien." O'Shea held the door open

wider. "I'm pleased you stopped by for this chat. Cooperation on the part of the public is an important part of solving any case."

When I stepped out onto the sidewalk, I thought about the murder weapon, the nature of the killing, and Jimmy Mahoney's business dealings. I knew exactly what I needed to do next. I straightened my knapsack, got into my car, and drove directly to the Round Tower at the old Turlough Cemetery.

CHAPTER 23

I didn't see a living soul in the cemetery. The flowers that
Aunt Georgina and Flann had left on their parents' graves
were still there, looking slightly wilted and beaten from nighttime showers. Pretending to be a tourist searching for ancestors, I walked around the rocky and hole-ridden grounds,
perusing headstones. I finally arrived at the tower's base.

It was still dead-quiet in the graveyard, so I proceeded to
examine the tower's fieldstone. As I neared, I glimpsed the edge
of a paper fluttering in the wind. I looked closer and could see a
loose stone. *That's interesting. The last time I was here, I didn't find
the hiding place.* I removed the stone and the paper. Sure
enough. Two columns of numbers, written in ink, separated by
a hyphen, cemented my hunch that neither Jimmy nor Allen
Skye was the mastermind in this shadow lottery game. But I
was surprised that someone continued using the same hiding
place.

From where I stood on the knoll, I could see the museum
grounds below me, the café, and the entrance to the greenway
walk, which began on the museum grounds and ended in
Castlebar. Whoever hid the hammer had a great vantage point

from which to watch the comings and goings and had obviously decided to hide the evidence in plain sight.

I scanned the area again. Satisfied that I was still alone, I replaced the betting slip with a blank sheet that I ripped out of my notebook. Next, I drove over to the museum grounds and parked my car. From there, I walked back to the round tower, where I positioned myself inside the stone-walled structure. I didn't know how long I'd have to wait, but I intended to confront whoever was playing this game—no matter how much time it took.

I didn't have to wait long. Just as twilight descended and the gravestones darkened, the gravel surrounding the tower crunched. I crouched in place. My breath came in quiet, short spurts, and I dared not move. Then, I heard the stone scrape.

"What the devil?"

I remained far enough in the shadows until I glimpsed the voice's owner. I smiled when I saw who it was. I snapped pictures, using the up and down volume on my phone's earbuds, which I texted to Lorcan with a message. *"I'm at the Round Tower. Call police. Numbers-running culprit."* Then, I moved out of the shadows.

There he was—Paul Shephard, the meat vendor from the open market in Cong.

"Making a special delivery?" I said. I'd been right about a mastermind, and his involvement made sense. With his meat distribution business, he had access to the pub owners. He'd already admitted he knew Jimmy. I wondered who else was involved. But I decided to leave that up to the police once this guy was under lock and key.

"You don't know who you're dealing with. You took private property. You'd better return it, or"—he smiled and waved his hand toward the graves—"you might find yourself in a deeper hole than you're already in."

"You're the one in the hole." I showed the picture to him.

"The police will be here shortly. In the meanwhile, you can tell me why you killed Jimmy. Were you angry because he decided to get out of the business?"

"Are you daft, woman?" He roared the words at me.

"You'll have plenty of time in prison to figure that out." I heard sirens in the distance. "You can make a run for it, but it won't be long before the police round you up."

"We'll see about that." Shephard grinned like the Cheshire cat and scrambled away. But when he got to the rusty turnstile gate, it refused to budge. Grabbing the gate with both hands, he tried to force it open.

"Your auntie should have heeded my note. You'll pay for this," he shouted up at me while continuing to rattle the gate open. Suddenly, it gave way to the street, and he fell out of the cemetery onto the pebbled verge. He jumped up, brushing himself off. "You're way out of your league. And not as smart as you think," he yelled. Then he jogged down the road toward the Turlough village shops, where I assumed he'd left his van for his clandestine cemetery visit.

I walked to the Hill family headstone—the resting place of Dylan's grandparents. I said a silent prayer for protection. Then, I raced back to the museum.

≈

I STOOD NEXT TO MY CAR IN THE MUSEUM PARKING LOT AND watched the blue flashing lights of a police car wind up the hill and stop near the cemetery walls. I dialed Lorcan.

"You got my message."

"Are you okay? Why didn't you tell me what you were planning? I'd have staked out the place with you." I held the phone away from my ear. It was the first time I'd ever heard Lorcan raise his voice. "I thought we were working on this case together," Lorcan continued.

I didn't know what to do. I felt upset that Lorcan might be angry with me. "I'm sorry," I said.

"Right. I'll meet you in town at the Davitt Restaurant. Meanwhile, I'll get over to the garda station and ensure they have this Shephard person under wraps. Promise me you won't make any detours between Turlough and Castlebar."

For once, I didn't feel like fighting. Instead, sudden bone-tiring fatigue flowed over me with the relief that Jimmy's murderer would soon be in custody and Georgina's life would go back to normal.

I REACHED THE DAVITT FIRST, WHERE I SETTLED INTO A BROWN velvet booth at the back of the restaurant. While I waited for Lorcan to arrive, I recalled the last time he, Georgina, and I had sat there. He'd offered to get me into the National Archives in Dublin. He'd also challenged me not to give up on the search for my mother. Relieved that Georgina was out from under a murder charge, I intended to focus on Evelyn Cosgrove and how she'd ended up with my mother's locket.

I'd just ordered a bowl of vegetable soup with brown bread and butter when Lady Marcella and Maeve walked in.

"Lorcan called and asked me to meet you here," Lady Marcella said. She waved her hand for me to move in so she could sit next to me. "He's still at the garda station, talking to O'Shea."

I nodded at Marcella and watched Maeve take a seat opposite us. She seemed to have increased her presence in Marcella's life since the deaths in Cong. I didn't like her, but then she wasn't my friend. The server arrived with pots of tea, raisin scones, and a serving dish with blackberry jam.

"Ah, I'm starving." Marcella broke a scone onto her plate and covered it with jam.

Maeve sipped her tea, quietly taking in the place. "I haven't been here in ages," she said. "I'm surprised you'd come back here, Marcella."

My ears perked up. Did Marcella have a history with this place? But then I dismissed Maeve's statement. As I'd learned, she had a way of misleading people. I had other things to worry about, like why it was taking Lorcan so long to show up.

Marcella shrugged and looked at me. "Have you spoken with Georgina?"

I shook my head. "No, I tried calling, but her phone went to voice mail. But knowing how connected she is to what goes on throughout the county, she's probably already heard the news. Besides, I want to be sure about this before I get her hopes up." I picked up my cell phone and dialed Georgina, but the phone went to voice mail immediately.

We'd just asked for another round of tea when my phone rang. "Star." Lorcan's voice sounded worried. "I have bad news. Shephard has an alibi for the night of Jimmy's murder. He was in hospital emergency for a gastro problem."

I clutched the phone in an effort to keep from throwing it across the room. "Are the police sure? I'm certain Jimmy was supposed to meet him that night. It all makes sense when you think about it. He drives the delivery van from pub to pub, dropping off meat provisions. He had the perfect cover for running a shadow lottery racket."

"I don't disagree," Lorcan replied. "He was supposed to meet Jimmy that night. But he got so sick he had to drive to Castlebar General Hospital. I'm sorry, Star. O'Shea checked his alibi immediately. That's why I'm late. Shephard is not the killer. I'll be there shortly."

I ended the call.

When my phone rang again, I glanced at the display and forced a smile onto my face before I said, "Hi, Georgina."

Georgina's voice shook. "Someone broke into the cottage."

"What!" I looked at Marcella. "Did you call the police? Where are you now? I'll be right there."

"Call the guards? When they think I'm a murderer? No way."

"Where's Terrence?" I asked, wondering where he was when this went down.

"Don't blame him. I sent him on his way early. Jesus, Mary, and St. Joseph. The place has been ransacked. Everything is thrown around. I don't know what they were looking for. I don't have anything of value. Just my design patterns. Some of my pictures with Jimmy are missing. Oh, Star. This is a nightmare." Georgina's voice cracked on her final words.

I glanced at my watch. "I'll be there in a few minutes. You're coming to French Hill with me tonight."

Marcella grabbed our belongings and ran to the counter to settle the bill. Maeve followed Marcella. Since Lorcan hadn't shown up yet, I figured he was still with the police. I wouldn't delay any longer. I strode over to Marcella.

"Wait for Lorcan. Tell him I'm on my way to Georgina's cottage."

Marcella nodded. Maeve stood off to the side. I exited the restaurant and got to my car.

~

GEORGINA'S CAR WAS IN THE DRIVEWAY WHEN I ARRIVED. I PARKED behind hers and ran to the front door. I knocked. No answer. It couldn't have been more than twenty minutes since I'd spoken to her. She knew I was coming, and I didn't waste time. I tried the door. It opened.

"Georgina?" Silence. My cell phone rang. "Lorcan, I'm at Georgina's, and she's not here. I'm going to look around."

"I'm already on my way. My mother brought me up to speed. Star, wait for me. Don't go in."

"I'll be here." I ended the call and walked through the open doorway. I quickly glanced around Georgina's cottage, taking in the mess someone had made of the place. Obviously, Georgina hadn't had time to tidy up after she'd called. Had someone been in the cottage all along while we were talking? But who could it be if the police had Shephard in custody? Obviously, he couldn't be the one stalking Georgina. Finally, I had to admit that something else was going on. My relentless pursuit of my shadow lottery theory might have put Georgina in more danger. But what else could it be? I walked back to the open doorway and waited for Lorcan. I didn't want to touch anything until I had another set of eyes to help me.

LORCAN AND I AGREED WE WOULDN'T HANDLE ANYTHING DURING the walk-through. Georgina's sewing basket was overturned— swatches of material strewn across the floor. A photo album lay open on the kitchen table, and several pages were ripped in the places where a snapshot might have been. Aunt Georgina had said that several photos of Jimmy were missing. More and more, this looked like whoever had been stalking Georgina was angry about her relationship with Jimmy. Nessa's name came to mind. But was she capable of murdering Jimmy? And, if so, did she have the strength to wield a ball-peen hammer at some-one's head and load his body into a wheelbarrow?

"We have to call the guards." Lorcan's voice interrupted my thoughts.

I nodded.

CHAPTER 24

I blocked O'Shea from moving toward Georgina's cottage before he'd even closed the door to his unmarked car.

"You were supposed to keep her safe." I glanced at the phone in my hand, hoping it would ring any minute and Georgina would be on the other end. Lorcan stood beside me.

"Hey, get back," Keenan shouted.

O'Shea held up his hand. Keenan stopped.

"You, Miss O'Brien, are impeding this investigation. If you don't move out of the way, I'll have to arrest you." O'Shea looked at his friend Lorcan as if to say, "do something."

Lorcan moved closer to me, creating a human wall. "We have every right to be angry. Georgina Hill is in danger. And, Tom, I'm in agreement with Ms. O'Brien. Something has been wrong with this investigation right from the start. An innocent woman has been falsely accused, who, I might add, may be in more danger now than she was when this all started. What are you going to do about it?"

O'Shea slammed his car door. Then he stepped around both of us. "Listen, man, we're doing our job. This wouldn't be the first time someone concocted his or her disappearance to draw suspicion away from themselves. Just let me and my men process this scene."

O'Shea waved to several police cars that had arrived. Uniformed officers emerged from their cars and walked toward the front door of the cottage. Keenan and O'Shea led the pack. When he got to the door, O'Shea turned around and said, "Don't leave the premises. I may have some questions for you."

I spun anxiously toward the sound of another car entering the driveway. I released the breath I was holding when Marcella and Maeve emerged. Marcella ran toward us, and Maeve hung back, watching the police.

"Lorcan, have you heard from Georgina?" Marcella's usually neatly coiffed blonde hair looked as if it had been blown around by a strong wind.

"No," Lorcan replied. "The guards and detectives are looking through the cottage now. We tried her phone, but it goes right to voice mail."

Marcella ran her hands through her hair and paced the driveway.

Maeve joined us; then she locked her eyes on me. "Do you think she's gone into town looking for you?"

I didn't answer. Maeve always seemed bent on creating a diversionary alternative to the current situation.

Maeve continued, "Do you think this has anything to do with Evelyn Cosgrove?"

I held my breath, containing my anger. "No," I replied through my gritted teeth. That's all I could bring myself to say to her.

Lorcan stepped between us. "We need to finish up here with the guards. Then, let's all go to French Hill, where we can regroup."

Lorcan's words made me think about where Georgina had gone when this nightmare erupted. I turned to face Maeve and

Marcella. "I hope you aren't hiding Georgina," I said in an accusing tone.

Marcella gasped. "Of course not. Georgina is my best friend. If she came to me, I'd tell you." Marcella looked up at Lorcan. "I'm as worried as you are, and I think we should check The Golden Thread. Sometimes, she goes there at night when she's running behind on a customer order."

"Marcella, I'm sorry. I didn't mean to snap, but I'm so worried." I pointed at Georgina's car. "No, she's not at The Golden Thread. She was in the cottage when she called. She knew I was coming to pick her up. Someone must have taken her. There's no way she would have walked into town in the dark."

Lorcan nodded. "I agree, but I think you and I should go by The Golden Thread, just in case someone dropped her there." He turned to his mother and said, "You and Maeve go ahead to French Hill and wait for us."

Soon after Marcella and Maeve left, O'Shea exited the cottage and approached us. "We will secure the cottage. In the meanwhile, please don't enter the premises again until we have finished with our work."

"Don't worry, Detective O'Shea. We'll be searching for the real killer," I replied. Then I got into my car and left.

LORCAN FOLLOWED CLOSELY BEHIND ME AS WE DROVE TO Castlebar. Red brake lights lined both sides of the street as cabs waited to take nighttime club-goers home. Lorcan and I maneuvered the narrow Main Street between the taxis, turned down Market Street, and parked in the lot behind Georgina's shop. I grabbed the key to the shop from my knapsack and ran toward the back door. Within seconds, I knew the place was empty. I walked through to the front of the shop and checked the locks.

They were in place, and everything looked as it should. Lorcan silently poked around the piles of fabric in the back room, where Georgina kept her design work but found nothing. I rang her cell again in case it was somewhere in the shop. But all I heard was the phone go to voice mail in my ear.

"Let's get to French Hill," I said, and I locked the door, and we drove out of town.

CHAPTER 25

Already at the cottage when we arrived, Marcella sat on the stone wall at the front of the cottage. Despite my concern for Georgina, I smiled at the sight of her "ladyship" seated on the side of the road. Maeve, smoking a cigarette, stood farther back in a corner of the garden. When she spotted Lorcan and me, she stubbed it out on one of the stones. I frowned. She might be Marcella's friend, but I couldn't get it out of my head that she was there for something else.

"I take it she wasn't at the shop," Marcella said. She rose and brushed off her linen pants.

"No," Lorcan replied.

"Let's get inside and get to work," I said. I unlocked the double front doors and left them open for everyone to follow. I wasn't in the mood to entertain, so I didn't offer tea. I turned on the lamps in the living room and gestured to the chairs. "Give me a minute. I need to call The Consulting Detective."

~

"Ellie, I have an urgent assignment for you and Phillie. I want you to drop everything else you are working on."

"Of course," Ellie replied. "What do you need?" Phillie's voice chimed in. I smiled. Ellie probably signaled for Phillie to jump on the call.

"I want you to profile Georgina Hill," I said.

"Your aunt, I mean, Dylan's aunt?" Ellie asked.

"Yes, I want you to treat her like one of the missing women's cases that we track for families." I squeezed my cell phone before I uttered my next words. "Because she is missing." I stopped and thought about how vague she'd sounded when I mentioned Jimmy's pub in London. "I want to know more about her background. Did she ever work or live in London? Was she ever married? And look specifically at the Smithfield area of London and the Smithfield Pub. Did she ever live or work in that area?" I paused. "Any questions?"

"No, boss. I'll get on it right away," Phillie assured me. I heard her hands already making keystrokes.

"Thanks," I replied and hung up. When I returned to the living room, Lorcan sat on the floor with a paper and pen in hand, asking Marcella questions about Georgina.

"And you're sure she didn't mention talking to anyone about Jimmy's murder?"

Marcella shook her head. "No, this was one time she didn't use her relationships with everyone to track down information." Marcella glanced at me. "Honestly, I think she was too scared about whoever was shadowing her, and she didn't want to put herself out there like she usually does."

"But she must have in some way—enough to end up missing. There is no way she ran from the police," I said, disagreeing with Marcella. "Georgina would do anything to help me with an investigation."

Maeve moved away from the table where she'd been looking at some pictures of Dylan and me. She held her phone in her hand. "I'm sorry, but I just got a message that requires my attention. I must leave."

Funny, I hadn't heard her phone ding, but I was glad to see her go anyway. I watched her walk down the front path until she cleared the gate. Then, I turned to Marcella and said, "Has Maeve been in touch with Georgina?"

"What? No. I don't think so. Maeve would have told me. She's as upset as I am, and she wouldn't keep that from me."

"You sure?" I asked.

"Absolutely. She's a good egg. Just a little surly around the edges at times. Probably all that history research she does." Marcella's eyes turned to look out the front door. Then, she continued, "Although I've been somewhat surprised that she's willing to spend so much time away from her books."

I nodded but didn't waste any more time on Maeve. "Okay, let's go over the timeline and what we know again."

Fifteen minutes later, we'd updated the list of potential suspects with the help of my notebook. No one person jumped out at me. We needed to look at this from another perspective.

"If we assume that Jimmy's murder had nothing to do with his shadow lottery activities, then it has to be something more personal," I said.

"The garda's stuck on his relationship with Georgina, but Nessa Bantry's been in the picture recently," Lorcan replied. "The question is whether or not she had the opportunity to attack Jimmy on the path."

"She was at the event that night," Marcella said. "Just like at Flann's event, she typically sits out of the way. Most of the time, I'll bet people don't even know she's there. She could have slipped out for a brief time."

I nodded in agreement with Marcella's thought process. "But it was raining that night. Could she have been unnoticed when she got back? She'd probably have been drenched."

"The café's main reception room is close to the restrooms. And there's a separate entrance from the outside into the restroom area. It would be easy to dash into one of the bathrooms and dry off," Marcella replied.

"Another thing," Lorcan added, "the bodhran drumstick is shaped like a ball-peen hammer."

I shook my head. I didn't even want to entertain the idea that the police had identified the wrong weapon.

"According to O'Shea, the examiner is sure about the weapon. But"—I looked at my cell phone to no avail—"Nessa doesn't like Georgina. Wrecking Georgina's cottage and taking her snapshots of Jimmy seems like something a jealous lover would do. Nessa could be the person stalking Georgina."

"We need to talk to her and tell O'Shea our theory," Lorcan said, holding up his right hand when I began to protest. "I know how you feel, Star, but O'Shea must be included. Agree or disagree, we have to work together. This is too serious to go it alone."

"Okay, why don't you deal with O'Shea. I'm going to find Terrence. He might be able to tell me if Georgina had any visitors this afternoon."

"And I'll head home," Marcella said. "Georgina may try to contact me." Marcella touched my shoulder. "Please, be careful."

Lorcan and his mother left together. I grabbed my knapsack and checked the charge on my cell. The office phone rang as I was about to leave.

"Hello." I held my breath.

"It's Phillie. I thought you'd want to know that Georgina Hill lived in Central London, right in Smithfield. She was a student at a local art school."

I connected this news with Georgina's vagueness when I mentioned Jimmy's pub in London. Suddenly, the potential intersections in this case increased exponentially. Could Georgina have known Jimmy years ago? And how likely was Grainne's and Deirdre's appearance in London purely a coinci-

dence? I had to chase this down. First, though, Terrence owed
me a conversation.

~

I HEADED TOWARD THE ADDRESS TERRENCE PROVIDED WHEN WE
hired him—Derryhick Lake, a fisherman's paradise located off
one of the byroads close to the Round Tower and Turlough.
Terrence lived in what appeared to be a one-bedroom cottage.
The evening's setting sun brightened the cottage's mud-splat-
tered yellow exterior. Two wooden kitchen chairs stood like
sentinels at the entrance. Empty but dirty beer glasses sat on
the muddy ground near the chairs. The door hung ajar,
swaying with the evening breeze. I pulled my phone from its
holster and loudly called, "Terrence."

"Who's there?" His voice came from farther inside the
cottage. Then, he appeared in the doorway. His face registered
surprise. "Is something wrong?"

"You tell me. When was the last time you saw Georgina?"

I didn't wait for the formalities. I walked right into the
main room. If Georgina were there, I'd know in a few minutes.
The open plan of the cottage included one sofa, a leather
recliner, and a stack of dirty dishes sitting on the side of the
sink. In addition to being a messy housekeeper and obviously
a major consumer of beer, Terrence liked to fish. The
numerous trophies hanging on every available wall space testified to that.

"Why, just a few hours ago. She told me she was heading
back to town. She mentioned her shop, and she said I could
leave for the evening."

"Do you have any idea why she decided to go back to the
shop?"

"No, she just said she had something to do."

"Why did you leave her? You could have gone with her." It

took every ounce of strength not to shake him. "What time was that?"

"About half six. I didn't think there was any harm in it. Why stay at her cottage if she wasn't there?"

"Because she's missing. That's why." In an effort to control my anger, I went outside and walked the cottage's perimeter. I thought about the conversations I'd had with Terrence, beginning with the one in the museum. He had found Jimmy's body. Could he be the killer? Was he the one stalking Georgina all along? Had she said or done something that threatened him?

"What are you doing?" Terrence asked, following me around to the concrete slab that was an excuse for a patio. More beer glasses and bottles cluttered the area.

"I've been hit hard by the recession," he said, watching me stop and look at the pile of alcoholic litter. "I lost my ancestral home, and this place is the best I can do for the moment. And I don't need anyone to know my personal habits. So, I'd appreciate it if you don't mention this to anyone at the museum, or to Lorcan, for that matter."

I ignored Terrence and completed my circuit. I arrived back out to the roadside and perused the area. Despite the few other cottages scattered along the road and its proximity to Flann Mahoney's farm, this stretch of road was isolated.

"I moonlight to save up a few extra bits here and there to get me through the hard times," Terrence continued as if I'd asked for an explanation.

I took a long look at his face and the shadows underlining his bulging eyes. Finally, I nodded.

"I can't keep you out of this. Georgina is missing, and as far as I know, you were the last person to see her. The police will want to speak with you."

"Oh, no," he said, his eyes bulging even more. "What can I do to help?" The words had barely left his lips when the sound of a car's engine barreling down the lane drowned out whatever

else he planned to say. The car looked similar to the one that
had sideswiped me on Cottage Road. The car's high beams
blinded me, and I couldn't see the driver.

"Where does this road go?" I asked.

"Ah, it's a narrow lane. No one uses it much. It cuts through
Parke and then out onto the road to the Round Tower and the
Turlough Museum. I use it myself to get to work most days."

I filed that bit of information away for potential later use.
"Let's get back to the last time you saw Georgina. Where were
you? And what was she doing?"

Terrence folded his arms over his belly. "Let's see. I arrived
at her place at about half five after I'd just gotten off my shift at
the Turlough Museum. She invited me in for a cup of tea and a
ham sandwich. We had a great chat."

"How did she seem?" I interrupted. I didn't need to hear
about their chat, but I wanted to know if Georgina acted any
different than usual.

"Arrah, she was grand. She had a pile of photo albums on
the table, and they were open like she'd been looking through
some of the pictures. I asked her about them."

"What did she say?"

"Now that I think of it, she didn't want to linger on that
topic. She just said, 'oh, some old memories from a lifetime
ago.' Then, she closed the albums and started talking about the
museum and the exhibits."

"Which exhibits?"

"The one where Jimmy's body was found." Terrence raised
his eyes to mine. "But mind you, she didn't ask me about
Jimmy. She wanted to know more about the actual exhibit. She
said she was doing some research about what women wore
back then."

I didn't believe it for a minute. Marcella had said Georgina
wasn't trying to investigate Jimmy's murder, but I didn't agree.
The Georgina I'd gotten to know in the last six months never let

an opportunity to gather information go to waste. She was onto something. But what? At this point, I had no idea.

"So, you had the tea, and then what?"

"I went outside to check the grounds. Then, she came to the door and said she had to go into town."

"Did you see her leave?"

Terrence shook his head. "No, she told me to go on home. She said she had a few things to do before she left. Like I said earlier, that was at about half six." Terrence's voice broke on that last word. "I'll never forgive myself if something has happened to her."

"What about the picture album? Did you see any specific picture?"

"She had a pile of photos with Jimmy in them. They were stacked up by themselves. They weren't in the albums."

"What did she do with them? Did she put them back in the albums?"

"No, she just left them there. I figured maybe she was planning to give them to his family as a kind of remembrance."

"Did you ever see Jimmy with Nessa Bantry?" I asked.

"Those two were quite a couple for a while there. In fact, I didn't even know Georgina and Jimmy had dated until recently. The times I saw Jimmy, he was always with Nessa, and you could tell she was really into him."

"How was that?"

"She always lingered around if he was at a gala or an event. She'd stay in the background, and then when the chat with everyone died down, she'd appear at Jimmy's side."

"You'd better get dressed. I'm going to call Lorcan, and I want you to go with him to police headquarters and tell them everything you've told me."

Terrence's bulging eyes widened. He took a long look at the mess and then walked back into his cottage.

I got into my car and went in search of answers.

CHAPTER 26

I bypassed the tourist parking lot and parked directly in front of the museum's exhibition hall.

"You can't park there, miss," the guard at the front desk said when I entered the building.

"Where is Grainne Canny?"

He rose to his feet, came from behind the desk, and blocked my path. "She doesn't meet with the tourists."

"I'm no tourist. Where is she?" I glimpsed a group of visitors walking toward the glass door entry. "If you don't tell me where she is, I'll make a scene right here. How will that go over with her?"

The guard stepped back and waved his hand. "She's downstairs in the rural craftspeople exhibit."

I took the staircase two steps at a time until I got to the exhibition area indicated by the guard. One of the exhibits replicated a typical Irish cottage. This area of the museum was dimly lit. By design, I assumed, to create the feeling of a time when candles, kerosene lamps, and firelight provided illumination.

I silently stationed myself in the open doorway to the cottage exhibit. Grainne, unaware of my presence, stood in the replicated kitchen. I watched her rearrange the artifacts on an oak table. She examined each piece she lifted and then carefully placed it back. Periodically, she paused and observed the curated scene, like an artist stepping back from a canvas, assessing the objects on the canvas and the light, color, and message.

"You must be a keen observer of history and culture," I said.

Grainne's hands momentarily froze. Then, the animation I'd just observed on her face flicked out, replaced with the stern, angry look I'd seen before.

"I'm just doing my job."

"Does your job include hiding information from the police?"

She brushed her steel-gray hair with an empty hand. The other wrapped around one of the candlesticks from the table.

"Who gave you permission to barge in here? This is one of Ireland's national museums, and I don't answer to you." She put the candlestick back down, dusted her hands on her skirt, and whirled past me toward an empty room at the back of the building.

"Who are you protecting?" I followed on her heels. "You were here the morning Jimmy's body was found. Terrence was here also. In fact, he's currently talking to the police because my aunt is missing." I paused to let that sink in. "So, if you don't want to find yourself ensnared in a murder and a kidnapping, you'd better tell me everything you know."

Grainne whirled and faced me. "I've worked here for twenty years. I know every inch of this building, and I've curated every exhibit in the place." She pushed one of the tables against the wall. "I have a right to keep the museum's affairs within its boundaries."

"Really? Someone didn't agree with you. Jimmy's killer brought the affair right here, under your nose. Why is that? Why would someone place his body here in this exhibit?"

Grainne sighed and sank into a folding chair. "I don't know," she said, shaking her head. "I've been trying to figure it out."

"Look, it's obvious you care about this place. But you are misguided if you think you can solve this on your own. If you know anything, you must tell the police."

I squeezed my cell phone case instead of shaking her. Aunt Georgina was missing, and this woman was more worried about a building of ancient artifacts than living, breathing people. I could see from her frown lines that her concern for the museum was heartfelt. I softened my tone. "Come on, Grainne; what's going on here?"

"I don't know. I truly don't know. But you're right, Terrence called me when he found the body. I'm this museum's guardian, and I love using my knowledge for the public to enjoy." She nodded her head toward the exhibit area. "Someone curated Jimmy's body." She stopped speaking as if she expected me to laugh at her, but I didn't.

"Go on," I encouraged.

"It's been bothering me since the beginning. Jimmy's body was posed in the tableau, which depicts local crafts and service roles." Grainne rose to her feet and commanded, "Follow me." Then she marched out of the cottage exhibit area and stopped where Jimmy's body had rested. The police tape had been removed. "Do you see?" she asked.

I looked at the rural postmistress and shop tableau. Then, I turned to face Grainne. "And..." I didn't finish because I still didn't see what she was getting at.

"His mother. Jimmy's mother was the postmistress in Turlough village. That's what I've been trying to figure out. There are three floors to this exhibit building, Miss O'Brien. Someone was trying to send a message. Someone posed Jimmy's body here in front of the postmistress display. It can't just be a coincidence."

"What do you think it means?" I asked.

Grainne shrugged. "I don't know. In rural Ireland, the post office was more than a place to post a letter. It was the social hub of a village. The postmistress knew everyone. Often, the post office was part of the local grocery shop, and the postmistress ran both. Most of the time, the role was kept in the family, passed from one generation to another." Grainne hesitated and then continued, "Jimmy's father himself was one of the guards back in the day. But Jimmy's parents are long gone."

"Have you mentioned your observations to the police?"

"Aye, they asked me if I had any thoughts about why the body was left there." Grainne's voice boomed through the empty area. "But I didn't have much more to add than what I've told you."

I perused the display. According to Lorcan, the police hadn't shared any information with him about why Jimmy's body was found here. I considered what Grainne had told me about Jimmy's parents. The exhibit was near a bay door that was large enough to enable artifacts into the building. It certainly would have accommodated a wheelbarrow if that was how Jimmy's body was transported into the building. Jimmy and his mother, though? What was the connection, if any?

"Have you mentioned this to Flann or Deirdre? Do they see any relevance to Jimmy's body being found here?"

"No, I haven't." Grainne looked around the vast room filled with artifacts depicting years of history. "I can't. The Mahoneys are wonderfully philanthropic friends of the museum, especially Flann. Jimmy was too. I don't want to add to their pain in any way." Grainne glanced toward the stairway when we heard voices and footsteps approaching. "Now, if you don't mind, I have a museum to run. I don't want to deal with the guards. I need things to be normal around here. If you want to discuss this further with them, well, that's your business. Just try to stay out of mine." With that, she walked away, her cane tapping the tile floor. Suddenly, she turned around and said, "If I were you, I'd talk to his girlfriend, Nessa. If anyone wanted to kill Jimmy, it was her."

Grainne melted into the museum shadows and the history it represented; the only evidence of her presence was the *tap, tap* of the cane. Since no one was looking, I stepped into the exhibit and examined where Jimmy's body had been found. The idea that someone had posed Jimmy seeped into my bones. That's the kind of thing that serial killers do—pose bodies. And usually, there's a message in their madness. What was Jimmy's killer trying to tell us? I shook myself out of my reverie. I needed to take action. It was time to confront Miss Bantry about Jimmy and, as I suspected, her stalking of Aunt Georgina.

Outside the building, I dialed Marcella. She answered on the first ring. "Any news?"

"No. What about you?" I asked, looking up at the sky, which was quickly giving way to darkness. I hoped Georgina was somewhere safe. Maybe her cell phone battery was dead, and that was why she hadn't called. *Stop it, Star,* I told myself.

"Lorcan called; he's still at the garda station with Terrence, but he wants you to call him as soon as possible."

I ended the call and dialed Lorcan.

"Star, they've debriefed Terrence and let him go home. Any luck on your end?" Lorcan's usually calm voice sounded shaky.

"None. What are the police doing?" I asked.

"I'm not getting anywhere with them. Sorry to say. This might be the end of a lifelong friendship with O'Shea. I can't believe they aren't taking Georgina's absence more seriously."

"I'm on my way to French Hill. Call me when you get done in town." I hung up and got into my car.

~

A DESERTED, COLD FEELING ENVELOPED ME WHEN I ENTERED THE cottage. I walked over to the kitchen window and looked at the broken ceramic teapot that Georgina filled with Margarites the last time she was there. Even the pot of flowers looked depressed. My stomach growled its hunger at me, but I didn't have the desire to feed myself.

Instead, I grabbed my notebook, sat at the kitchen table, and outlined everything I knew about this case again.

Jimmy Mahoney dead. Murdered on the greenway between Turlough and Castlebar. Jimmy involved in numbers-running. Georgina discovering Jimmy's entanglement with said shadow lottery. A string of local pubs between Turlough, Castlebar, and Cong. Allen Skye, known local drug dealer, probably in on the numbers-running, murdered in his own bar. Police supposedly had that person in custody.

I sat back and looked at what I'd written. In a moment of anger, I ripped out the page. I'd already been down this path. So, what then? There was Jimmy's pub in London and a missing girl. Georgina's vague response when I'd asked her about it. Phillie saying Georgina had been a student in London at the time. I started a new page with another series of questions.

Did she know about the missing girl? Georgina would have been about the same age. Had Georgina known that Jimmy owned the pub? I stared at the page again. Was there a connection? And if so, what was the connection between something that happened almost forty years ago and Georgina? Police are not interested in old cases out of their jurisdiction.

I kept writing questions. Georgina's stalker? Who and why? Georgina had taken it upon herself to intervene in Jimmy's life. Who was impacted by her involvement in Jimmy's death? Allen Skye had been at the top of my list. I listed out the potential suspects again. I circled Nessa's name. She'd been pretty steamed about Jimmy's friendship with Georgina. She'd been at all the museum's money-raising functions. Flann hired her for his events, and she was a frequent musician at Jimmy's pub as well as others in the Castlebar area.

Then, there was Grainne. She, too, would have been at the museum the night Jimmy was killed. But, thinking about her fierce dedication to the museum and the fact that she liked the donations she received from the Mahoney twins, I didn't think she murdered Jimmy. Besides, she wouldn't have wanted to defile one of her exhibits. That left Jimmy's siblings, Deirdre and Flann. Both of them had been at the museum the night of the murder. Deirdre seemed to hate her brother, but she kept turning up in places that overlapped with his life—places I didn't expect to see her, first in Cong and then in London.

I put Deirdre on the list right after Nessa. She could have left the gala and come back. I recalled our first meeting. She didn't want to admit she'd been at the event. She also probably knew all the access points into the exhibit building. And the police had found the murder weapon in a wheelbarrow outside in the café garden. So, she had the opportunity, but why would she have wanted to kill Jimmy?

Then, there was Flann. He, too, had been at the event and had access to the greenway. But I didn't think he would have keys to the exhibit hall. I dropped my pen onto the table and thought about Flann and Georgina. I respected Georgina's judgment of people, and I needed to talk to him as soon as possible about the last time he'd spoken to her.

The knock at the back door jolted me out of my chair. Lorcan's face peered through the glass panes, and I waved him in.

"I see you have your notebook out again."

"Yeah, but I'm hitting a brick wall." I shook my head. "I have to admit that my persistence in pursuing the shadow lottery theory may have cost us time in uncovering what's really going on here."

Lorcan pulled out a chair and sat down. "No. Don't do that to yourself. You pursued the most obvious thread. You, we will figure this out, Star." He retrieved a piece of paper from his breast pocket, where he usually kept a pencil or some graph paper related to his patents and inventions. "Look, I took some notes when the guards met with Terrence. According to him, he had seen Nessa Bantry following Georgina."

"Where?"

"At the museum for one," Lorcan replied.

I turned my list around to show Lorcan. "Nessa keeps coming out on top. But we can't stop there. We have to talk to everyone Georgina's been with in the last few days."

"I agree, but I want to add the new owner of Jimmy's pub in Cong to the list."

"Why? I've already spoken to the staff several times. I don't want to waste more time."

"Something Terrence said. He mentioned that Ciaran has been around the museum. Terrence saw Nessa there the day of the murder in the parking lot, and it looked like a heated discussion between Nessa and Ciaran."

I considered what Lorcan said, picked up the pencil, and wrote Ciaran's name next to Nessa's.

"Okay, I see your logic. But I want to go back to Georgina's cottage first. I don't trust that the police did a thorough search."

"I'll drive. Let's go," Lorcan said.

I locked the kitchen door behind me and followed Lorcan.

CHAPTER 27

Georgina's cottage looked forlorn. I checked for the spare key hidden in one of her flower pots near the front door. "The key is gone," I said, wanting to kick myself. "I should have checked earlier. Do you think Georgina moved it, or did whoever ransacked her cottage take it?"

Lorcan reached forward and turned the handle. The door swung open.

"Yeah, the police did a thorough job, didn't they?" I remarked. "Let's split up. You take the kitchen, and I'll take the living room."

I went to Georgina's sewing basket, mannequin, and other clothing design tools. The earlier mess looked even worse since the police had rifled through things.

"Right." Lorcan moved quickly into the kitchen, where I could hear him opening cabinet doors. "Any ideas about what we are looking for?"

I perused Georgina's supplies, thinking about where, if she wanted to hide something, she might put it. "I always have something up my sleeve," Georgina had said to me about the anonymous note. I walked to the mannequin and began removing the dress draped over it. This dress form didn't have sleeves, but I noticed stitching up the entire length of the linen-covered body. I thought of ripping the stitching but decided against it when I didn't feel anything out of place.

I stepped back to think. Someone had been in Georgina's cottage, searching for something. I looked at the overturned sewing basket. I picked through the jumble of material on the floor. Mostly remnants, but interestingly, there were two men's shirts. A needle and thread were stuck into one of them next to a buttonhole, and the opposing button was missing. Obviously, Georgina had mended some of Jimmy's shirts. As far as I was concerned, this evidence solved the mystery of how Georgina's blood got onto Jimmy's clothing. I refolded the shirts and put them on a table to take with me.

"I'm heading into the bedrooms," I said to Lorcan.

"Does this look familiar?" He walked toward me from the kitchen, a green diary in his hand.

I reached for it. "Yes, Georgina had one like this before." I turned to the last few pages. "Look, these words are written in her scrawl." I turned the diary for Lorcan to read the words. *London and forgiveness.* "Georgina sounded vague when I asked her about Jimmy's pub in London. I think she knows something." I glanced up at Lorcan. "Do you think her disappearance has anything to do with the London pub?"

"I don't know, Star. Her car is here, so the logical assumption is that she's been taken. Does that have anything to do with an old missing person's case or Jimmy's previous business? We won't know until we talk to her."

"We've got to find out more about what happened in London," I replied, pressing the book between my fingers.

"We've got to find Georgina. If she's stumbled into something else that Jimmy might have been involved in before he came back to Ireland...well, then she may be in even more danger than we know," Lorcan replied, prying the diary from my grasp. "Let's finish up looking around the cottage."

I nodded. We split up again to search the cottage's two tiny bedrooms but didn't find anything more. The bathroom, including the medicine cabinet, yielded zilch. Back in Georgina's living room, I picked up the two shirts but then decided to leave them. I didn't want the police accusing me of tampering with evidence.

"Ready?" Lorcan asked.

"No." I pulled my cell phone from its case and dialed Marcella.

"When was the last time you saw Georgina?" I asked when Marcella answered.

"We just had lunch a few days ago. While you were in London, actually."

"Oh, did she mention my call?"

"No, she seemed fine. She suggested we meet at the museum café."

"Did she mention my trip to London?"

"Not really; she seemed like she wanted to talk to Deirdre about something. Georgina stopped by the kitchen door and asked one of the prep chefs if Deirdre was in."

"Did she speak to Deirdre?"

"No, Deirdre came out of the kitchen and walked right past Georgina. Walked past me as well." Marcella sighed. "I didn't think anything of it at the time. She is always so jumpy around people. Even friends. Do you think she knows Georgina's whereabouts?"

"I intend to find out. Anything else different about your lunch or your conversation?"

"No." Marcella paused. "We bumped into Maeve while we were there...."

"What!" I almost threw my phone across the room. "What was she doing there?"

"The exhibit hall is open. She'd just come from a tour, and I think she said something about how fascinating it was, and the three of us should do it together someday."

Yeah, right. Like the historian who'd lived in Ireland all her life needed a tour. When it came to Maeve Baldwin, I didn't believe in coincidences.

"Anything else you think I should know?" I said to Marcella.

"No, but listening to the sound of your voice, I'm worried. I'm sorry I didn't mention the luncheon. But we do this all the time, and I didn't see anything out of the ordinary." Marcella's voice started to crack. "I'll never forgive myself if something has happened to Georgina."

"It's okay," I said. "Lorcan's with me, and we're going to visit Jimmy's place in Cong. Call me if you hear from Georgina." I didn't want Marcella to fret, but I doubted she'd hear from Georgina anytime soon.

"You look worried. What did my mother say?" Lorcan asked. He'd been standing, looking at the shirts and Georgina's sewing paraphernalia while I was on the phone.

"I am. More than worried." I held up my hand. "Just a second. I've got to call The Consulting Detective." I didn't waste any time on niceties when Ellie answered. "Ellie, have Phillie find out what she can about a woman named Maeve Baldwin. She's an historian, lives in Cong, County Mayo. Don't hold back on anything. The slightest bit of information may be critical."

"Of course. Have you heard from your aunt?" Ellie asked.

"No, Georgina is still missing, and I'm sure it's not voluntary. I've got to go. Call me as soon as you can." I looked up at Lorcan. "Do you know where Maeve Baldwin lives in Cong?"

"Sure. I've been there lots of times with my mother. What's going on?"

I looked Lorcan in the eye and said, "I know she's an old friend of your mother's, but I don't like her. My gut tells me she's hiding something. I want to talk to her, and we can stop at

Jimmy's pub on the way back." Then, I walked out the cottage door to Lorcan's car.

We drove to Cong in silence. Lorcan kept his eyes on the narrow roads while I thought about all the moments Georgina and I had shared a cup of tea. Her arrivals at the cottage with her homemade blackberry jam and brown bread. I didn't know what I'd do if I lost her. But I knew what I'd do to whoever had hurt her. I just hoped that wouldn't be the case.

Lorcan pulled up outside a modest-looking cottage on a wooded road not far from Ashford Castle. Electrified candles lit each of the front windows. The door, painted black, sported a pinecone wreath sprinkled with fake red berries. When we opened the gate to the cement walkway, a large Irish blood-hound charged at us from the back of the house. The front door opened.

"Lorcan and Star, you are welcome." Maeve, dressed in her usual black slacks, black fishnet pattern sweater, and pearls, held the door so we could enter. She didn't look surprised to see us.

"Were you expecting us?" I asked.

She didn't answer immediately. Instead, she called "Mid-watch" to the bloodhound, which responded and settled on the cement walk outside the door. "Midwatch is a great watchdog," she commented, waving us into her living room.

I glanced around the place; ceiling-to-floor bookshelves covered every available wall. A barrister's writing desk nestled inside one of the breaks in the shelves. Some of the room's end tables held piles of papers. The video camera over the door didn't escape me either. So, that was how she'd known who was at the door. I nodded at the device. "Have you had trouble with intruders?"

Maeve's eyes traveled to the camera. "Oh, that. I guess I look like a vain old woman, but I thought it important to have some security in the place." She swept her hand in the direction of her desk and the bookshelves. "Not that I'm famous or anything, but I own several rare reference books." She laughed. "So, it's Georgina, isn't it? Have you had any word?"

"When was the last time you saw her?" I asked.

Maeve pursed her lips and fondled the pearls hanging from her neck. "Let's see. I think it was a few days ago. She was having lunch at the museum café with Marcella." Maeve smiled. "I have to admit I was a little perturbed that they didn't include me."

Lorcan walked around the room, which seemed cavernous compared to how small the cottage appeared from the outside.

Pretending to be surprised, I said, "That's odd. You and Marcella are good friends, aren't you?"

"Yes, but we're not joined at the hip," Maeve retorted. "So, what is this visit about? It can't be about a silly lunch date."

"I'm following up with everyone who might have spoken to Georgina recently." I didn't want to tell Maeve too much. "So, what were you doing at the museum that day when you bumped into Marcella and Georgina?"

"Research. I wanted to look at some of the paintings that have been installed on the lower level of the building." Maeve paused and then continued, "Now, it's my turn to ask the questions, Ms. O'Brien." I nodded, expecting to hear something about Georgina and the exhibit. "Have you spoken with Evelyn Cosgrove?"

"Let's get back to Georgina. Have you heard from her?"

I looked around at Maeve's living quarters and wondered if there was some kind of professional rivalry with Evelyn. But I didn't have time for that. Nor was I going to let her distract me.

Maeve smiled again. "No, I haven't, but she's a smart cookie. I'm sure she's all right."

"You were going to chat with Ciaran and Rosaleen at the

pub in Neale? How did that go?" Lorcan asked from the other side of the room where he was perusing the bookshelves.

Maeve moved closer to Lorcan. "Oh, yes. I did drop in on them for a visit and a few words. But there's nothing much to tell. They claimed they hadn't been aware of Jimmy's money schemes. Please, tell your mother I'll give her a call later." Then Maeve turned back to me. "If that's all, I'll call my canine protector in so you two can get back to your car."

She walked to her front door, opened it, and patted her side. Midwatch ran into the house while Lorcan and I moved along the path and through the gate.

As soon as we were back in Lorcan's car, he remarked, "I've never seen Maeve like this. I'd almost say she's hostile to you."

"Hostile. That seems like the right word. But why? Why is she so interested in the search for my mother?" I banged my hand on the dashboard. "Let's go. We have to get to the pub and talk to Ciaran."

Lorcan took the hand that I'd crashed on the dash panel and held it in his. "Look, I know this is getting to you. But we'll get through this."

"I'm all right," I said, taking a deep breath.

"Let's try to slow down for a few minutes. The pubs don't close until the wee hours of the morning in Ireland."

I nodded. "Do you think Maeve is involved with Jimmy's death?" For once, I wanted to hear Lorcan's opinion. It didn't matter to me anymore how independent I wanted to be. At this moment, I knew I needed his calm and methodical mind.

Lorcan shook his head. "No, she's not involved with Jimmy. But she sure is focused on you and Evelyn."

"I agree, and it has got nothing to do with Jimmy or Georgina." My other hand reached for the locket. I didn't know yet what Evelyn's purpose was, but I knew this locket was as real as Maeve Baldwin's interest in me.

"You are quite the mystery, Star O'Brien." Lorcan smiled, squeezed my hand, and started the car.

Once again, we drove in silence as if we'd already said everything we needed to say. I found it comforting.

CHAPTER 28

C ars, trucks, and Jeeps filled the pub's parking lot and lined the road across from the establishment.

"Geez, we'll never get anywhere with this crowd," I said to Lorcan as we walked toward the entrance.

"Not to worry," Lorcan replied. "Why don't we split up when we get in there? You take Nessa, and I'll take Ciaran."

I agreed. We pushed our way through the throng at the door and surveyed the room. Already familiar with the layout, I forged ahead to the area near a fireplace where a row of kitchen chairs held musicians playing traditional music. Nessa sat at one end, her bodhran and drumstick in her hands. Her feet tapped along with the music. She didn't see me approaching until I was well within earshot.

"You," her voice rasped. "I've got a gig here. What do you want?" She kicked one of her feet up in the air, almost hitting me in the shin.

I leaned forward and whispered, "I want to talk to you about Georgina Hill. If you refuse, I'll make a big fuss here in front of all your friends."

The hand on my shoulder squeezed hard enough to make me turn my head. A tall, burly man with salt and pepper hair shoved his face into mine. "What do you want with Nessa?" he demanded.

"Who are you?" I asked in response.

"I'm her husband, Pete, and her bodyguard." The big brute squeezed my shoulder a little harder. "She told me about you. You'd better clear out of here, or I'll have to do something you won't like."

"Go ahead and try. But you'll find yourself on the inside of a jail cell if you don't drop your hand." Lorcan's voice interrupted the man's threats. "Be a gentleman and walk away, now. I won't repeat my instructions again."

Nessa's husband, if he really was her husband, shrugged and moved over toward the bar.

"Star, are you okay?" Lorcan's face seemed to reflect the red-hot heat emanating from the fireplace.

"I'm fine. But let's go. I don't think we'll get anywhere here at the moment."

Lorcan agreed. "Good idea." Lorcan tilted his head toward Nessa's husband. "After a few more pints, that oaf may decide to create a ruckus. I spoke to Ciaran, and I'll fill you in when we get outside."

Back in the parking lot, I noticed a dark sedan. The driver-side door panels were covered with musical stickers of bodhrans and drumsticks. I stopped and used my cell phone flashlight to highlight the scratch I'd seen when the car was parked outside Nessa's condo.

"Did you see something?" Lorcan asked.

"Yes, that"—I pointed at the car—"looks like a twin to the one that tried to run me off the road," I said, remembering the flash of a car whooshing by and lines of silver along its side. "And I'm sure it belongs to Nessa." I turned off the flashlight and faced Lorcan. "You said you had something to tell me."

"Yeah, Ciaran confirmed that Nessa came to the bar often, not just as part of a musical gig. Jimmy had gotten worried about her, and she kept harassing him about Georgina. It seems she has seen the two of them together more than once lately. It wasn't to Nessa's liking."

I didn't like what I was hearing. Stalking cases never ended well. I determined to have it out with Nessa Bantry once and for all.

~

"You're unusually quiet," Lorcan remarked. I sat, observing the lights in the homes we passed on our way back through Ballinrobe, Partry, and Ballyhean.

"I can't help but think that Jimmy's murder is tied to something or someone he was involved with. You know, a personal relationship."

"I agree. But with whom? Ciaran told me the guards cleared him and Rosaleen of any connection to the murder. The guards didn't think there was much to explore related to the pub as a motive. Seemingly, Jimmy didn't leave a will. The assets flowed directly to Flann and Deirdre, and Flann handled the transaction."

I nodded. "Yeah, you're right. Phillie emailed the Irish succession legalese information to me. That's probably how the pub's ownership transferred so quickly."

"Besides," Lorcan continued, "the guards are so focused on Georgina, it's difficult to press them on anything else." Lorcan glanced over at me. "We will get to the bottom of this, Star. Don't worry."

"But I am. A day has come and gone with no sign of Georgina. What if she's lying dead somewhere? What if she's fallen and broken her leg and her phone is dead? I have to find her."

"I wish I could say something to relieve your concerns, Star, but I'm just as worried as you. We just can't give up; that's all."

LORCAN WALKED ME TO THE COTTAGE'S KITCHEN DOOR. "I'M NOT coming in," he said. "You look exhausted, and I want to speak with my mother again. I'll see you first thing in the morning." Back in the cottage, I checked the landline and computer for any messages—nothing. I knew I wouldn't be able to sleep for a while, but I also knew there wasn't much I could do until the morning. Finally, after a warm shower, I sat in the living room, reviewing my notes. Nessa Bantry remained at the top of the list. Even more so since I'd heard she'd been harassing Jimmy. It wouldn't have taken much to turn her anger and jealousy onto Georgina. But had Nessa killed Jimmy? Someone had moved his body from the greenway to the museum exhibit. Nessa would have needed help to do that. I jotted Pete's name onto the page. The landline interrupted my ruminations. I ran to the kitchen, picked up the receiver, and said, "Hello."

"I don't have much time," said the voice on the other end.

I immediately recognized the caller's voice. "I'm finished playing hide and seek with you, Ms. Cosgrove. What do you want? What do you know about my mother?" I twisted the phone cord in my hand.

"I don't know where your mother is. I'm only trying to fulfill a promise to my father." Evelyn spoke in a hushed tone.

"So, you've handed me the locket. You've kept your part of the promise. Why should I spend any more time on you, especially when you keep running away? What are you afraid of?" I had so many questions for this Evelyn Cosgrove, who may or may not be a blood relative. But I couldn't, wouldn't allow her to string me along.

"I...I have a lot to tell you. To show you, but I have to be careful."

"Yeah, scammers are always careful. Either put up or shut

up, Miss Cosgrove. You have ten seconds before I hang up this phone."

"I'll be at the Turlough Inn the day after tomorrow at nine p.m. I have something else to show you."

She hung up before I could reply. I put the phone back on the receiver and turned out the lights. I'd had enough for one day.

CHAPTER 29

L orcan's knock on the door came shortly before 9:00 a.m. "Any updates?" Lorcan asked.

"Nothing regarding Georgina. I had a call from Evelyn Cosgrove, though." I shook my head. "I don't know what her game is, but I'm done playing. She wants to meet me tomorrow night at nine near the Turlough Inn."

Lorcan pushed his glasses up the bridge of his nose. "I can go with you."

"No. I will handle her."

"Then, why not let me go ahead of you? I can be nearby, unseen. Just in case. There's too much at stake to chance something happening to you."

I liked his idea but didn't want to admit how vulnerable I felt at the moment. I shook my head. "We can't allow ourselves to get sidetracked with my issues. Georgina is the focus." Impatient for action, I glanced at my cell phone. "I've got to go through some emails from The Consulting Detective. Then, I plan to drive by Georgina's shop again just in case we missed something."

Lorcan nodded. He reached forward and touched my arm.

"Be careful, Star. We—" Lorcan paused and then continued, "I can't afford to lose you."

I didn't move away from his touch; instead, I nodded and waved him out the door. As soon as he left, I packed up my knapsack, made sure my phone was charged and headed for my car. I'd told him I intended to stop at The Golden Thread. That much was true, but I hadn't mentioned my other plan for the morning.

THE SHOP REMAINED CLOSED. I CONTACTED BETH, GEORGINA'S assistant, reminding her to phone me if she heard anything at all and to take a few days off. Since Georgina's shop wasn't far from Nessa's condo, I walked there.

By the time I arrived, a light drizzle had smeared the condo's windowpanes. The window's drapes were closed. I guessed a nightlife career necessitated darkened rooms. Good, maybe I'd catch her off guard. I knocked on the door and waited. When there was no answer, I knocked again. The drapes moved. Then, the door opened. Nessa Bantry stood there in a full-length dressing gown. During the night, her eye makeup had run, creating a vertical line halfway down her face.

"What do you want?" she demanded.

I didn't wait for an invitation. I moved quickly past her into the living room. "I know you tried to run me off the road."

"That's some Yank bull you've got there. Gee, you Hill women just don't give up, do you? Get yourself out of here, or there'll be more than a dent in your car."

"I'm sure the police will be interested in that scratch on your car and the matching paint chips they took off mine."

I glanced around the room while Nessa rubbed her eyes and seemed to stall for time before answering. Next to an ashtray on one of the end tables, I caught a glimpse of photographs of Jimmy.

"I see you've been reminiscing about Jimmy," I said, nodding to the pictures. At this point, I didn't care how angry she got, and I wanted to see if she'd blurt out anything that led to Georgina's whereabouts.

Nessa screamed primordially and lunged to grab one of her drumsticks. She swung at me with the mallet but missed when she tripped over the bottom of her dressing gown.

"Nessa, what's going on?" The husband, Pete, emerged through an open doorway on the other side of the living room.

"This one just won't give up. I want to kill her."

Pete approached Nessa and wrapped a swarthy arm around her. "Listen, babe; she's not worth it. Give me the drumstick. I'll take care of her."

As Nessa slumped against him in tears, her hand dangled at her side. He took the stick in his beefy paws. Then, he glared at me. "Get the hell out of here and stay away from us, or you won't be so lucky the next time."

Knowing I wouldn't be able to best both of them, I left. When I heard the door lock behind me, I turned and saw the drapes pulled open. Although Nessa and Pete still watched me, I remained standing on the sidewalk, considering my next move. With her husband's help, Nessa could have moved Jimmy's body to the exhibit hall. Together, they had the strength to do it. The sideswiping of my car and the photos of Jimmy that probably came from Georgina's cottage justified asking the police to question Nessa and her husband. I pulled my phone from its holster, but Lorcan's name flashed on the display before I could dial.

"Star, where are you?"

"I'm in town. Why?" Lorcan's voice sounded hurried. I touched my locket, bracing myself for bad news.

"The guards have Jimmy's killer in custody."

I looked back at Nessa's front door. "Who?"

"Willem Block."

"What? Of all the people I've considered, Willem has been at the bottom of the list."

"Yeah, he walked into garda headquarters while I was there and confessed to killing Jimmy with the hammer. He admitted using a wheelbarrow to move Jimmy's body to the exhibit."

My head spun at the revelation.

Lorcan's voice continued, "Star, listen, the good news is that O'Shea has agreed to drop the charges against Georgina."

"That's great news, but what is O'Shea doing about finding her?" I asked.

"Let's meet at French Hill cottage. I want to collect my mother, and we can discuss it all there. This place is a zoo, and the press is outside." Lorcan ended the call.

I took one last look at Nessa Bantry's apartment and ran to my car at The Golden Thread. As I raced to exit town and get to French Hill, a million questions ran through my mind. Why had Willem killed Jimmy, and why pose his body in the museum exhibit?

◈

As I pulled up to the cottage, I spotted Lorcan and Marcella. I parked my car and ran toward them. Marcella threw her arms around me and squeezed tightly. "Thank God, this horrible nightmare is over. I'm sure if Georgina is hiding somewhere, she will hear the news and get in touch with us."

I shook my head. "I don't know. She wouldn't have put us through something like this if she were okay."

Marcella nodded, and the three of us walked into the cottage. Marcella put the kettle on and began throwing tea bags and mugs onto the table.

Lorcan took a slip of paper from his pocket and adjusted his glasses. He sat at the table and reviewed the notes he'd taken while at the police station.

"I want to know everything," I said once Marcella had poured hot water into each of our mugs.

"There isn't much to tell. As I said, Willem arrived at garda headquarters and asked to speak with the detectives in charge. I was with O'Shea when the desk sergeant came into O'Shea's office with the message. I waited in his office while he followed the sergeant out. A few minutes later, O'Shea returned and declared they have their man."

"But why?" I asked. "I still can't fathom a motive for Willem to kill Jimmy."

"That's an interesting point. Willem won't tell O'Shea why he did what he did. He only said he's the murderer and was offering himself up to the guards."

"He's covering for someone," I said.

"But who?" Marcella asked. "From what I've seen of him at the museum, he's a loner. I don't think he's friendly with too many people."

"I agree with you, but for one exception, Deirdre. He's always with her." I pounded the kitchen table with my fist. "I should have seen it sooner. When we were at Flann's event, Deirdre's dislike for Jimmy was on full display. And Willem is always in the background, helping her. But why would Deirdre kill Jimmy? And why let Georgina take the fall? Willem and Deirdre have a lot to explain."

Lorcan folded the paper he'd been looking at and returned it to his breast pocket. "I agree, but there's no way you're going to get close to Willem if that's what you're thinking. O'Shea has him locked up tight as a drum."

I nodded. "But you can talk to O'Shea, Lorcan. And Willem probably has a lawyer by now. You've got to get something out of them." I clenched the cell phone in my hand. "You've got to, and I'll talk to Deirdre."

"If you think Willem is covering for Deirdre, that could be dangerous for you, Star. Maybe Deirdre is holding Georgina someplace in the museum." Marcella shuddered at her words. "God knows that place is centuries old. There could be all kinds of tunnels we don't know about."

I didn't want to consider Marcella's ideas. "Yeah, but if that's the case, Georgina is in even more danger than before. With Willem taking the rap for Jimmy's murder, Deirdre might want to get rid of Georgina, especially if Georgina knows who her abductor is."

The phone interrupted our conversation. I jumped up to answer it, but the line was dead by the time I reached for the receiver. I turned to Lorcan and Marcella. "I'm going to talk to Deirdre."

"We'll come with you," Marcella and Lorcan said at the same time.

"No, I want you to go back to Georgina's cottage and wait there for me. If we have to, we'll tear the place apart. We've got to figure out where she is."

The phone rang again.

"I heard the news about Willem. Have you heard from Georgina yet?" Flann Mahoney asked when I answered.

"No, nothing." I didn't mention my suspicion of his sister.

"If it is of any help, I'll offer a reward for knowledge of Georgina's whereabouts," Flann said.

"That's a generous offer, but I don't think it will bring us any closer to finding her. Actually, it may just get her killed. The last time you spoke with her, did she say anything about meeting up with someone?"

"Well, now that you mention it, she said something about wanting to talk with my sister."

"When was that? Did she say what she wanted to discuss?" I pressed the phone's receiver to my ear and looked over at Lorcan while I waited for Flann's response.

"No, just something about London. Georgina mentioned that you'd seen Deirdre there." Flann paused before continuing, "I didn't think anything of it at the time. But now that there's news about Willem and Jimmy, I guess it is a good idea to talk to Deirdre. Do you want me to meet you at her place?"

"I think it's best I speak to her alone. Look, I have to go. Please, call me if you hear from Georgina. Do you have my cell phone number?"

"No, hold on. Let me get a pen and paper." I heard a door closing in the background, and then Flann was back on the phone line. "Go ahead."

I recited my number slowly, giving him time to write.

"That's grand," he said. "I'll ring if I hear anything."

"Thanks, Flann." I ended the call and said to Marcella and Lorcan, "Georgina planned to meet with Deirdre about London and Jimmy's pub there."

"Oh?" Marcella's eyes widened in surprise. "Why in the world would Georgina want to talk to anyone about that?"

"Georgina must have thought it was important." I picked up my car keys from the counter. "I've got to go. Can you go to her cottage? I'll meet you there later."

My feet flew over the cement pavement to my car. I could hear Lorcan calling my name, but I didn't answer. I had to get to Deirdre.

CHAPTER 30

*N*o! The driver's side front tire lay flat in the grass.

"What's wrong?" Lorcan said as he caught up with me, drawing back from the angry look on my face.

"Let's go," I said and moved over to his car.

He took a quick look at where I'd pointed. Then, he opened his passenger door. "Hop in," he said.

"Don't worry about me," Marcella said, pulling a cell phone from her bag. "I'll call one of the neighbors and have them drop me home. It's probably best for me just to wait there. And Star, I'll get someone out here to fix the flat."

For the third time in almost as many days, Lorcan and I drove in silence until we reached Deirdre's house in Turlough's Rockfield section, not far from Georgina's cottage and the greenway between Turlough Museum and Castlebar.

The one-level ranch was set back in a large field. The size of the gate and fence around the property seemed to be overdone for the smallish bungalow. A dark-colored sedan sat in the driveway, and Lorcan pulled into the small lay-by outside the gate.

"Don't turn off the car," I said. "I'm going in alone."

Lorcan's face registered his surprise, but he complied." Are you sure?" he asked.

I nodded.

"I'll be right here," he said.

"No, I want you to go on to Georgina's cottage. I think we have to give it one more search, and I'll catch up with you later."

"This isn't a good idea, Star," Lorcan said, turning off the engine. "If Deirdre helped Willem kill Jimmy, she will be desperate, and she might even be holding Georgina in there."

"I don't disagree with you, but if I'm wrong about Deirdre, then we've both wasted precious time. We've got to split up. Please, just do as I ask." Then, I opened the car door, jumped out, and strode toward Deirdre's front door.

I heard Lorcan's car pull away.

"WHO IS IT?" DEIRDRE'S VOICE ASKED FROM THE OTHER SIDE OF the door.

"Star O'Brien. I need to speak with you."

"Who?"

"Georgina Hill's niece. I need to talk with you. Now."

"Give me a minute."

I heard scratching on the other side of the door like a piece of furniture was being moved. Then the footsteps returned. Deirdre opened the door. The blotchy red marks on her cheeks and the puffy bags under her eyes telegraphed all I needed to know. She must have heard about Willem.

"What can I do for you, Miss O'Brien?" She tried to smile, but it didn't reach her eyes.

"I can see you've heard about Willem's confession. The charges against my aunt have been dropped, but I'm unable to reach her. I thought she might have come by to see you."

I pushed myself through the front doorway into the foyer area. The odors of cooking food wafted through the house.

"Your aunt? No, I haven't seen her." Deirdre rubbed her sleeve-covered arms as if giving herself a hug.

I pressed farther into the house, scanning each of the two rooms that opened from the main hallway. "Are you sure? I believe she planned to speak to you about Jimmy and the pub he used to own in London."

Deirdre stepped back. "I don't know anything about that." She stopped rubbing her sleeves and put one of her hands into the pocket of the apron she wore.

"I saw you. You and Grainne. In London. Close to Jimmy's former pub. Are you sure you know nothing about what Georgina wanted to speak with you about?"

As if looking for an escape, Deirdre glanced around the hallway. "No, that's ridiculous." Her words were spoken more confidently than the puzzled look on her face. "Grainne and I are thinking about a collaborative cooking exhibit that would coincide with some cooking lessons and recipes in the café."

Was she lying or telling the truth? I continued pressing her. "I found some notes at Georgina's concerning London. A young woman went missing when Jimmy owned that pub. Do you think Willem had anything to do with that? Perhaps that's why Georgina wanted to speak with you?"

"No. Stop." Deirdre placed both hands over her ears. "Please, stop. That poor man has suffered enough." The tears ran down her face like sheets of rain. She paced up and down the hallway. "It's all my fault. It's all my fault."

"What is? If you have information that the police don't already know, you'd better tell me. Did you help Willem murder Jimmy? If you're involved, the police will find out eventually. It will go better for you if you tell me what you know." I stepped closer to her. "Where is Georgina?" It was difficult to keep the desperation out of my voice.

Maybe she sensed my distress, or perhaps she'd gotten control of herself. Deirdre wiped her face clean with the edge of her apron. Then, she walked back to the front door and opened it. "I appreciate your situation, Miss O'Brien, but I don't know anything about your aunt. Please, leave me be. I have to go see what I can do for Willem."

I stood my ground for another few moments, but she didn't budge from her station at the front door.

"I hope for your sake that you are telling me the truth," I said.

WHILE I RAN TO GEORGINA'S COTTAGE, I SIFTED THROUGH THE disastrous thoughts circulating around my brain. I considered all the suspects thus far in Jimmy's murder and Georgina's disappearance. After speaking with Deirdre, I was more certain than ever that Georgina was kidnapped.

What was Deirdre hiding? She blamed herself for Willem's behavior. Willem was not talking to the police about his motives, and I could only deduce that he was protecting Deirdre. But from what? And what did Georgina have to do with that?

Lorcan's car was in the driveway when I arrived at Georgina's place, and her cottage door stood open. I strode in and found Lorcan lifting sofa cushions and piles of cloth remnants.

"Star, I hope you never do that to me again," Lorcan said as soon as I entered the cottage.

"I'm sorry, but I am so worried about Georgina."

"We all are, but it doesn't mean that we take unnecessary risks. How did your talk with Deirdre go?"

"She's upset about Willem, and she claims she hasn't spoken with Georgina. I tried, but I couldn't get her to say more," I replied, looking around the room. "Find anything?" I asked.

"Nothing, but I spoke to O'Shea again about Georgina. He's going to put everyone he can on finding her."

"I'm glad he's finally seeing things the way we do."

As much as I wanted to rant and rave about the police and O'Shea, I didn't. Every focus needed to be on finding Georgina.

"He also plans to interview Nessa and her husband. They may not have had anything to do with Jimmy's murder, but I don't like the way they've behaved toward you and possibly Georgina."

"There's got to be something here," I said to Lorcan as I searched Georgina's living room and kitchen again, looking for some other hiding place where she might have kept notes, photos, or any information about why she wanted to meet with Deirdre.

"I looked everywhere but didn't find anything. Let's go back to French Hill. I'll call O'Shea for an update."

"No, I'm not stopping until I find her." While I was talking, I noticed that one of the paintings hanging just inside the front door was slightly askew. I pulled the frame away from the wall, revealing the letter G followed by a phone number scrawled across the painting's backing in Georgina's handwriting.

"What do you make of this?" I held the piece up for Lorcan to see.

"That's an odd place to store a number." Lorcan took the frame in his hands and brought it closer to examine the back. "This is a Turlough exchange."

I pulled my cell phone out of its holster and dialed the number.

"You have reached the Turlough Museum of Country Life. We are currently closed. Please dial back during normal business hours."

I didn't wait to hear the rest. "Let's go," I said, taking the picture with me and striding out the door to his car.

"Where to next?" he asked.

"Back to the museum. I want to talk to Grainne again. Grainne, Deirdre, and Willem all work at the museum in one capacity or another. Willem is covering for Deirdre, and I should have seen it sooner. The way he acts as if he is her bodyguard. Grainne and Deirdre were in London, supposedly for research, according to Deirdre. I want to hear what Grainne says."

"But the museum is closed. How do you propose to get in there?"

"From what I've seen of Grainne, she's a workaholic. She'll be there."

"Right."

LORCAN PARKED HIS CAR ON THE GRAVEL CURB OUTSIDE THE museum gates. We climbed over the stone wall and walked up the drive to the Fitzgerald House, where the museum staff had their offices. Lights shone in several of the windows on the second floor. I looked at Lorcan and pointed upward. I rang the doorbell and used the brass knocker to announce our presence.

When the door finally opened, Grainne looked from Lorcan to me and then stepped outside onto the driveway.

"What are you doing here?" she demanded. "And how did you get in here?" She glanced behind us as if looking for one of the security guards.

"Your museum isn't very secure, is it?" I asked. Then I turned the painting, which I'd brought with me so that she could see the museum phone number on the back. "Why did Georgina Hill call you?"

Grainne's face froze. "What are you talking about? I have nothing to do with your aunt."

"This is the museum number, isn't it?" I said while taking

my cell phone out and dialing. I heard a phone ringing through an open window above us.

"So?" Grainne shrugged. "That doesn't mean I was on the other end of whomever your aunt was trying to reach. She gets involved in some of our exhibits with clothing and things of the sort. It could have been any of the staff. How long ago was that number written on that frame?"

"Come on, Grainne. Jimmy is dead, Willem is in jail, Deirdre blames herself, and my aunt is missing. Do you really want the publicity and whispers this can bring to your museum?" I waited for what I'd said to sink in and then continued, "What were you and Deirdre doing in London?"

Surprise washed over Grainne's face. "Have you been following us? That's against the law. I'll have you arrested."

"There's no need for that," Lorcan said quietly. "The best way to settle this is for you to tell us everything you know about what happened the night of the gala and why Georgina might have wanted to talk to you."

A huff of exasperation escaped Grainne's pursed lips. "Deirdre and I were in London researching a collaborative cooking and artifact exhibit. Working together, we thought we'd get more of the local youth involved in history and healthy food." Grainne glanced over at the garden's hothouse. "Willem was involved too. We were planning a new vegetable garden at the side of the café. We want to have the school children plant the seedlings and then watch the garden grow."

"What about the night of the gala?" I asked.

"Your aunt asked me the same thing. I didn't see what happened if that's what you're getting at. I'm as surprised as anyone to hear that Willem confessed."

I wanted to grab Grainne at that point and shake it out of her but realized that Lorcan's approach was best. "So, Georgina did call you," I stated quietly.

Grainne shook her head. "Yes, she asked about the gala and

whether I'd seen anything unusual. Like I just said, I told her I didn't see anything out of the ordinary. Then, she asked me about the exhibit where Jimmy's body was found."

"That seems like a curious question," I said. "Especially with her knowledge of the area's history. What did she want to know?"

"She asked me to describe what the exhibit represented. She wanted to know if I'd used any local papers or family artifacts to research the display."

"And did you?"

"Yes, as a matter of fact, I interviewed some of the local families, including the Mahoneys."

"The last time we spoke, you mentioned funding provided by the Mahoneys for the museum," I stated, waiting for Grainne to elaborate.

"Yes, they contribute. But your aunt was more interested in the family history. I already told you that Jimmy's mother was the postmistress, and his father was a member of the garda."

Georgina must have made some connection between the exhibit and Jimmy's body being placed there. But what was it? I'd have to talk to Flann and Deirdre again—especially Deirdre. She was involved, but how, I didn't know yet.

"Anything more to add?" I asked Grainne.

"No, nothing else. Now, if you don't mind, I've got paperwork to catch up on." She turned to Lorcan. "I trust you will keep our conversation as private as possible. My administrator in Dublin is asking questions, and I don't want to lose my job."

"I can't make any promises, but I'll speak to Detective O'Shea in private," Lorcan replied. "And thanks for your help. This may assist the guards in figuring out Willem's motive."

Grainne stepped back into the building and slammed the door.

Lorcan and I moved quickly back to his car and drove to French Hill.

CHAPTER 31

J ust as Lorcan hung up from his call with O'Shea, the
cottage's landline rang. I ran to answer.

"Are you planning on meeting with me tomorrow
night as I asked?" Evelyn's voice came across the line.

"Of course. That's provided you show up."

"Good, I'll see you then." She ended the call before I could
say anything else.

Lorcan glanced at my face and asked, "Bad news?"

"I committed to the meeting with Evelyn at the Turlough
Inn. I don't have time for this, but based upon her behavior, I
believe I have to make one last try to meet with her." I touched
the locket that hung from my neck. "I don't know why she's
playing this cat-and-mouse game, but I've got to find out." I
didn't say how conflicted I felt about taking time for the
meeting with Georgina missing.

"I'll meet with her," Lorcan stated.

"You can't do that," I replied.

"I hate to remind you, but you were the one who said we
don't have time to waste. Listen, Star, you are an independent
woman. And I admit it is one of your most endearing traits. But

just this once, let's work together. Besides, I want to meet this mysterious woman."

I didn't let on to Lorcan, but I felt heart-warmed by his acceptance of my feisty independence. And I considered that he had been instrumental in getting me into the National Archives. He'd handled Grainne well, and his calm demeanor might prove beneficial in meeting with someone as flighty as Evelyn.

"Okay," I relented, "but only because I can't be in two places at once. And I want to follow up on why Georgina was so interested in the museum exhibit."

"Good," Lorcan replied. "O'Shea is planning to talk to Willem about what Grainne told us. I don't think there's any more we can do tonight. I recommend we both get some rest and start fresh in the morning."

I glanced out the window at the fading daylight and had to admit he was probably right. My insides crumbled at the thought of another night passing without finding Georgina, and my gut told me she had been onto something that had gotten Jimmy killed and maybe even her.

"I'll call you when I get home," Lorcan said. "Be sure to lock up." His blue eyes crinkled with his smile. "Don't worry; we'll find her." Then, he was gone.

I sat in the living room, staring at the cold fireplace. Ever since I'd arrived in French Hill, the furniture and artifacts that belonged to Dylan's family made me feel safe and secure from the pain of losing so many of the people I loved. Then, as I looked around, I realized it wasn't our belongings that defined us. It was the people who populated our life's journey. Georgina, Lorcan, and Marcella had all become a part of my life. I didn't think I'd be able to deal with the pain of losing Georgina. She was the closest I'd come to having family since Dylan's death. I got up and paced the living room floor. Every road seemed to lead to Deirdre and Willem.

Lorcan kept his promise and called a few minutes after he left. "Everything okay there?" he asked.

"Yes, how's your mom doing?" I asked, realizing this must be as tortuous or even more for Georgina's lifelong friend.

"She's fine. I persuaded her to get some sleep. She's wrung out and blaming herself for not keeping Georgina at our house."

"Thank her for getting the flat tire repaired."

"You don't have to thank us, Star. We are your friends. You need to get some rest, too, so I'll say good night," Lorcan said. Then, we ended the call.

In times like this, we all had regrets and what-ifs. Finally, I realized I had to get some sleep if I were to confront Deirdre again tomorrow.

~

THE NIGHT PASSED, AND WITH IT ANY SENSE OF HOPELESSNESS. By 5:00 a.m., I laced up my sneakers and took a long walk along Cottage Road. Moving quickly, I mapped out my day—first the museum to speak to Deirdre and then on to Flann's place. Back at the cottage, my cell phone rang, and Lorcan's name popped up on the display.

"You're up early," I said, glancing at the time. "Is everything okay?"

"You're not the only lark around here," Lorcan said before continuing, "O'Shea sent me a text message earlier. He thought I'd want to know that the guards brought Nessa Bantry and her husband in for questioning yesterday."

"Did you talk to O'Shea?"

"Yes, I just got off the phone before I rang you. The Bantrys have alibis for the time of Jimmy's death. The husband, Pete, moonlights at the Castlebar movie theater in the ticket office, and there's video of him in the cashier's booth all evening until the place closed."

"What about Nessa? She was at the gala."

"According to O'Shea, verifying her story was a bit trickier, but the waitstaff at the gala claim she never left the corner of the room where she set up her instruments. According to the servers, people kept engaging Nessa in conversation whenever there was a break in the entertainment. So, O'Shea doesn't think they had anything to do with the murder or Georgina's disappearance."

I could hear Marcella's voice in the background, asking Lorcan if she could speak with me.

"Star, I'm going to Maeve Baldwin's place today. Between the two of us, we may be able to figure out where Georgina is."

I didn't want to burst Marcella's belief in her childhood buddy, Maeve, but I doubted she wanted to do anything other than ushering me out of the country, something she'd made abundantly clear several times. "Okay, just keep your cell phone with you in case Georgina shows up. Oh, and ask Maeve if she's spoken with Evelyn recently."

"Of course. But I don't think Maeve's been doing much with the historical society since, you know, the murders in Cong."

"Thanks, Marcella," I said, not wanting to get into a conversation about Cong. Phillie's research into Maeve hadn't found anything unusual other than Maeve moved around a lot, living in London and New York for brief periods before moving to Cong. "Can I speak to Lorcan again?" I asked.

"Yes, what else?" Lorcan asked when he got back on the phone.

"I'm heading over to the museum to talk to Deirdre. Will you check out Georgina's cottage again and the shop? Her assistant should be back in today."

I knew I was reaching for straws, but reaching was better than doing nothing. Lorcan and I agreed to meet later that morning in town at police headquarters. After my conversation with Deirdre, I expected to have some updates as well as questions for Detective O'Shea.

~

THE MUSEUM'S GATES STOOD OPEN, AND I QUICKLY DROVE UP THE winding driveway to the parking area. The lot stood empty this early in the morning. But by lunchtime and late afternoon, tourist buses would line the sandy parking area. Tourists usually flooded the gift shop and café after alighting from the bus. I expected to find Deirdre in the café's kitchen, preparing the day's menu. If I understood one thing about Deirdre and Grainne, it was their persistent, workaholic personalities.

I entered the building through one of the side doors that led past two bathrooms: one men's room and the other for women. Once through that corridor, I came out into the gift shop. Several staff members stood in a circle, shaking their heads. Another staff person was on a phone located near the cash register. When they saw me, the conversation stopped. One in the group, a woman with a name badge that read *Naomi* stepped forward. "I'm sorry, but the café is closed momentarily."

"What do you mean it's closed?" I asked. I'd expected to find Deirdre there and so, too, had the staff, judging from the concerned looks on their faces.

"I apologize for any inconvenience. But we can't serve anything right now—maybe if you take a walk through the museum. We think the manager must be delayed." Naomi pointed to the woman on the phone. "Our supervisor is checking with her now. But until she gets here, we can't unlock the doors to the kitchen."

My gut immediately reacted to the news, confirming my suspicion of Deirdre. I didn't believe in serendipity. And it was no coincidence that the day after I confronted her, she hadn't shown up at work. I wondered if Willem's lawyer had arranged a meeting for his client and Deirdre. I pulled my business card from my knapsack and handed it to Naomi.

"Thank you, but I'm not a visitor to the museum. I'm a friend of Deirdre's, and I wanted to speak with her about an urgent matter."

Naomi turned the card over in her hand and then pointed to the woman on the phone. "It's probably best if you speak with our supervisor."

I nodded and walked over to the female Naomi had pointed out. The woman hung up the phone just as I arrived.

"I'm looking for Deirdre Mahoney," I said.

The supervisor pushed past me toward the group of waiting staff. "Naomi, put up a sign on the door indicating that the café is closed."

Naomi rushed off; I assumed to get a pen and paper. The supervisor continued speaking to the rest of the group. "There's no need for ye to stay. You can go home. The director says you'll be compensated for your time, but it's no use sitting around here at the moment."

The group moved quickly, gathering up belongings. They exited via the same door through which I'd entered. The supervisor turned and walked back to her station at the cash register. She looked surprised when I followed her. "Yes? How can I help you, miss?"

"Where is Deirdre Mahoney?" I asked, not waiting to get through the niceties. I flashed my business card again and threw out Flann's and Deirdre's names as friends of my family.

The supervisor laughed and said, "If you think you can use your Yankee pushiness here, you are mistaken. I'm sorry, but I'm not authorized to discuss museum staff or their families, for that matter." She moved around me and walked toward the administrative office section of the museum. "If you wish, I can have the director speak with you," she said as she drifted away.

"Thank you. Just tell Grainne that Star O'Brien was asking for her," I replied. I took off back to my car.

As I drove back down the winding driveway, I considered why Deirdre hadn't shown up at the museum. If she were involved in Georgina's disappearance, she might have gone on the run. After all, it was only a matter of time before Willem realized what he'd done when he confessed in a cover-up for Deirdre. I immediately dismissed that idea. Whenever I'd seen Willem, he'd seemed protective of Deirdre, and I doubted he would change his mind about shielding her. I wondered if Deirdre had gone to see Willem. If she were involved in Jimmy's murder and Georgina's disappearance, she'd want to ensure that Willem stayed true to her. That seemed like a more realistic scenario. With that in mind, I drove to police head-quarters in Castlebar.

∽

MY CELL PHONE RANG AS I NEARED THE STATION DOOR.

"Anything at Georgina's cottage?" I asked.

"No, nothing here. How did it go with Deirdre?" Lorcan asked.

"It didn't. She is a no-show at work. I'm in Castlebar, and I'll bet she's either taken off or she's with Willem. I'm sure she killed Jimmy, and Willem is covering for her. I've got to get to her before she does something to Georgina."

"I'm on my way," Lorcan said and ended the call.

∽

THE DESK SERGEANT WOULDN'T PERMIT ME TO SEE O'SHEA. SO, I loudly shouted O'Shea's name over and over. All they could do was arrest me. Within minutes, the sergeant picked up the phone. Keenan appeared.

"Don't worry, Sergeant. I'll take it from here," Keenan said. He escorted me to a seating area in a nearby room. "Miss O'Brien, to what do we owe the pleasure this morning?"

"I need to talk to your boss, O'Shea. Has Willem Block given you a motive for killing Jimmy?"

Keenan compressed his lips.

"Just what I thought," I continued. "You don't have a motive. He didn't kill Jimmy; Deirdre Mahoney did, and Willem is covering for her."

Keenan's head reared back, and he laughed. "Of all the wild."

"It's not crazy at all. Listen to me. Deirdre is not at work today, and no one can find her. Georgina is missing. And the last time someone spoke to her, she planned to go talk to Deirdre. Georgina's life is in danger. Someone has to listen to me."

"What's all the commotion about?" O'Shea's voice boomed into the room. The scar on his face throbbed.

I jumped up from my chair. "I know we've had our differences, and you think I'm a meddling American, but you've got to hear me out this once, please."

Lorcan appeared at the door, the desk sergeant at his side. "Sir, Mr. McHale would like a word with you."

O'Shea threw his hands up and surrendered. "Okay, everyone, take a seat. I'm listening, but I don't make any promises. Go ahead, Miss O'Brien."

I took a deep breath and plunged in.

"First, I've been working on a different set of assumptions than you from the beginning. Georgina Hill is innocent." I held my hand up when O'Shea opened his mouth to speak. "I know you thought you had proof of guilt in the blood DNA evidence. But I found several men's shirts at Georgina's cottage in her

sewing basket. Seemingly, she mended Jimmy's work shirts for
him. She probably pricked her finger and got blood on one
shirt." I stopped to let that sink in.

Lorcan added, "I asked my mother about the shirts, and it's
true. Georgina told Marcella she often mended clothes for
Jimmy when they were dating. My mother thought it was
ridiculous, and that's why it stuck in her mind. She told
Georgina several times to let him take his mending to the
tailors."

"When you took Georgina into custody, did you check her
for wounds?" I asked.

When O'Shea didn't answer, I answered for him. "If she had
no wounds, then there's no way the blood you found happened
on the night Jimmy was killed."

I continued putting my case before O'Shea, "Now that you
have Willem Block in custody, you will admit, won't you, that a
drop of blood on a shirt does not an entire case make?"

"Okay, let's say that is the case," O'Shea said. "How do you
come up with the idea that Willem Block is covering for
Deirdre?"

"Process of elimination. First, I admit that I wrongly
pinpointed Allen Skye as Jimmy's killer. And, after Skye's
death, someone continued to stalk Georgina." I counted off on
my fingers as I outlined the shadowing examples. "First, there
was the anonymous letter left at Lorcan's home."

"Paul Shephard admits that he wrote the letter," O'Shea
said before I could continue.

"Yes, and for some time, I believed the numbers-running
person was Georgina's stalker, but you have Shephard in
custody."

"Has Shephard confessed to the vandalism at Georgina's
cottage or the dead animals left at her shop?" Lorcan asked
O'Shea.

"He denies the other incidents," O'Shea responded.

"And he has an alibi for the night of Jimmy's murder. That leaves us with the other incidents, including the ransacking of Georgina's cottage, hours after you arrested Shephard."

"Tom, Star, and I went back to Georgina's cottage," Lorcan added. "We couldn't find the house key she leaves hidden outside. You have to admit that, with Shephard locked up, someone else might be responsible for these other incidents."

"So," I continued, "with Skye and Shephard eliminated, the remaining suspects are other people in Jimmy's life who were at the gala that night."

"There's a hole in your case right there," O'Shea said. Keenan smiled.

"Why?" I asked.

"You assume the killer was at the gala," O'Shea replied.

I shook my head. "I'm right. Jimmy was seen at the gala. He was dressed for a special event. Grainne, the museum curator, admitted to me that Jimmy was a major philanthropic contributor to the museum." I emphasized what I said next, "*Someone at that event* followed Jimmy out onto the greenway and bludgeoned him."

"And Willem Block admits that is exactly what he did," O'Shea moved to get up from the table.

"I'm not finished," I said. "You have no motive, and you have no fingerprints on the murder weapon. How do you expect to bring a successful case when you have only circumstantial evidence? Circumstantial evidence is not enough to convict, as you know."

"Hear us out, Tom," Lorcan said.

"Whoever killed Mahoney did so in a rage. Your aunt had motive," O'Shea said, "and we have her DNA. Perhaps Mr. Block is covering for her."

"Georgina Hill doesn't get into rages over men. No. I think she's been investigating on her own, and Deirdre Mahoney has kidnapped her."

I hadn't planned just to blurt that out. But I was getting antsy, trying to lead O'Shea through my logic.

"Deirdre Mahoney didn't arrive at work this morning," Lorcan said to O'Shea.

"And I saw her in London a few days ago near the pub where a girl went missing—a pub Jimmy owned. Don't you think that's too coincidental?"

"That's a cold case," Keenan interjected. "Detective O'Shea had me follow up after your last visit, and there's no connection to here."

"But there has to be." I shook my head. "Georgina went to school in the same area. She's been looking through old pictures. She went to talk to Deirdre at the café. But according to Marcella McHale, Deirdre brushed her off. Then, someone broke into Georgina's cottage. Now, she is missing, and so is Deirdre. What if Georgina discovered something that incriminates Deirdre? What if Deirdre is holding Georgina somewhere? Do you really want to face the public if what I'm saying is true?"

"Let's say you are correct," O'Shea said. "What is Deirdre Mahoney's motive?"

"Anger. She admitted to me that she didn't like her brother."

"That's not really a motive," Keenan piped up. "A lot of people don't like their siblings."

O'Shea's scar crinkled when he cast a frown at his partner.

Ignoring Keenan, I continued, "I caught her in a lie. She claimed she wasn't at the gala, but Terrence O'Shaunessy, the security guard, one of the café servers, and even Willem said she was there that night. When I asked her about Jimmy, she called him her "cursed brother" and wished he'd never come to the gala. She hasn't made her dislike of Jimmy a secret. Nor has she expressed surprise that he was involved in an illegal scheme." I looked around the room in frustration. "Willem Block follows her around everywhere. What if she killed Jimmy and Willem helped her move the body to the exhibit hall? What if Georgina was onto something? Both women are missing. All I'm asking is for you to consider the possibilities. Block has got to tell you if Deirdre killed Jimmy." I stopped talking. I felt my heart pounding in my chest, waiting for O'Shea to speak.

O'Shea glanced out the room's window before he answered. "I will speak to Mr. Block again, but I can't guarantee anything. In the meanwhile, I will put out an alert for your aunt and Miss Mahoney."

I heaved a sigh of relief. "I have an appointment to keep. Thank you for listening."

"Tom, if you don't mind, I'd like to stick around until you talk to Willem," Lorcan said.

O'Shea nodded his approval, and he and Keenan left the room.

"You look exhausted," Lorcan said. "Do you want to wait here with me?"

"No, I hope O'Shea keeps his word, but I cannot rely on his promise. I still have work to do. Call me if you hear anything."

"Where are you going?" Lorcan asked.

"Looking for answers," I replied and left the building.

CHAPTER 32

B efore I entered the library, I rang Flann Mahoney. I'd
almost given up when he answered.

"Star, my dear, any news?"

"Yes, as a matter of fact. Deirdre is missing, and she hasn't
reported to work today."

"Oh, dear. Her old melancholy must be back. I suppose
she's upset about Willem. I'll have to have a chat with her."

"You haven't heard from her?" I asked.

"Why, no. I've been busy here on the estate. You know she's
done this before. She disappears for a few days and then comes
back as if nothing has happened. Not very reliable at times."

"I don't agree with you. She's hiding something about
Jimmy's death and Georgina's disappearance. I'm worried she
may do something desperate to herself or Georgina," I said,
watching the cars move around the traffic circle by the library.

"Ah, now, no worries. Where are you?"

"In Castlebar. I've just met with the police, and they've
agreed to put out an alert. Look, I have to go. If you hear from
either one of them, call the police." I ended the call. It was
getting late, and I had two more stops to make.

~

AFTER SEARCHING THE ARCHIVES ABOUT TURLOUGH VILLAGE'S history, I exited the library building. Grainne had stated that Jimmy's mother and father came from the area. Many of the photographs and articles featured Jimmy's mother because of her postmistress duties. But I really had to dig to find anything about his father, a member of the police. One article, buried in the back of a paper, gave me pause. Disciplined for drunkenness and aggressive behavior, his suspension was lifted at the end of the inquiry. Friends and family vouched for him at the hearing.

From the library, I drove to the Turlough Museum and parked my car outside the exhibit hall. I waved at the security guard and ran down the stairs to the rural postmistress tableau. I reread the placard that went with the exhibit. Sure enough, the description supported my hunch. *The rural postmistress often came from a strong family history of dedication to the community. Self-employed, they held an elevated standing among the people they served.*

Once back outside, I called Lorcan. "Anything new from O'Shea?"

"No, I'm still here. Willem's lawyer showed up. There might be a delay before O'Shea can speak with him, but they're going to tell him that Deirdre's gone missing. Maybe when Willem realizes he's been left in the lurch, he'll be more willing to talk. Where are you?"

"At the museum. I had something I wanted to check."

"And..." Lorcan seemed to wait for me to tell him what I'd found.

"I have one more thing to do. You said you'd meet with Evelyn for me. Are you still willing to do that?"

"Yes, but where will you be?"

Not wanting to alarm Lorcan about my hunch, I didn't tell

him where I intended to go. Instead, I told him a partial truth. "I'm going back to Deirdre's house this evening. I think I know what she's hiding."

"What?" Lorcan's voice practically hissed. "After trying to convince O'Shea that Deirdre is a murderer, you are going to confront her? Don't do that, Star."

"Lorcan, I need your help with Evelyn. I'll have my phone with me, and I promise I won't go inside. If I see any movement, I'll call you and the police immediately. Thanks."

I ended the call, got into my car, and prepared for what I had to do.

CHAPTER 33

The sun had dipped below the horizon when I pulled a black sweatshirt over my head. Even without the hood, I didn't think my pixie-cut ebony hair would be an issue. But I wasn't so sure about what to do with my lifeline to the world—the almost umbilical connection—my cell phone. I knew I couldn't risk a shred of light to permeate the inky shroud cover I needed to pull off what I was about to do. My decision made, I turned off the phone and tucked it down into the side leg pocket of my capri pants. Finally, I laced up the black sneakers I'd bought earlier in the day.

Before turning out the lights, I took one last look around the kitchen. My eyes went to the oak table where Aunt Georgina and I shared many a cup of tea, and I pictured her arguing with me about what to do with my life while her steady hands sliced homemade brown bread. My hands trembled when I closed the back door behind me.

I parked my car at Georgina's cottage on the Old Turlough Road and ran the mile to the Turlough Castlebar greenway. Stray bits of crime scene tape hung lopsidedly at the place on the walkway where the police believe Jimmy was killed. I wondered how much Jimmy had seen of the ball-peen hammer before his skull shattered. I shivered in the cold, damp air but kept on going until I reached the N5.

Earlier in the day, I'd driven along the N5 and noticed a stone stile where I could cross from the highway into one of the fields that lay beyond. I ran across the highway, squeezed through the narrow opening, and moved toward the ring of oak trees standing sentry around the house. As soon as I reached the shelter of the trees' canopy, I hunkered down to wait. Even though it had been years since I'd attended a church service, I prayed that my hunch was correct. I believed that although Georgina may be held captive in that house, she was alive. Normally, I grasped my phone for support. Tonight, all I had was faith.

The prayers caught in my throat when I heard the crack of a branch right behind me. I held my breath and slowly turned toward the sound. I didn't know what to expect. Sunset brought out things we didn't or couldn't see in the light. The eyes staring back mirrored my fear. Then, with the whoosh of a reddish tail, the eyes disappeared—a fox. I allowed air to escape silently through my pursed lips. Then, what I'd been waiting for happened. The moon disappeared behind the predicted cloud cover—plunging the entire area into an abyss of darkness.

Without a cell phone flashlight to guide me, I thought of Ashford and how he had rushed into danger the last time I faced a vicious murderer. At this moment, I desperately longed for Ashford to appear.

Finally, I half rose from my crouched position and moved toward the structure's back door. The unlit windows didn't give any clue as to the occupants. I paused, trying not to make a noise or sudden movement. My eyes scanned from side to side as I eased again along the ground.

The air smelled of animals, but the night was so eerily silent that the only sound I heard was my heart beating in my chest. I dreaded what I'd find when I reached the door. But with the moonlight obscured, I stood to my full height and picked up the pace.

I heard a sudden rustling behind me and instinctively dropped to the ground. My breath came in short bursts. A line of sensor lights flashed on, illuminating the patio. I held my breath and cursed the beating of my heart, watching for someone to emerge from the house. But the lights snapped off as quickly as they'd come on. *Ah, he definitely doesn't want anyone to see him,* I thought to myself. *Or he knows I'm here and wants to be the pursuer instead of the pursued* was the other terrifying scenario. I scrambled back to the safety of the tree line and lurched forward when my foot missed a step and caught in a jumble of twisted branches. I ignored the pain that shot through my ankle. From the corner of my eye, I glimpsed a human silhouette and a flashlight beam at one of the windows farthest from the door. I couldn't wait any longer; I made myself move forward, creeping toward the door again.

"Get into that car now." Flann's voice pierced the air as he opened the farmhouse's kitchen door and shoved Georgina out onto the gravel driveway.

My stomach recoiled in revulsion. I stepped back into the shadows. I wanted to scream, "Run" to Georgina, but the words froze in my throat when he grabbed her arm and dragged her toward the car. The gun in his hand jabbed her back, and he forced her into the trunk.

Frozen in place by fear, I reached my hand for my phone, my connection to the world, but I stopped. I had the element of surprise, but I *couldn't, wouldn't,* risk Aunt Georgina's life.

I remained hidden in the shadows.

"Don't move, or I'll have to kill you here." Flann lowered the trunk lid and returned to the house.

I didn't know when Flann would reappear. I guessed how long it would take me to reach Georgina and get her out of the trunk—too long—long enough for Flann to shoot both of us.

At that moment, he emerged, dragging Deirdre out by the hair. He reopened the trunk and threw her in on top of Georgina. The trunk lid slammed shut, and Flann got into the car and drove away.

I didn't wait to see the car's rear lights fade into the gloom. I launched from my crouched position and ran in earnest toward the direction I'd come from earlier. The house's sensor lights flashed on. I kept moving, hoping Flann was so focused on killing his passengers that he wouldn't notice. Time seemed to pass like an eternity as I raced through the darkness, thinking about every possible place Flann would go to kill Georgina and Deirdre. In my mind, there was only one location to bury a body. When I reached my car, I pulled out my phone and turned it on. Then, I drove to the Round Tower and the old cemetery.

CHAPTER 34

I hit the *accept* button as soon as my phone rang and Lorcan's name popped up. "Lorcan—"

"Star, why has your phone been off? I've been trying to call you for the last forty-five minutes!"

"I'm sorry, but—"

"Flann's been abusing Deirdre," Lorcan interrupted again. "Willem thought he was killing Flann that night, but Willem got confused."

"I know. Lorcan, listen to me. Flann has Deirdre and Georgina. Call O'Shea. I'm on my way to the Round Tower. I think that's where Flann is headed, and I've got to stop him before he kills them."

I ended the call and floored the accelerator.

When I neared the cemetery, I turned off the headlights and engine, allowing the car to coast down the hill. Then, I exited quietly before stealthily moving to the stone wall, which surrounded the graveyard. Instead of entering through the gate, I vaulted over the wall, landing in a tuft of grass. Ground fog hovered over the graves. Cloud cover, obscuring the earlier moonlight, cast a dark pall over the boneyard.

From my crouched position, I watched Flann march

Deirdre and Georgina to the place where this entire nightmare had started—the base of the Round Tower. He thrust Georgina forward, forcing her down onto the ground. Then, he kicked her. I didn't see her moving, but I heard her crying.

"Oh, lose the tears, woman," Flann growled at her. "It won't be too long now."

Deirdre chose that moment to struggle with him, but he shoved her into the collapsed crater of a grave. I couldn't see her anymore, but I heard a thud.

I had to get his attention. "I read about the investigation into your father's drunkenness and aggressive behavior. The violence and abuse must have been horrible when you were growing up. What did your mother, the postmistress, do about it? As a matter of fact, she didn't do a thing. Friends and family testified on his behalf, so the suspension was lifted," I shouted from a standing position, below the rise.

"It had to be covered up—buried here along with the family," I yelled, louder this time, running nearer to where Flann stood, shovel in his hand, poised over the caved-in grave. As I got closer, I glimpsed Deirdre's hands, clawing at the crater's edge.

"The family standing had to be protected no matter what," I shouted again. "But you, you are the worst kind—a bullied child who is a bully. Deirdre became your target, didn't she? That's why she wears the long-sleeved blouses and jumps when a door opens suddenly and never engages with people. She's afraid, and you like it that way."

"You're next, Miss O'Brien." Flann's laugh exploded in an uncontrollable cackle, echoing off the silent stones. He held the shovel over his head in his clenched fists, and I could see the craziness burning in his eyes as he spun toward me.

"Really? You'll have to catch me first. I'm much faster than you are." I raised my hand so that he could see my phone. "I've recorded everything. You may kill me, but someone will find the phone. The video will be seen. What will people think of the Mahoney family then? Flann Mahoney has been living a lie all his life—that's what everyone will know."

He growled, charging toward me, brandishing the shovel.

I threw the phone as far as I could into the mess of broken headstones and cratered graves, farther away from the tower.

Flann paused, his head swiveled, looking from me to where I'd thrown the phone. When he refocused on me, rage contorted his face. He raised the shovel and lunged toward me.

"Run, Georgina, run!" I cried. My feet carried me toward the steeper, older part of the cemetery. Tufts of grass, sunken graves, and half toppled headstones littered my path. I veered away from where I'd thrown my phone.

"Over here," I taunted.

He spun in the direction of my voice. His eyes, bulging with fury, wildly scanned the collapsed gravesites.

"Now you see me, now you don't," I shouted, running toward an even older section of the cemetery, close to a tangle of trees and bushes. But before I could get there, I tripped and fell into one of the collapsed resting places.

"Never mind, Miss O'Brien. I'll tend to you later." Flann's laugh roared through the air as he turned back toward Georgina and Deirdre. "I'll just finish up my little project. Then I'll come for you."

I could see him turning back to where he'd left Georgina and Deirdre. I tried to rise from the crater, but my hands and feet slipped on the wet grass. *Oh, no,* I thought when I felt the throb of pain in the ankle I'd twisted earlier. *I won't get there in time.*

"Fooled you, didn't I, Miss O'Brien?" Flann screamed from above me. He raised the shovel and swung it at my head, but I ducked out of its way. He swung again, but his entire body shook, missing me by a wide margin. I grabbed onto the base of a broken headstone and pulled myself out of the crater.

Once again, Flann raised the shovel above his head, but a sudden gusting wind, wailing through the graveyard and rustling the nearby trees, captured his attention.

"No, no," he shrieked, "you won't catch me."

I could see his eyes rolling from side to side as he peered wildly into the darkness.

I stood up, steadying myself on the half-missing headstone. Ignoring the pain that shot through my ankle, I propelled myself at him.

My movement caught his attention, and he leaped toward me, shovel swinging. I raised my hands, preparing to grab the handle. But at that moment, on the shovel's downward arc, I bent forward and hurtled my body at him. Closing the gap between us, I shoved him as hard as I could. He stumbled, fell, and hit his head on a stone marker. Then, his body rolled into the collapsed grave I'd exited.

I picked up the shovel from where it had fallen and looked down at Flann's motionless body. He was either unconscious or dead, and I didn't care which one. I went in search of Georgina. She hadn't run, and I found her where I'd last seen her, ministering to Deirdre, who rested against the Mahoney family headstone.

I couldn't get to Georgina fast enough. My ankle twinged with each step, but I didn't care. I threw my arms around her and squeezed as tightly as I could.

"I love you, Aunt Georgina," I whispered.

"And I you, Star O'Brien," Georgina replied.

I stepped back, wiping tears from my eyes. "Now, let's get this mess cleaned up," I said as the police cars rolled up on the scene.

CHAPTER 35

T *hree weeks later*
Georgina and I walked along the greenway between
Turlough and Castlebar. She carried a Belleek China vase of
crushed purple hyacinths.

"How is your ankle doing? It's a bit of a walk," Georgina
said.

"My ankle is fine. I'm just grateful for all the walking and
running I do. It came in handy that night," I replied.

"Did you hear the cries in the cemetery?" Georgina asked.

"I heard something. I thought it was the wind blowing
through the trees and echoing around the headstones." I hadn't
wanted to bring up the wailing sound, but, I admitted to myself,
it had sent chills up and down my spine.

"You were near the part of the cemetery that borders a
copse, weren't you?" Georgina asked.

"Yes," I replied, wondering where she was going with this.

"It is said that the banshee sits crouched near the base of
the trees, wailing and warning of someone's death—even
someone far away. I think we heard the banshee."

"I don't know anything about the banshee, Georgina. What
I do know is that my taunts enraged him. Then I shoved him,

and he fell." I changed the subject. "Do the flowers have a specific significance?" I asked.

"They symbolize forgiveness and sorrow."

"I hope you don't blame yourself for what happened to Jimmy."

There was a long silence, then Georgina said, "No, I wish I'd known more about his internal demons. I might have been able to help him. But he made his choices. And"—Georgina smiled—"they weren't all bad. After all, he was trying to get himself out of the illegal lottery scheme."

There was another long silence as we walked the remainder of the way. When we neared the place where Jimmy had died, Georgina sprinkled the petals around the bases of several oak trees. Then, she bowed her head and murmured something. I didn't hear what she said, and I didn't ask. She deserved to keep the moment to herself. When she finished, she looked up and smiled. "I want to go to the old cemetery before we have lunch."

I nodded, and we turned back toward the Turlough Museum. Georgina didn't speak again until we neared the gardener's cottage. "That poor man. His life is in ruins."

"It's unfortunate that Willem took justice into his own hands."

"He should have reported Flann to the guards."

Once more, my thoughts returned to how often the police didn't listen to me. My mother's case was an example. Would the police have listened to Willem, especially when the accusations were against a highly respected member of the community? Would Deirdre have admitted that she was the victim of sibling abuse? We would never know.

"I'm surprised you're willing to return to where you were almost killed," I remarked as we made the steep climb to the cemetery gate.

"Star, if there's one thing I've learned in this life, it's to respect and remember the past." Georgina stopped walking and took my hand. "I also know how important it is to draw upon our roots to deal with the present. Unfortunately for Jimmy, he didn't try to come to terms with his life until it finally caught up with him."

Roots, there's that word again, I said to myself. *When would I know about my roots?*

"What did you say when you scattered the flower petals?" I asked when we'd gotten some distance from the solemnity of the moment on the greenway.

She smiled. "Oh, the final verse from one of St. Paul's letters. It goes something like, 'love bears all things and endures all things.'" Georgina sighed. "I'm just sorry I didn't see his hurts sooner. I might have been able to save him."

We reached the cemetery, and Georgina moved through the gate first. I fell behind, allowing her time to lay the bouquet of violets she'd brought onto her parents' resting place.

While I waited, my thoughts turned to what Georgina had said about our pasts and our present. I wondered why she'd never married. Did it have anything to do with her past? I realized I didn't really know much about Georgina's life. I could say it was because I'd been so focused on finding my mother that I'd been letting the present slide by me. But truthfully, I was afraid. Afraid of what allowing myself to become immersed in this circle of people I'd come to know would mean. Afraid it might change my life in ways I couldn't control. But after almost losing Aunt Georgina, I made a promise to myself not to let my fears hold me back any longer.

Georgina blessed herself, gave a look around the cemetery, and said, "Let's go have lunch."

∾

I ALMOST DIDN'T RECOGNIZE THE WOMAN WHO WALKED FROM THE café's kitchen to our table with a plate of chocolates. "Georgina, don't get up. I'm more than happy to take your order and bring your plates to you. It's the least I can do." Deirdre's eyes shone like the bright-blue sky after a violent thunderstorm had wiped the heavens clean.

"I'm glad to see you here." Georgina swung one end of her scarf behind her shoulder before continuing, "I hope you've thought about what we discussed the other day."

Deirdre nodded in agreement. "Yes, I called Karen Greene, and I've an appointment for later in the week." Deirdre turned to me and said, "Your aunt suggested I seek counseling, and I've agreed. I need to release my past and move on with my life." She looked around the room at the crowded tables. "I'm determined not to lose my business—pouring myself into this place and my catering is how I've coped all these years."

"Have you gone to see Willem?" Georgina asked.

"Yes, the poor soul," Deirdre replied, taking a seat at the table. "He knew about the abuse, of course, because I'd confided in him. Willem had been trying to get me to go to the guards about Flann."

"Why didn't you go to the police?" I asked.

"Fear. Abuse was a common thing in our house when I was growing up. Our mother was domineering and abusive, and the wooden spoon was her favorite weapon. Then, Flann turned out to be the bully among the three of us." Deirdre rubbed one of her arms as if trying to soothe herself.

"What about your father? He didn't do anything to stop the abuse?" I asked.

"He was just as abusive as our mother, and he would have beat us twice as hard if we told anyone about our home life. The family reputation had to be protected."

"But Jimmy must have known. Why didn't he do something?" I asked.

"I don't think you understand, Miss O'Brien," Deirdre replied. "Our family history, our reputations, and our place in the community were more important than admitting what really went on in our family. I just coped with it rather than speak out. Simply said, I was intensely afraid."

"I'm so glad you'll be seeing Karen," Georgina interjected, reaching out to touch Deirdre's hand. "Many times, when someone grows up in a violent environment, the abuse becomes normalized."

"I never thought Willem would take it upon himself to kill Flann," Deirdre stated.

"He told the guards that when he saw the bruise on your arm, he lost it and followed Flann out of the building," I stated.

"For once, the bruise wasn't the result of Flann laying his hands on me. I'd slammed one of the kitchen fridge doors on my arm." Deirdre's eyes filled with tears. "If only Willem had asked me about it." She shook her head. "Then again, he probably wouldn't have believed me. I should have gone to the guards long ago, but in all honesty, I just couldn't face the shame of it all."

O'Shea had shared with Lorcan the theory that Jimmy and Flann had crossed paths somewhere between the café's dining room and courtyard. Maybe Willem started following Flann but then ended up walking after Jimmy. We'd never know. One way or another, Jimmy had ended up at the end of Willem's rage.

"Georgina, I'm so sorry." Deirdre's voice quivered. "Willem let you take the blame for Jimmy's death because he didn't want to reveal my family secrets. It was only when I went missing, too, that he finally told the guards about Flann."

"But why did he pose the body in the exhibit?" I asked.

"Willem knew about the abuse in our family. When he realized he had killed the wrong person, he put Jimmy into the exhibit. Willem thought that would serve as a warning to Flann to stay away from me."

I took a deep breath and thought again about my past with

Dylan Hill and French Hill cottage. I'd learned that secrets had a way of living parallel lives. I looked at Georgina and realized how lucky I was that I'd put the pieces together about Flann on time.

Georgina must have guessed what I was thinking. "When you told me about the missing girl in London, I pulled out some old photo albums. Her name was Susan. She was a pal of mine from school. I was in the London pub you visited on the night she disappeared. I had no idea, of course, that Jimmy owned the pub until you told me. Or that Flann was there the night Susan went missing. But he didn't know that. One of the evenings he was at my cottage, he saw the old photos. He was worried I'd remember something that connected him to the pub that night."

"Obviously, he was unnerved enough to kidnap you, but realistically, if he hadn't panicked, that case would have remained a cold case," I said.

"When you mentioned your trip to London and Jimmy's pub, he got worried you'd unearth something—that the case might be reopened." Georgina stopped and gazed out the café's window before continuing, "We were just schoolgirls out for a fun evening."

"You don't have to say anymore," I said to Georgina. Lorcan had already told me about Georgina's meeting with O'Shea after Flann was taken into custody. According to O'Shea, Georgina had courageously recounted Flann's tormenting words. "I hope the police in Britain can tie him to the case. It's been a long time. Nevertheless, he will pay for what he did to both of you."

"I'm so sorry, Georgina," Deirdre said. "After Willem was arrested, I went to Flann's place to beg for his help. I wanted to hire a good lawyer for Willem. But when I arrived, Flann was in a rage. He grabbed me and marched me down into the base-ment, where he had already placed Georgina."

Georgina nodded. "When Flann took me to his farmhouse, he took great pleasure in recounting what he'd done that night in London, including where he'd buried Susan's body." Georgina looked at Deirdre and said, "He was out of his mind, and I saw the monster that he was. I understand why you were terrified."

"I'm just grateful that it's all out in the open now," Deirdre replied.

Georgina sighed and said, "Not to worry, we will get through this. Now, let's have lunch." She squeezed Deirdre's hand before turning over the menu to look at the list of baked desserts.

Georgina didn't mention Nessa Bantry. Nor did I. According to Lorcan, O'Shea had let Nessa off with a stern warning about what would happen if she ever came near Georgina again. It turned out that she had left the dead animals at Georgina's shop, thrown the beet juice at Georgina's cottage door, and sideswiped my car. Lorcan hadn't agreed with O'Shea, and neither did I, but then I accepted O'Shea's decision.

I gave Deirdre my order of vegetable soup, brown bread, and butter just as Lorcan came through the café door. Marcella, Maeve, and a third female followed close behind him. Large-framed sunglasses hid most of her face, and the blonde wig was gone. Instead, ebony-colored hair hung to her waist. Then, she removed her glasses. Chills ran up and down my spine as I recognized her hazel eyes and pale skin scattered with freckles. I saw my face in her face, my eyes in her eyes.

I got to my feet, walked over to Lorcan, and almost threw my arms around him. Instead, I reached out and touched his hand. "You convinced Evelyn to come," I said, smiling into the beautiful blue eyes behind his glasses.

Lorcan's eyes held mine. "Of course, I did. You're not the only persistent person around here, Star O'Brien."

"Thank you, Lorcan," I replied, my thoughts turning to how much I'd come to value his friendship.

Then, out of habit, I reached for my connection to the world, tethered to my capri pants. But I stopped myself. Instead, my hand went to the tiny, gold locket at my neck. Taking a deep breath, I turned to Evelyn and said, "We need to talk."

ABOUT THE AUTHOR

MARTHA M. GEANEY is the author of the amateur sleuth Star O'Brien mystery series which starts with *Death on Clare Island*. The series is set in real places in County Mayo, Ireland where Martha has been visiting since she was four years old.

Martha is the President of Citrus Crime Writers, Sisters in Crime (SinC)'s Central Florida chapter. She has been a member of SinC and Citrus Crime Writers since 2017.

Martha earned a Ph.D. in Interdisciplinary Studies, and before turning to the mystery life, served as dean of a business college in the Pennsylvania State University system.

Martha, her partner, Bill, and their puppy, Turlough, live in Sumter County, Florida.

AND A FINAL NOTE FROM MARTHA—

Thank you for reading *Death at the Turlough Museum* and for following along with Star as she unravels the mysteries of her life. If you have time, please leave a review on Amazon or Goodreads. You can also like my Facebook author page at *https://www.facebook.com/mgeaneyauthor.*

And if you have questions or feedback that you'd like to share, please contact me at www.martha-geaney.com. I'd love to respond to your comments.

Made in the USA
Las Vegas, NV
16 April 2023

70687437R00138